I0670784

AN INCONVENIENT WEDDING

Brigit Stacey

2

www.BOROUGHSPUBLISHINGGROUP.com

AN INCONVENIENT WEDDING

ISBN 978-1-951055-89-9

For my two sweet babes—I can't wait to meet you this summer

AN INCONVENIENT WEDDING

Chapter One

Lauren

"That kid is going to grow up to be a whole lot of trouble," an amused voice said behind Lauren as she stood at the pen fence surrounding her animal enclosure.

She looked over at her best friend and farmhand, Sage, whose emerald eyes crinkled as she smiled. They stood together as Lauren stifled a laugh at the antics taking place before them.

It seemed the little goat Jackie had gotten loose again. She was jumping from haystack to haystack, knocking over troughs of water along the way, bleating in delight.

"Jackie," Lauren called out. Jackie heard her name and cocked her head as Lauren approached her. "Jackie, you better get down right now. I'm giving you one more chance." The little goat ignored Lauren completely. Frustrated, Lauren furrowed her brows and frowned at the goat, attempting to look stern.

"Jackie. Come here. Now."

The goat ran past Lauren, knocking her over. On the ground, Lauren picked straw out of her hair, then reached into her pockets. She held out her hand, revealing pellets and seeds. Jackie ran to Lauren, face planting into her palm, devouring the pile of food. Within seconds, Lauren threw Jackie's leash around her neck, tugging her as she reluctantly followed Lauren back to her pen.

"Gotcha," Lauren said, looking down at Jackie fondly. The kid was a four-month-old Saanen goat, pure white, but with a wild streak of brown hair down the top of her head and back. Now unleashed in her pen, Jackie ran up and jumped off the logs Lauren had put in the pen as a goat jungle gym.

"Speaking of trouble, the Lone Loon Brewery crafted a new beer. What say ye to a rewarding brew?" Sage asked, smirking.

Lauren shrugged. "Maybe…but I have a lot of work to do. I need to do more work advertising the homestead as a wedding venue before fall comes and goes."

"We can do that tomorrow." Sage's encouraging look was enough to bend Lauren.

"Well, okay." Lauren brought her finger to her thick, long chocolate brown hair, twirling a lock around her index and middle fingers.

The noise of crunching gravel and booming bass shifted Lauren's attention to the driveway between the highway and her small, two-story craftsman home. A white Mercedes sped up the drive, stopping abruptly in front of her house.

"Who could that be?" Lauren wondered.

"More importantly, who do they think they are?" Sage rolled her eyes, following Lauren, who was already headed toward the car.

The goats' pens were forty yards from the front porch of Lauren's home on her seventy-acre farm called Big Heart Homestead. It was a little over a year ago that Lauren Anderson closed on the property, beginning her journey into the great unknown. Yes, she was nervous, yes, she was inexperienced and hated spiders, but also yes—she believed in herself or at least liked to think so. Her cheerful spirit could be easily mistaken as confidence, but she'd gladly accept it.

Please be a client, Lauren thought as she approached the shiny luxury car. Farming hadn't reaped the dividends she'd needed, and if she didn't get some form of income soon, she'd have to turn to her parents for financial help—something she'd do anything to avoid. It was why she'd started renting out the farm as a venue.

Ever since the age of ten, Lauren had imagined owning her very own farm, growing fruits and vegetables, gathering eggs from her hens, milking goats for cheese and cream. Her mother owned a confectionary and ice cream shop in town, called I Scream, and her father owned the town's successful restaurant and inn, Lakeside Inn. Lauren knew the best chocolate and caramels were made with goat milk. She wanted to be the one who milked those goats, made the chocolates and caramels. Of course, she'd also imagined her homestead would be a vast, beautiful space where she could happily host all sorts of people for weddings, birthday parties, and other celebrations. From a young age, she'd loved planning her birthday parties, working with her mother to bake the perfect cake from scratch, and concoct delicious fruity punches to make her guests feel special and welcomed.

And now, here she was, standing on acres of farmland that were all hers.

I need to make this work on my own.

A woman exited the car, her long, tanned legs swinging to the ground with ease. The enormous diamond ring on her left ring finger sparkled blindingly in the sunshine.

Bingo.

Lauren beamed.

"Hi, welcome to Big Heart Homestead," she said, waving her hand at the statuesque woman.

"Hi." The woman removed her dark sunglasses, revealing sparkling blue eyes, her lips pursed in a half-smile. She was a svelte blonde, wearing a pink blouse, a tight white miniskirt, and hot pink pumps. It didn't take Lauren long to realize she was a) gorgeous and b) not from town. Women in Pine Lake, Wisconsin knew how to put together an outfit and were naturally beautiful—no doubt—but there would be no reason a woman from Pine Lake would dress that way unless she was trying to sell a mansion on the lake. And Lauren knew this woman was not one of the fancy-dressing realtors in town.

"So, long story short, I'm looking for a wedding venue, and the town paper listed your property as an option. Is that true? It doesn't look like—"

"Yes," Sage exclaimed. She stepped forward, her muck-covered jeans and sweat-soaked t-shirt in dire contrast with the woman's attire. "We are the number one wedding venue in Sawyer County."

"Really?" the woman asked.

Really? Lauren thought. *Massive lie, Sage.*

"And this is Lauren Anderson. She owns the homestead. I'm Sage Fischer, her farmhand." Sage stuck out her hand, and the woman shook it.

"Gemma Turner." Gemma then shook Lauren's hand. Her grip was firm, and Lauren felt intimidated by Gemma's confidence.

Lauren brought her fingers to her hair, and as Gemma turned to grab her purse, Sage slapped Lauren's hands away. "Stop," she mouthed to her best friend. Purse in hand, Gemma looked at Sage and Lauren.

"So? A tour?"

"Oh, yes, yes. Follow me." Lauren walked past her adorable home, which she'd spent loads of time and money remodeling last autumn. She'd painted the siding cobalt blue, its shutters bright white, and planted indigenous grasses, plants, and wildflowers around its perimeter. Inside had been remodeled into a three-bed, two-bathroom home, inspired by all the trendy farmhouses Lauren had seen in magazines. There were lots of white walls, dark pine hardwood floors, a farmhouse kitchen sink, and rustic furniture. She loved her little home.

One hundred yards across from her home and its matching one-car garage sat a huge, two-story white-painted barn. A driveway connected the barn to the other buildings. In front of the barn's massive doors was a neglected lawn.

"So, this is the barn and the main venue. You can either have your wedding inside the barn, outside, or both," Lauren said, her voice hopeful.

Sage heaved open the massive barn doors, unveiling a dark, primitive space. Gemma took off her sunglasses again as the three women entered the barn.

Gemma winced. "This is unfinished."

Clearing her throat, Lauren replied, "Well, yes, that's true, but—"

"Renovations begin tomorrow, and it will be ready for events as soon as next week," Sage interjected.

Lauren nearly gasped. Sage was at it again. Her audacity never ceased to amaze Lauren.

"Imagine a bright, tall space, hanging fairy lights, white vintage chandeliers, massive pine tables with mid-century modern chairs, benches, and tin pots overflowing with hydrangeas and peonies. Burlap table runners," Sage paused to think, "and the most delicious organic, farm-to-table meals, made straight from the farm. Fresh vegetables and fruit, free-range chicken raised right here, and the best part? Homemade decadent caramels and chocolates made from our farm's very own goat milk, made in Lauren's very own kitchen."

Gemma's mouth hung ajar. Was she salivating? Lauren hoped so.

A pause. Then, "Oh my gosh, that sounds amazing." Gemma beamed. She looked around the barn. "With some natural pine wood floors? And walnut and goat cheese salads. And maybe even a funny biography about each chicken on the menu?" Gemma chuckled.

"Oh, that's not very nice," Lauren murmured to herself. Sage nudged her, nodding.

"Hilarious." Sage smiled at Gemma.

"Um, so, Gemma. Tell us a little bit about your reasons for choosing Pine Lake as your wedding destination and um, also..." Lauren couldn't stop thinking about her precious little chickens being mocked by cruel guests. She tried to snap out of it. "Oh, and the wedding date? Things like that."

"We're planning on November third. But I want to be clear. I want a fall wedding, not a winter one. It won't be all snowy up here by then, will it?" Gemma asked.

"No. Of course not," Sage said.

Lauren's heart began to pound. She couldn't keep track of Sage's lies. Of course, it wasn't *exactly* a lie—the weather was unpredictable. But Wisconsin, especially this far north, was known for its harsh winters, which often came as early as Halloween. Odds were it would snow rather than not the first weekend of November.

"Wonderful. I can't wait. Now, where do I sign?" She smiled, showing perfectly straight and blindingly white teeth. Lauren wondered if they were veneered.

She smiled back at her first client. At last she was headed toward realizing her dream.

***

Lauren and Sage stood on the front porch of Lauren's house, watching the white Mercedes turn onto the highway and disappear into the distance.

Lauren turned to Sage in a panic. "One week? We'll get the barn renovated in one week?"

Sage smiled an exaggerated grin and shrugged. "It's possible."

"And you promised it wouldn't snow before November?"

"It's possible," Sage said.

"And you said our wedding venue is the number one wedding venue in the county?"

"It's possible."

Lauren narrowed her eyes, and Sage laughed.

Sage smirked. "Lauren, haven't I ever shared with you my marketing wisdom? Lie to them, and they will come."

"I don't think it's right, Sage. She'll find out sooner than later, and it won't be good for our branding in the long run—"

Sage raised the contract before Lauren's eyes. "But look at this. She's paying three thousand for the venue and another five thousand for the food. That's amazing. Our first client is bringing in eight thousand dollars in one day. I gotta say, I'm pretty proud of myself and all those *white* lies. They're more like opinions."

Lauren nodded. "Well, maybe you're right. Regardless, that means we have to renovate the barn, create a menu, harvest, and buy some chickens in less than six weeks."

Sage looked closely at the paperwork, zeroing in on the date.

"Wow. September twentieth already?" She smiled. "Hey, it's almost fall equinox time. We're gonna have a party, right?"

Lauren sighed. "Maybe."

"We always have a party."

"Fine. We'll have a party." Lauren took the paperwork from Sage's hands. "I mean, it is pretty cool we got our first client. And right when we needed that money. Her deposit will help so much." She read the contract. "Gemma Turner. From New York City."

"Makes so much sense," Sage said.

"And she's in advertising. Not surprising. Says here her fiancé will be paying the remainder of the balance. Contact information: Ash—"

Lauren's heart quickened its pace. Her eyes froze on the name on the contract, written in beautiful handwriting.

"What?" Sage stepped closer to Lauren, trying to get a glimpse of the contract. "Oh. My. Gosh. Asher Wolf?"

Lauren blinked.

"Like, *the* Asher Wolf? Like your ex-boyfriend Asher Wolf? Like the worst breakup in your life Asher Wolf? Like—"

"I don't know," Lauren yelled. She calmed herself, taking deep breaths. "I mean, maybe not. She's from New York City. There are, like, a billion people living in that city. There could be more than one guy named Asher Wolf in that city, I mean, don't you think?"

"But why would not-your-Asher-Wolf happen to want to get married in your-Asher-Wolf's hometown of Pine Lake, Wisconsin? It so happens that another Asher Wolf randomly chose the farthest town in northern Wisconsin to get married? The odds of that are slim to none."

"It's possible," said Lauren faintly. Her hand shot to her hair, wrapping a lock around her finger.

"What are you going to do if it is your Asher?"

"He's not *my* Asher. He's Gemma's Asher. What can I do? That ship has sailed. It's ancient history. I mean, I haven't thought about him in ages."

Sage raised an eyebrow at that.

"Besides, it doesn't matter. She's our first client, right now our *only* client, and we need her money. Her business is the only thing stopping me from defaulting on the farm's mortgage. So, unless we can miraculously book another wedding—or five weddings—before November third, we can't say no."

Sage shook her head. "That's not true. You could easily ask your parents for a business loan. They'd be happy to help. You haven't asked them for a cent."

"I'm not doing that, Sage. You know how important it is for me to do this all by myself. When my parents opened their businesses decades ago, they didn't have any help from their parents. I can do this on my own," Lauren said. She frowned, adding, "I hope." She shook her head. "No, no. I *will*." She looked at Sage, whose arms were now crossed.

"I know you think you can't say no, but—"

"It's not even that. You know what?" Lauren took a deep breath, steadying her voice. "I don't want to say no. That's unprofessional. And I am a professional. Asher and I ended a long time ago, and I'm not one to hold grudges."

"Everyone knows that. You've got a big heart. But that's the problem, Lauren. Even if you weren't over Asher and even if you didn't need the money, you'd still say yes to his wedding because you're so afraid of disappointing other people."

A slicing, stabbing pain shot through Lauren's body after Sage said that. Sage frowned, looking as if she immediately regretted her statement. She extended her hand to Lauren's forearm.

"I'm sorry. That was mean, and I didn't mean it to be. I mean, wow, I said mean three times in one sentence." She shook her head. "I don't want to hurt you. But it is true."

"Well, who *likes* disappointing other people? That's ridiculous. Of course I don't like disappointing other people."

"Right, right," Sage said, letting it slide. She looked at her feet, then back up at Lauren. "So, how about that beer?"

"Heck yes," Lauren said, speed walking to her car, leaving Sage grinning in her wake.

***

The Lone Loon Brewery was quite crowded for four o'clock in the afternoon on a Saturday. Lauren tried to remind herself not everyone was a homesteader like her, working sunup to sundown, and eschewing fun activities until all their tasks were completed. But she was glad Sage had suggested visiting the brewery, and right now, she needed an ice-cold beer.

"I'll try the new Oktoberfest beer you guys unveiled," Lauren said to the bartender and co-owner of the bar, her childhood friend Jacob Carlson. His gray-blue eyes twinkled as he ran his hand through his scruffy beard.

"Great choice," he said, pouring her a pint. "How's the farm?"

Lauren took a sip of the crisp, spicy beer. It tasted like fall—her favorite season.

"Homestead," she corrected him with a coy smile. "It's not exactly a farm… yet. I refer to it as the homestead."

"Okay, sure. What's the difference?" Jacob asked.

"Well, I guess a homesteader sells crops and livestock to make a profit like a farmer, but also their main goal is to be as self-sufficient as possible and live off their land completely."

Jacob nodded. "I hope that doesn't mean you're a prepper."

"Huh?"

"You know, one of those people who thinks the rapture is coming, or the zombie apocalypse or a government conspiracy."

Lauren frowned. "Jacob John Carlson. You know me better than that."

He laughed. "You're right. I do. You're too sweet to be a prepper. And if you did, you'd welcome everyone in and make sure they were all fed and happy before the world ended."

She smiled. "That's sweet." As Jacob stared at her, Lauren grew uncomfortable. Was he flirting with her? She smiled again and sipped her beer. "Anyway. It's going well. My hens are laying more eggs than I can count, our goats are happy and producing milk, and the crops are slowly but surely coming in. And," Lauren stopped herself. She was a private person—should she tell Jacob about her new client? The last thing Lauren wanted was to spread gossip or start drama or be the center of attention in any way whatsoever so she kept her mouth shut. "And, yep. Doing okay for our first year."

"So, your goal is to be self-sustainable, live off your land as much as possible, and make extra income by bountiful harvest?" Jacob reiterated. "Cool." He smirked. "But you'll always rely on me for your brews, right?"

Lauren chuckled. "Of course, Jacob. You're my number one."

That made Jacob blush. After, he nodded, walking away toward a customer at the bar.

Alone at the bar now, Lauren looked around for Sage, who had spotted her boyfriend Will when she first walked in. Although the bar was small, it wasn't dark or dreary. Its floor-to-ceiling windows and exposed brick fireplace, soothing paint colors, and cozy booths and chairs made the bar seem stylish, chic, and welcoming. Jacob had done a great job renovating his father's tavern, and his craft brews were nothing short of delicious.

Like Jacob, other grown children in town were beginning to renovate and rebrand their parents' businesses. Pine Lake, Wisconsin, once a sleepy, forgotten lakeside town up north, had entered its renaissance, and people between the ages of twenty and forty who had moved away to start college had now moved back, contributing to its economic rise and fixing its infrastructure. It remained a sweet, simple place, focused on the natural beauty of the surrounding forests and lakes, but it had new life breathed into it. Its children had reclaimed it. Now adults, they loved the town so much they wanted to make it beautiful and relevant again.

Born in the four-stoplight town, Lauren spent her childhood and adolescence contributing to her parents' businesses. After earning her degree in agricultural science, minoring in business, Lauren had spent her early twenties gaining hands-on experience with them.

And there was no other place on earth Lauren wanted to live out this dream than her hometown of Pine Lake with her very own homestead.

Things were near perfect and Lauren was living her dream. She'd saved enough money to put twenty percent down on a large mortgage. She was able to make payments, pay her bills, and somehow not collapse of fatigue from running a farm. So, there was nothing to complain about or yearn for.

Except...

Well, she didn't want to raise only goats and chickens. She also wanted to raise children. She'd turned thirty, which was still young. Lauren was a natural nurturer.

She shuddered. Because of that fact, it was why she hadn't bought chickens to slaughter yet. The thought of it...well. It wouldn't be happening anytime soon.

She took a sip of her beer, enjoying her solitude. Sage was the one naturally skilled at starting up conversations and filling awkward silences, and Lauren was happy to let her.

She looked around the bar. Where was Sage, anyway? Her best friend could get on her nerves but was also her sidekick. It was difficult for Lauren to meet new people and socialize without Sage by her side.

Lauren stood up, grabbing her beer, weaving through the clusters of people who stood, chatting, enjoying their craft brews. She spotted an empty booth by the fireplace, heading that way.

Sidling up to the fireplace, Lauren tried not to look lonely. She took a sip of her beer, now half-drunk. A chilly wind breezed by her, and she looked toward the open front door to see who was entering the bar.

It was Gemma, sunglasses on, and her thick, shiny hair still perfectly curled at the ends. Lauren felt her body lurch forward, her arm stick up, and her mouth open. But Gemma's head turned as Lauren was about to say hello. She shoved her hand back under the table, acting as though she hadn't been ignored. Lauren reassured herself with the thought that Gemma probably hadn't seen her anyway. She *was* wearing sunglasses.

Lauren began to twirl her hair. Until she felt another gush of wind and looked to the front door again.

Oh my. No, no, no.

A tall, raven-haired man entered the bar. His jaw was chiseled, his sideburns thick, and his eyes a sapphire blue. He looked around the bar, then saw Gemma across the room, and approached her.

Without thinking, Lauren dipped sideways, bending her body at the waist to lie down across the long booth seat. She faced the bottom of the table, eyeing crumbs and puddles of sticky beer on the floor. Her heart raced.

Asher's here. Of course he would be here. His fiancée is here. Why wouldn't *he be here with her, scoping out the town, the venue? That makes sense. Why wasn't I prepared for this?*

Lauren reached for her cell phone, wiggling so that she could text with one hand while keeping the cell phone hidden under the table. She thumbed through her text messages, looking for Sage. Finding her, she started a text message. "Asher is here" was as far as she got until she heard her name.

"Lauren?"

Lauren reflexively lifted her head, bumping it on the table. "Ouch." She awkwardly slid her neck back, until her head was out from under the table, her body lying, still bent at the waist, on the seat of the booth.

"Oh, hey there," she said, unable to see whoever it was who'd said her name. She sat up, her thick, dark hair covering her eyes. She pushed it aside to see Gemma with Asher standing next to her, looking puzzled.

"Lauren?" Asher stared at her in disbelief.

"What were you doing?" Gemma asked, her one eyebrow rising.

Lauren shrugged, stalling. "What was I doing? Oh, you mean under the table? Yeah, I was, um, looking for my cell phone." She waved her phone in the air. "Found it."

Gemma smiled politely, then pointed to Asher.

"This is my fiancé, Asher. Asher, this is Lauren, the girl I told you about, who owns the farm."

Asher nodded. "Hi, Lauren."

Lauren smiled. *Awkward.* Was Asher pretending not to know Lauren? Should Lauren go along?

"And you went to high school together, or something, right?" Gemma asked, looking at Asher, then at Lauren.

"Yeah, we went to high school together. We know each other. Everyone in this town knows each other," Asher said.

Lauren nodded. "That's true. Small town."

"Cool." A pop song came on the radio, and Gemma's face instantly lit up. "Oh my gosh, I love this song." She bopped her head along to the beat. "I'm going to get a beer. Want one, Ash?"

Lauren's stomach dropped to her feet. She watched Asher nod, pulling his wallet out of his back pocket, and handing his credit card to Gemma.

"Thanks, babe." Gemma kissed Asher's cheek, walking away.

Lauren cleared her throat, taking a sip of her beer. She looked up to see Asher staring at her. "How are you?"

"Great," Lauren said. *Too chipper,* she told herself. She lowered her voice an octave. "How are you?"

"Good, good." Asher looked around the bar, then back to Lauren. "Can I sit down?"

"Oh, sure. Sorry," Lauren said, scooting over, closer to the fireplace, feeling the warmth of the dwindling fire against her skin.

"So, you met Gemma," Asher said.

"Yes, I did. She's beautiful." Lauren's face was beginning to hurt from her polite smile. She reached for her beer to take another sip, realizing there was only a drop left.

Furrowing his brows, Asher looked at Lauren. "I guess it's kind of weird to have our wedding at your farm."

"No. Don't worry about it. That's what my farm is for. I love hosting weddings," Lauren reassured him.

"Oh, okay. That's good, I guess. So, how many weddings have you hosted?" Asher's cool eyes gazed into Lauren's. He had *not* lost his looks, she noticed. He had faint crow's feet around his eyes, and his stubble was a bit more pronounced, and she noticed a few silver hairs in his jet-black hair, but other than that, he was as handsome as she'd remembered.

"How many weddings have I hosted?" she mumbled. "Er..."

"Ten." Lauren looked up to see Sage standing next to the table.

"Sage." Asher smiled, rising to hug her. "How's it going?"

"Going swimmingly, thanks for asking. And how's the Big Apple treating you?"

"Treating me very well," Asher said.

Sage crossed her arms. "What are you up to these days, you know, besides getting married on our farm?"

Asher looked at Lauren, then again at Sage.

Lauren leaned in to explain. "Sage is my farmhand. My assistant, too. I guess she works with me, well, I suppose she works for me." It had always felt strange to admit she was her best friend's boss.

"Oh, nice," he said. "Yeah, Gemma picked the spot. My mom somehow convinced Gemma to have our wedding in Pine Lake, and Gemma's dad told her he couldn't afford a New York wedding, so Gemma started researching venues, and I guess she fell in love with yours. I think her exact words were 'sweet and simple.'"

"Interesting," said Sage.

Lauren smiled. "Well, I'm delighted that she did. It will be so beautiful."

She saw Sage shift her eyes her way, but Lauren ignored her. Asher nodded.

"Yeah, I think it will be."

Nodding, Lauren looked at Asher. "Yeah."

"Yeah..." Asher said, looking for Gemma. "Well, I'm gonna go find my fiancée. But I'm sure we'll see you around. We'll be in town for a while." He smiled, then walked away.

Sage widened her eyes at Lauren. Lauren pretended not to see, bringing her pint glass to her mouth, forgetting again that it was empty.

Chapter Two

Asher

Asher found it difficult to focus on what Gemma was saying, knowing that Lauren was only a few feet away. Every few sentences, he flicked his eyes over to where Lauren sat with Sage and Will, sipping pints of beer. Asher reached for his pint glass, finding it empty. *Hey, who drank my beer?* Then he realized it'd been him.

"Babe? Are you listening?" Gemma asked as her head cocked to the side, disappointed.

"Yeah, yeah. You were talking about the wedding," he guessed, watching Gemma's smile as she continued whatever she'd been saying.

"Well, I think that because we're saving so much money on everything since we're not having it in New York, even though I'd prefer to have it in New York but my dad has made it loud and clear we won't be having it in New York—well, I thought maybe we could go to Bora Bora for our honeymoon, and maybe my dad will even give us some money for that, you know—"

Asher nodded along, noticing she hadn't taken a breath during any of that.

"How much is that again?" Asher asked.

"Flights and hotels for a ten-day honeymoon in Bora Bora are minimum of ten thousand dollars."

"Minimum?"

"Yeah, but you only have a honeymoon once."

"Gemma, we talked about saving money for a house," Asher said, a knot beginning to form in his stomach.

"A house? Do you mean a condo? I don't want to move out of Manhattan, Asher. We've discussed this."

"But we talked about Brooklyn Heights or maybe even—"

"Don't say it. We may be having our wedding in the country, but we are *not* moving there."

Asher shut his mouth.

"Besides," Gemma added, "you would hate it. You love the big city. I bet you'll be so tired of your hometown by tomorrow you'll want us to go back to the city immediately."

Asher shrugged. It was possible.

An irritating ringing sound startled Gemma, and she reached into her purse, pulling out her phone. "I have to take this, B.R.B.," she said, getting up and exiting the bar.

Asher sat at the table, looking at his empty glass. He and Gemma had arrived last night after an excruciatingly long road trip from New York to Wisconsin. They'd stopped for a night somewhere in Ohio—or was it Indiana?—and stayed at a cheap motel. Gemma had tossed and turned all night, waking Asher up because she thought she felt bugs crawling on her, or she could hear someone trying to break in. They'd been pure flights of imagination, so he'd been exhausted when they'd finally arrived in Pine Lake yesterday evening. He was also tired of listening to Gemma's playlists, never realizing the difference between their tastes in music. She'd been a good sport, though, and shared driving responsibilities equally. She had endless stories to tell, and also didn't mind if Asher worked a bit on his laptop or took business phone calls, since she was as dedicated to her career. In fact, Asher would venture to say she was even *more* dedicated than him to her job. She was driven, serious, and cutthroat. Sometimes her passion for her work made Asher feel insecure about his lack thereof. He tried not to think too much about it.

Heidi Wolf, Asher's mother, had welcomed them both with open arms as soon as they'd arrived, insisting they sit down and eat. She'd had a variety of meat and vegetables roasted and drizzled with butter dished out on her finest china. Even though she worked tirelessly as a teacher at the local high school, when it came to her three sons and husband, Heidi had continuous energy to give. Asher's father was kept busy with his plumbing job, and had zero energy by the end of the week due to his aching joints. So his lack of enthusiasm over their wedding wasn't much of a surprise to Asher.

His parents were financially comfortable after living frugally for so many years, but their four-bedroom Victorian house wasn't exactly suited for the wedding Gemma and Asher had in mind. So Heidi had suggested Gemma check out Big Heart Homestead owned by "an old friend" of Asher's. When Gemma had mooted the idea, Asher had no idea Lauren owned the property. He'd have nixed that idea immediately. He had his suspicions that his mother had, though.

Asher hadn't gotten a chance alone with his mother since he'd arrived, but he was going to confront her at some point. He knew his mother, and he knew his mother loved Lauren Anderson.

Asher stood up, walking to the bar to refresh his pint of beer. Without turning his head, he looked over to Lauren, who sat smiling as Sage dominated the conversation. *Nothing's changed there,* he thought.

"Another brew, buddy?" Jacob asked.

"An Oktoberfest. Thanks."

Jacob nodded, pouring the pint. "So, back in town. Hear it's for your wedding?" He looked at Asher with a smirk.

"That's right. My fiancée is from New York. She was in here a minute ago," Asher said, turning to see Gemma pacing outside, still on the phone.

"Congratulations. I'm happy for you, man." Jacob handed Asher his beer. "This one's on me."

"Really? Thanks, man," Asher said, watching Jacob smile and leave, tending to other customers.

Pleased, Asher headed back toward his table. *That was nice of him.* Asher had never seen Jacob so kind, come to think of it. He had always gotten a weird vibe from Jacob, like he secretly hated Asher. He couldn't think of a single reason why Jacob would hate him. Asher had always been kind to Jacob on the rare occasion they interacted. Asher had been a baseball player, golfer, and was now a business guy. Jacob had been a musician, poet, and was now hipster-artisanal-craft-beer-brewer guy. They never ran in the same circles, never competed for the same roles, and never got into any conflict. Yet, Asher could feel Jacob's daggers on him—he could feel his rays of burning disdain. It was a mystery to Asher, who concluded he would always respond with kindness, for the simple reason he hated drama.

Gemma loved drama. The advertising world was full of it. You needed drama to sell things. And Gemma was talented at it, together with the selling part. As long as she kept it at work, Asher decided he could deal with it. And for the past three years they'd been together, she'd had done a good job at living up to her end of the deal.

Asher leaned over the table to take another look outside. He couldn't spot Gemma. She'd probably begun walking down the street, passionately lost in a deal, an idea, or a work conflict, as she often did. Was he beginning to look like a loser? Sure, he'd been living in New York City for seven years, but he wasn't unrecognizable. Plus, he'd been home every year for Thanksgiving, Christmas, and Easter. Had he become irrelevant in Pine Lake?

Once the most popular guy at PLHS, there was a time Asher couldn't keep track of all his friends. Throughout high school and college, he was known as the guy who could simultaneously carry the team to playoffs and volunteer for every charity event in town. He had a big heart. But the person who encouraged him to put his words into action was the person with the biggest heart he knew—Lauren Anderson.

He glanced over toward her booth again for a quick look. She was texting or looking at something on her cellphone, and she was smiling. He felt a tiny shiver. What was she looking at?

Taking a sip of his beer, Asher snapped out of it. He was a good man, and he knew it wasn't right to think about his ex-girlfriend, even if his thoughts were innocent. He loved Gemma and he wanted to be a good husband to her. If he expected her to be a loyal, loving wife to him, he should reciprocate.

It wasn't a big deal, anyway. It's not like he'd thought about Lauren much, not since he'd met Gemma, anyway. It'd been seven years since they'd broken up. He'd moved on. She'd moved on. And this wedding wasn't going to change anything. Aside from this weekend and the actual wedding itself, Asher wasn't going to be in Pine Lake again. And he certainly wasn't going to plan the wedding. Gemma was on top of that, and Asher didn't care much about the details. As long as he could invite everyone he cared about, and as long as they served his favorite Wisconsin cheese and beer, and they had a live band, Asher was good with anything. He didn't want to wear pink, though, in any way, shape, or form, and he knew that was Gemma's favorite color. So, maybe he had a few preferences. Gemma could plan the wedding perfectly, and Asher was confident of that. He was certain he couldn't. So, on Sunday evening, Asher would fly back to NYC and Gemma would stick around for a while finding vendors in town.

"Wolfman." Asher heard at his left arm as he felt a slap on his back. He turned to see a face with smooth, olive skin framed by long, straight black hair. The man's eyes were warm and youthful, smiling along with his smile.

"Lukas?" Asher almost couldn't believe it. Little Lukas Blackstone had grown up quite a bit since he'd last seen him, which was Christmas, four years ago.

"How are you, brother?" Lukas threw his arms around Asher, bringing him in for a warm embrace. *Another big heart,* Asher thought.

"I'm good, man. I'm good. How have you been? You look great."

"I feel great. I took over my dad's lumber business. He's retired and living on Lake Superior. The first year was a little scary. But it's better now. I'm more experienced," Lukas said.

"That's awesome. Good for you."

"You're going to be a husband?" Lukas asked, putting his arm around Asher's shoulder. "I'm so happy for you." He released his grip.

"I appreciate that," Asher said. "Are you still with Cora?"

"We're engaged."

Asher shook his hand. "Congratulations." Asher took a sip of his beer, watching Lukas sip his beer, too. "How long have you two been together?"

"Freshman year of high school. We met at your homecoming party." Lukas smiled wistfully. "The luckiest night of my life, running into her. I would never have had the courage to talk to Cora, but Lauren introduced us."

Asher nodded. He remembered that night. The party was innocent. His parents were there. It was a bunch of awkward teenagers celebrating the football team's win, even though Asher was a baseball player. He and Lauren, a year older than Lukas and

Cora, had been dating for a year by then. They were so young, yet so in love. And that's how the next six years of their relationship continued, up until their abrupt end.

"Can I say something honest? Straight from the heart?" Lukas asked, which made Asher nervous. Asher looked around to make sure no one was listening.

"Uh, sure, go ahead."

"You know, I always pictured you and Lauren getting married. You two were role models for me, Cora too. An example of a successful high school sweetheart story."

After a swig of his beer, Asher shook his head. "But it *wasn't* successful, Lukas. It ended."

Lukas frowned. "I know. I'm sorry I brought it up." It was impossible to be mad at Lukas. He was such a pure soul, a gentle spirit. He was like the smiling Buddha. A skinny version.

"No worries," Asher said, as he looked up to see Gemma flying through the front door, shooting straight over to where Asher and Lukas sat.

"Oh, my gosh, Asher," she screamed, not even looking at Lukas, who'd risen to meet her.

"Uh, Gemma, I want to—"

"You will not believe this."

"Gemma," Asher said, standing. Gemma looked at him. Asher turned her attention toward Lukas. "This is Lukas Blackstone, an old friend of mine. Lukas, this is my fiancée, Gemma."

Gemma smiled, sticking her hand out, but Lukas embraced her.

"I am so happy to meet you, Gemma," he said. She reluctantly returned the embrace, raising her eyebrow at Asher. He shrugged.

"Nice to meet you," Gemma said, finally able to pull away. She smiled at Lukas, then turned to Asher. "Asher, guess what?" But before Asher could guess, Gemma blurted, "We're opening a new ad agency in Tokyo, and the company wants me to oversee the process."

Asher smiled wide, nodding, unsure of what this meant. All he knew was that he should be proud. And he was. "Wow, Gem, that's great. Congrats."

"I mean, that is a *huge* deal, you know? The CEOs want me to lead the opening, set up the company, run things. It's like a huge promotion. Imagine that on my resume. It's amazing."

"Congrats." Lukas beamed. Gemma smiled at him. She stared at Asher, who nodded, reaching his hand out, pulling Gemma in for a kiss.

"So proud of you, baby," he said. "So, I imagine this means you have to fly to Tokyo for a few days?"

Gemma took a breath. "A few days? This is going to take months."

"Oh," Asher said. The gravity of the situation fell upon him. Gemma often took business trips, but they never lasted more than a few days every month. A day or two away from Gemma was fine, even welcomed by Asher, but Asher didn't like the idea of his fiancée being gone for months. He liked having a partner by his side to share his days with, as mundane as they might be. "So, like after the New Year or... when?"

Gemma bit her lip. She looked at Asher, sheepish. "This week. We're starting up the new company this week."

Asher blinked. "Wow, that's fast."

"Yeah..."

Suddenly, it hit him. "Wait, so the company is starting up this week... and it will take months... and you're opening it... in Tokyo..."

"I'll be back for our wedding, obviously."

"Wait, what?" Asher's heart began to race. "Whoa, wait, I didn't realize—you mean, you're leaving this week and you'll be gone for the next six weeks—in Tokyo?"

Gemma nodded. "It's the most amazing career opportunity ever, Ash."

"But what about the wedding?"

Poor Lukas is caught in the middle of this, thought Asher, watching his buddy standing awkwardly next to them.

"It's still gonna happen, duh," Gemma said. "I'll need you to be around physically to check out vendors, do some tastings, book some stuff. You can FaceTime me while you're doing it and it will be like I'm here with you."

"But I don't want to do that. You were going to take total control of planning the wedding. I don't know anything about weddings. I mean, seriously, Gem, you want *me* to plan our wedding for us? I'd buy a keg and order pizza for everyone," Asher said. He was beginning to panic. The idea of planning a wedding by himself was overwhelming.

"Oh my gosh, it is not that hard, Asher." Gemma rolled her eyes. "And your mother is here to help you. And Lauren. Ask her, I mean, it's what she does for a living."

Asher looked over to where Lauren sat. Lauren looked up, her eyes meeting his. He swiftly looked away. "I can't do that."

"Why not?"

"Because I can't."

"I'm sure Lauren would be happy to help. We can even pay her to be our wedding planner. I'll be getting a raise with this promotion," Gemma said, beaming. "Money is no object." She seemed to take pleasure in saying that. This career news was a dream come true to her, Asher could tell. How could he force her to give up the biggest opportunity in her career because he was afraid of planning a wedding?

"But what if I screw it up?" Asher asked.

"You won't. As I said, you've got plenty of women who will walk you through it, and I'll be approving of everything before you sign any contracts," Gemma said. "Your company is so flexible, they won't mind if you spend a few weeks working remotely in Pine Lake." She smirked. "You have to make sure the Wi-Fi works at your mom's."

Asher took a deep breath. Lukas put his hand on Asher's shoulder. "I can help, too."

Asher smiled at Lukas. "Thanks. I appreciate that."

"See, Ash? You've got the whole town behind you. Everyone's here to help," Gemma said. "It's actually pretty sweet."

Asher nodded. His gaze shifted over to Lauren. She must have felt it upon her, turning to stare back at him. A slow, soft smile radiated her face. Asher looked away, back to Gemma.

"I can do this. Don't worry about me, Gemma. This is a huge deal, and I wouldn't want anything to stand in the way of you pursuing your dream."

Gemma's face crinkled, her hand shooting to her chest, as if stopping her heart from falling out. "Aww, thanks, babe." She leaned in, kissing him.

He glanced back to Lauren, who wasn't looking, and he wasn't sure how to describe his feelings at that moment. All he knew was that this was going to be more difficult than it seemed.

***

"Well, isn't that something," Heidi Wolf said, placing a serving bowl of buttery mashed potatoes on the dining room table. She looked at her son. "What bad timing to receive such good news."

Gemma shrugged. "I'd prefer not to think of it as bad timing. It's the way things are. I don't want to assign a negative value to it," she said, which caught Fred's attention. He frowned.

"A man planning a wedding? Asher, don't you have other important things to do at work?" Fred asked.

Asher shrugged. "Well, yeah. Of course I do. But Gemma's right. With technology these days, working remotely is no big deal."

"Then why can't Gemma open up that company remotely, using the Internet or what have you?" Fred asked.

"Good point." Heidi finally sat down. She looked out at the dining room table, at the many bowls and platters of food. "Okay, dig in."

"Okay, because there's a difference between working at a company that's already established and logging in remotely and starting up a new company. I have to physically be there," Gemma said.

Heidi smiled warmly. "I think that's wonderful, honey. Congratulations. It's quite a professional leap, isn't it?"

"Yes, it is," Gemma said.

"It's fine, Dad. I can fly back to New York every couple weeks for important meetings when they need me," Asher said, knowing his dad would never understand anyway.

Fred asked, "What else is there to do for a wedding, anyway? You pick your spot. The date. Order some food."

Gemma looked at Heidi. Heidi looked at Gemma. They burst out laughing.

"Honey," Heidi said to Asher, "thankfully, you have the date set. The rest will fall into place, but it's going to take a lot of work. We should start on the invitations tomorrow."

Asher looked at his mother, wondering what she was truly thinking about this situation.

"I feel like it's in good hands," Gemma said.

Heidi smiled, placing her hand on Gemma's forearm. "It is, dear. You have nothing to worry about." Then she looked at Asher with a loving smile.

Asher was ready to jump out the window, but instead, he scooped a huge chunk of potatoes onto his fork and shoveled it in his mouth.

***

Sunday morning, Asher and Gemma attended church with Heidi and Fred. Asher was able to introduce Gemma to more of his childhood friends, distant family members, and favorite locals. Gemma flashed her perfect smile and knew all of the most polite, interesting things to say and the most thoughtful questions to ask for the town to fall in love with her. She was gorgeous, smart, successful, and charming. Asher felt proud showing her off. He didn't mind the looks from other men after they'd taken a look at Gemma. Men's faces expressed, "Wow, buddy. Good job on snagging a hot wife-to-be."

He was proud of her, yes, but he couldn't shake the feeling of resentment that was beginning to settle into his bones. How could she leave him with such an important event to plan without her? Weren't women supposed to be dying to plan their own weddings? The bottom line was that Asher couldn't do anything about it. He was stuck in his hometown planning their wedding while his fiancée moved to Japan for six weeks starting up a company. He had to suck it up, as inconvenient as it was.

On their walk to the church parking lot, Gemma spotted Lauren as she headed to her minivan. Asher recognized the van as Lauren's parents' minivan they'd given her when she graduated college. It was about fifteen years old, maroon with rusted bottoms. He was surprised it was still running and that Lauren hadn't upgraded. But if Lauren was still the same woman he knew years ago, she'd probably kept that car because she'd always thought cars weren't worth spending money on. No doubt it was being used for some practical reason, like hauling produce from the farm to the markets. Lauren had always been practical.

"So, I don't know if you've heard, but I was offered this amazing career opportunity, and I'll be in Japan for the next six weeks getting a new company off the ground—" Gemma took a breath, allowing Lauren to figure out it was the moment she should congratulate her.

Lauren's doe eyes blinked, then she said, "Oh. Oh, wow. Congratulations, that's so impressive."

Gemma smiled, continuing, "So, that means dear husband-to-be here will be the one meeting with the florist, photographer, baker, etcetera. And that also means we'll need to hire a wedding planner to help him." Gemma's face lit up as she stared at Lauren. "How would you like to be our wedding planner, too? I'll pay whatever you'll ask in addition to our already agreed-upon contract. Amazing, right?"

Lauren's mouth fell open, her big, honey-colored eyes stared at Gemma.

"Your... your wedding planner?" Lauren blushed. "I've never planned a wedding before."

"Yeah, but you've hosted a dozen weddings," Gemma said, at which point Asher noticed Lauren flinch, shake her head, "so you know how they work. And you live in town, which means you know the best of the best." Gemma softened her voice. "Lauren, Asher needs help. Would you please promise me you'll help him?"

Lauren looked at Gemma like a scared rabbit backed up against a wall. "Work with Asher?"

Asher wasn't sure if Lauren was filled with disgust or fear at the thought of working with him. She'd probably hoped she'd never see him again after their breakup. Isn't that why she broke up with him in the first place?

"I'll pay you double. Triple. Whatever. I need this wedding planned, and I can't do it myself," Gemma said forcefully.

Asher shot her a look. "Wait, I thought you said you'd be calling me every step of the way—approving stuff before we set it in stone?"

Gemma laughed. "Asher, I didn't mean that literally."

He frowned, confused. "What *did* you mean by it?"

"Like, sometimes I'll be available. But I'll be starting a company, and the time difference will be, like, crazy. So you *can't* expect me to be with you every step of the way." Gemma looked at Asher, then pursed her lips, taking his face in her hands like he was a puppy dog. "Aww. You'll be okay, babe." She kissed his lips. He wiggled out of her grip.

He looked at Lauren, whose mind seemed a million miles away. She was twirling her beautiful long hair in between her index and middle fingers. Asher smiled at that. *She still does it. She must be nervous.*

"So you'll do it, right?" Gemma asked Lauren, although it was more of a demand. She was standing so tall and confident, her voice strong and assured. Lauren snapped out of her trance, looking at Gemma. She nodded.

"Uh-huh," she said faintly.

"Great." Gemma turned on her heel and walked toward her white Mercedes. "Talk to ya soon, Lauren. Asher will call you tomorrow." Asher looked at Gemma. *I will?*

He followed Gemma to her car, turning to look at the still-frozen Lauren, her hair being twirled faster and faster by her dainty fingers.

***

Early Monday morning, Asher pulled to the curb of the airport, pushing the hazard button while he double-parked. He got out of the car, pulling Gemma's luggage from the trunk, meeting her on the sidewalk.

"So, I guess I won't see you for six weeks?" Asher asked, distressed.

Gemma smiled sympathetically, throwing her arms around him, pulling him close. "Not until our wedding weekend." She kissed his neck. Asher closed his eyes, memorizing her smell. She wore a floral, citrusy perfume, one of her many expensive bottles. It was potent and didn't smell natural, although it was a feminine, pleasant scent. "Who knows, I might surprise you one weekend in between. I love you so much, babe." She pulled back, face to face now, and kissed his lips. "Have fun, okay? Don't get all mopey-Asher on me, okay?"

He nodded, taking it in stride. He knew he could be a bit of a wet blanket sometimes.

"Are you sad to be leaving me?" Asher asked. "I mean, you'll miss me, right?" He couldn't help it. It bothered him that Gemma was so excited at that moment.

"Of course, babe. Of course." She kissed him again, hugging him tightly. "Okay, I gotta go. Love you." She grabbed her luggage, winking at him right before she turned around.

"I love you," he called, watching her enter the airport. She was gone. He sighed, standing there, staring at the closed glass doors. His phone buzzed in his pocket. He pulled it out. A text from Gemma. He smiled, sliding the screen to read it.

I almost forgot. Be good to my Mercedes. Regular car washes, park it in your parents' garage, and *no eating* in the car.

Asher's heart sunk. That's what she cared about? Her stupid car? He texted her back. **Of course babe. Love you**.

She replied with a kiss-face emoji.

Asher grumbled to himself as he got into the car, turned off the hazard button, and shot away from the airport.

***

Pine Lake's natural landmarks looked the same, but the town looked remarkably different. As Asher drove past cranberry bogs, cornfields, and dairy farms, he recognized the familiar beauty of his hometown. As he drove past the farms and toward the national forest surrounding the town's beautiful lake, tall red pine and balsam fir trees sprouted, sheltering bald eagles, crows, and herons. Yellow birch and white ash trees were already beginning to turn, displaying bursts of gold and saffron. Glimmering lake waters reflected the soft sun rays of autumn. Familiar birdsong and critter sightings comforted Asher. The natural splendor of Pine Lake was constant. As Asher entered the town, he spotted changes.

Jacob Carlson had transformed what was once a run-down tavern into a hip brewery and bar, and his sister Rachel had redesigned the tiny diner into a chic coffee shop. New boutiques, restaurants, and renovated buildings breathed life back into his hometown. He noticed a sign for a storefront gift shop, previously a bakery, now called Simple Pleasures. Its window display looked like the perfect snapshot of Pine Lake. Quaint, simple, beautiful, natural, and cozy. The shop was filled with cranberry candles and soaps, stunning stoneware and pottery, wool sweaters and handmade jewelry. He thought about Lauren, how she would love a shop like that.

Would Gemma? Asher wasn't sure. She preferred brand names. Department stores. Fashion Week. But maybe she would like something from that shop. Asher was more uncertain about Gemma's preferences than he was certain. But Lauren—or at least the Lauren he used to know—was simple, transparent about her likes and dislikes.

Stop thinking about Lauren, he told himself, a heavy dose of guilt sinking inside of him.

It wasn't normal for him to think of Lauren this often. In New York City, he never gave her a thought. Why would he? Nothing in the city reminded him of her. Being around Gemma, he only thought of Gemma. He was a faithful and loyal partner to her. He valued fidelity and respect and wanted to be married. As a man of course he noticed attractive women, but he'd never thought about those women the way he was now thinking about Lauren.

It's because you're in town and you're forced to think about her, Asher rationalized. No other reason. It made perfect sense.

I shouldn't beat myself up about it. But I should stop. I should.

As Asher pulled up to his parents' driveway and parked, his mom flung open the front door of her home, dressed in a navy blue cotton dress, suede ankle boots, and a jean jacket. At sixty years old, she was attractive, fit, and energetic. When people complimented her, she'd reply that being around young people all day long made her feel young, although Asher couldn't see the logic there. Regardless, he thought his mother looked lovely. She also looked determined as she galloped down the porch steps and toward the car.

"Off to school a little late, aren't you, Mom?" Asher asked, checking his watch. It was already nine o'clock. She walked around the Mercedes and opened the passenger-side door.

"I'm not going to school. I took the day off," she said, buckling her seat belt.

Asher furrowed his eyebrows. "What's going on?"

"We're going invitation shopping," she beamed. "But let's stop for coffee first." She reached over and kissed his cheek. "Some mama-son bonding time. I'm so excited."

"But—"

"Did you eat? Probably not. We can grab breakfast too. Do you need to use the bathroom? Well, you can hold it until we reach the restaurant, right? I'm glad you didn't drive Gemma to the airport in your pajamas," Heidi said. She looked at Asher, who was frozen, puzzled. "Well? Let's get a move on."

"Were you going to ask me first? I didn't ask for the day off. I only sent an email last night explaining this situation to my bosses, and I haven't even seen their response yet. I can't take a day off, too," Asher said, although he knew that he probably could.

Director of Business Operations sounded important, but Asher never felt that important. He worked for a nonprofit, so he wasn't paid as well as directors in the corporate world. This didn't mean his work wasn't meaningful or difficult. It only meant he could easily work from home for the next six weeks, and he could take the day off today. But he didn't want Heidi knowing that.

"Oh, they'll understand," Heidi said. She smiled. "Go." Her teacher's voice commanded him. Asher obeyed, reversing the car down the driveway, and returning to the small town roads.

He had a feeling it was going to be a long six weeks.

Chapter Three

Lauren

By nine-thirty Monday morning, the twenty-second of September, Lauren had already milked goats, collected hens' eggs, and harvested ripened tomatoes, cucumbers, bell peppers, spinach, sweet potatoes, and apples. Tomorrow morning would be more of the same. She'd wake up with the sunrise, shower, dress, and begin moving.

Lauren preferred to eat her breakfast after her morning farm tasks, once she'd worked up an appetite. She sat at the farmhouse kitchen table eating eggs she'd hard-boiled the day before, some goat milk yogurt she'd made, sprinkled with frozen raspberries she'd harvested in June. Sliced tomatoes with goat cheese, cucumbers, carrots, and spinach supplemented her breakfast. *Nothing like nourishing your body with food you've grown outside your door.* Lauren delighted in the crisp, fresh, flavorful produce and dairy from her farm.

When she finished her breakfast and cleaned up the kitchen, she brewed herself a cup of lavender tea, continuing with her morning ritual. Sitting in a rocking chair on the front porch, Lauren sipped her tea, looking out at her property—the stretching green crop fields, chicken coop, goat pen, and fruit trees and bushes. She pulled the blanket over her lap as a crisp breeze blew past. Summer's humidity had officially dissipated. The sun's rays were weaker, the sun itself lower in the sky. Today was the autumn equinox, and nature was making it clear. Autumn had arrived.

It took thirty minutes for Lauren to drink a cup of herbal tea. She used this time to rest, think, meditate, observe—to simply *be*. Thirty-minute tea break was a time Lauren cherished. It was the solace between intense morning chores and continued afternoon labor. Months ago, Lauren had promised herself she would begin daily rituals to help ease her anxiety. Owning and managing a farm was difficult, stressful, and laborious. As a natural worrywart, Lauren discovered she needed to implement coping mechanisms for these difficult emotions. Taking time out every day to sip tea, and do nothing, helped her.

It was also her coveted alone time. Every day at ten a.m. Sage would arrive to assist Lauren in daily farm tasks. Weeding, watering, planting, pulling, hauling, cleaning, maintaining, feeding—the list was endless. Soon, Lauren hoped, when the farm's produce and animals multiplied, Lauren would have to hire more help.

For now, Lauren relied on Sage, whose diligence, tenacity, and nonstop chatter Lauren knew was steadfast.

It was nine forty-five when Lauren spotted a white Mercedes turn off the road and onto her driveway. She sat up straighter, the blanket falling from her lap. *Gemma?*

No, that can't be Gemma. She left. Asher's here. Lauren stood up, spilling steaming hot tea onto the porch. She pulled her hair out of its ponytail, ruffling it up so she could look more presentable. She looked down at her dirt-covered jeans and Wellingtons, unbuttoning the top button on her flannel shirt.

I look like a farm girl, that's for sure. A cute one, I hope. Lauren tried to scrape off a crumbly white stain on her jeans. *Goat's milk. Eww.* Her heart quickened its pace.

Breathe. She did, reaching for her tea. She held it in her hands steadily, taking sips to calm herself. Usually Lauren welcomed unannounced visitors with open arms, ushering them inside to have a cup of tea and a slice of homemade pie. But Asher Wolf? Arriving unannounced when Lauren looked like a field mouse? Not so much.

The car pulled up to the garage, parked. An excruciating moment elapsed before the car doors opened, and Lauren saw Heidi Wolf pop out of the passenger's side, holding two cups of to-go coffee.

"Good morning, Lauren, dear." Heidi waved from the car. She marched to the house, up the stairs, and threw her arms around Lauren, somehow without spilling liquid. Returning Heidi's embrace, Lauren watched Asher amble up the porch steps, hands in his pockets, uncomfortable.

"Good morning," Lauren said. She mustered a weak smile at Asher.

"I hope you don't mind we showed up unannounced?" Heidi asked.

"Oh no, not at all. That's my motivation always to keep my home tidy," Lauren said.

"Your house is a dream. You've got it painted and decorated like I see in all the magazines. You're so talented," Heidi said, handing Lauren a to-go cup. It felt hot and smelled like coffee. "I got you a French roast. Black. Not sure if you wanted to add your own milk."

"Oh, thanks." Lauren held the coffee in one hand and her tea in the other.

Asher still hadn't said a word. He looked lost in thought.

"So, what brings you to the farm this morning?" Lauren asked as warmly as possible. She could feel a burning sensation in her gut. Worry started to climb up each organ in her body. It began in her belly, twisting her insides to make her feel nauseated, and then wrapped itself around her lungs, squeezing her heart. Then it gurgled up like bile into her esophagus, until her eyes and head hurt. No one would ever know it, though. Lauren had perfected the cheery smile, calm surrender of "sure," "no problem," "of course you can." On the outside, she looked perfectly composed. Inside, she was a mess.

"We're not going to stay long—" Asher began, but his mother interrupted.

"Is it all right if we sit down and chat a bit?" Heidi asked.

Lauren looked quickly at Asher, then nodded at Heidi. Heidi opened the front door, stepping inside the foyer, marching into the living and dining rooms. Asher shook his head, slowly following behind Lauren.

"Beautiful. I love it. So simple, so clean and cozy. You're such a good homemaker, Lauren," Heidi said.

"Mom, please stop," Asher said.

"I can't help it," Heidi said, finding the dining room table. Thankfully, Lauren had tidied the house last night. The sturdy, reclaimed barn wood table was cleared off. The tall beeswax candle in the middle was lit. It was another morning ritual. Heidi took a seat at the head of the table. Lauren waited for Asher to find a seat, and then sat across from him, next to Heidi. She planned to avoid eye contact with Asher as much as possible.

"Can I get you something to drink? Or eat? I have some leftover chocolate cheesecake I made two nights ago. Experimenting with the goat milk," Lauren said. Heidi raised her coffee, shaking her head.

Asher shook his head. "I'm good on the stimulants."

Lauren chuckled. Asher's eyes flicked to hers. He smiled back.

"So, we don't want to take too much of your time, but we're hoping you can help Asher plan the wedding. Certainly, I want to help as much as I can, but I have five classes of seniors—two AP English and three honors classes—so as you can imagine the next six weeks will be quite busy teaching them to write their college essays while also writing hundreds of recommendation letters. I simply don't have the time to hold Asher's hand as he plans his wedding. That's why I was hoping *you* could hold his hand," Heidi said.

Asher's eyes went wide as Lauren started to laugh nervously.

"What?" Lauren asked.

Heidi giggled, smacking her forehead. "Oh, you know what I mean."

But Lauren caught Heidi's smirk, and she cleared her throat. "Well, I suppose, I mean... I know Gemma asked me to help yesterday, but... The thing is—I've never planned a wedding before."

"Oh honey, you manage a farm. You can do anything."

Lauren looked at Heidi. Did she truly believe that?

Asher sat up straighter, his eyes dead set on Lauren. "Lauren, listen, you don't have to do this. We're happy to get married on your beautiful property in the first place. So, thank you. But please, don't feel bullied into planning Gemma's—and my—wedding." He stared intensely into Lauren's eyes. She blushed. He blinked, continuing, "And for the record, my mom basically kidnapped me and forced me to drive over, so I'm sorry that we barged in like this."

Heidi gasped, incredulous.

"No, no—not at all," Lauren heard her reflexive response. She'd been irritated, but as soon as Asher apologized, guilt replaced her frustration. *Did I look irritated? I hope they didn't think I was angry.*

"I'm sure I can figure this out on my own. It can't be that hard," Asher said. He looked at his mother, who pursed her lips and looked away.

Lauren looked at them both. "I can help you. That's fine. Harvest season this year won't be too much work. Plus, I could use the extra money." She wondered if she shouldn't have said that. *Was that rude?*

"Yes, they'd pay you for it, Lauren," Heidi said.

Asher nodded.

"Great. Okay. Well, then, sure. I'll help you. I mean—I'll be your wedding planner," Lauren said.

"Lauren, you know that means you and I have to work together. Plan it together." Asher's gaze burned into Lauren.

Her heart thumped wildly. "I know," Lauren said. "If you don't want to—"

"I'm fine with it," Asher said. "But are you sure you'll be?"

That last sentence kicked over Lauren's heart from nervous to angry. Yes, this unfamiliar emotion was certainly anger. *What's that supposed to mean? Will I be fine? And why would he be fine, but I wouldn't?*

She nodded, smiling. "Oh, absolutely." She gritted her teeth, then shifted her gaze to Heidi. "When do we start?"

Heidi beamed, clapping her jewelry-laden hands in victory.

***

When Sage arrived ten minutes later, Heidi had flown the coop, leaving Lauren alone with Asher. Asher waited at the dining room table while Lauren ransacked her office's desk and closet, gathering notebooks, pens, highlighters, and a calendar.

Lauren returned, arms full, into the dining room to see a confused Sage staring at an emotionless Asher.

"Uh… what…?" Sage asked Lauren, who froze, her big eyes wide.

"Oh, hi, Sage. Um, I'm gonna need you to be a team player today. Think you can get a lot of the work done without me?"

Sage stared at Lauren, blinking rapidly. "You mean you want me to clean the coop, the pen, the barn, pasture the hens and goats, and irrigate, pull, plant, and weed by myself? Before nightfall?"

She is so dramatic. It was the last thing Lauren needed at a time like this.

Lauren nodded. "Only for today."

Sage blinked rapidly. "It's the autumn equinox tonight."

Lauren smiled. "Oh wow, that sure arrived fast."

"We're having a party."

Asher's eyebrows raised in surprise, and he chuckled. Lauren looked to Sage, shooting her the stink eye. "Fine. But I'm not gonna plan it—you can."

Sage dropped her drama act and smiled. "Great. Well, then, I better get to work. You two enjoy whatever it is that you're doing." Sage nodded, smiled, and turned on her heel out the door.

Asher shook his head. "She hasn't changed a bit."

"As my grandmother would say, 'She's a card,'" Lauren said, splaying her arms-full of stuff onto the dining room table and sitting down.

"How is your grandma, by the way?" Asher asked, genuinely interested.

Lauren shifted her gaze to the table, pulling out the calendar. "She passed away last summer."

"Oh, wow. I'm so sorry, Lauren." Asher intuitively reached his hand across the table but stopped short of touching Lauren's hand.

She looked at him. "Me too."

Silence filled the room. Lauren thought of her grandmother. She had adored Asher. The old version. Lauren realized she had no idea who Asher had become in the past seven years since he'd moved to New York. He could be a different person now. It seemed that way if he was with someone like Gemma. Her grandma had often said, "Find a boy who treats his mother well. If he's good to his mother, he'll be good to you." And Asher was a good son, even when Heidi overstepped her boundaries as she did that morning.

"How are your parents?" Asher asked.

"They're good, still working. The businesses are doing well. I sell my goat milk chocolate at my mom's confectionary."

Asher raised his eyebrows. "Wow. You can make chocolate from goat milk?"

Lauren laughed. "And yogurt and cheese."

"You do that?"

"I do a lot of things." Lauren opened a notebook to a clean sheet of paper. "Okay, so first things first..." She looked at Asher. He was staring at her.

"You look... older." He was studying her face.

Lauren blushed. "Um, thanks a lot. Way to make me feel bad."

"No, no—I didn't mean it as an insult."

"Well, you know, aging in our society is apparently the worst thing that can happen to a woman." Lauren rolled her eyes.

"Yeah, that's terrible. And couldn't be further from the truth."

He was still staring at her. Lauren cleared her throat, reaching for her hair, twirling a strand between the fingers on her left hand as she started to write a list with her right hand. "Anyway," she said.

"That's so funny," Asher said.

"What?"

"You still do that. I saw you do that the other day, too."

"Do what?"

"Twirl your hair."

Lauren dropped her hand to her side. "It's a bad habit. I've done it since I was six."

"I know," Asher said, smiling. His eyes scrunched when he smiled. It was almost like they sparkled. Lauren hated that she thought he was so handsome at that moment.

Is he flirting with me? This is bad. Very bad.

"What I meant was, you look more mature. Womanly," Asher said. Then, he waved his hands. "No, no, I don't mean... I'm not talking about... you know." He gestured toward her chest and torso. "I mean, you've grown up. But you look great."

Lauren bit her lip. "Thanks. So have you. I mean, you look great. And grown-up, too."

"Thanks. Stop biting your lip," Asher said.

She stopped immediately. "I have a lot of bad habits."

Asher laughed. "Do you do drugs? Steal? Get into bar fights?"

"What? No." Lauren sounded horrified.

"Then biting your lips and twirling your hair doesn't seem to be too bad of a habit to me." He smiled.

Lauren nodded. Beginning her list, she wrote the number one on the piece of paper, then looked up. "Wait. Do you do drugs or steal or get into bar fights?"

Asher chuckled. "No." He thought for a moment. "But it's not uncommon for some of the people I know to do that. Anything goes in the city."

That made Lauren feel weird. Old Asher was pure and innocent. They used to drink underage—sure. Who didn't? But looking back, Lauren realized how pure and good they were, especially for kids who'd grown up in a small town with nothing to do. She imagined a scene in New York—grimy, smelly, dark, scary. Why would Asher want to live there when he could live in a place surrounded by beauty and goodness?

"Aren't you going to ask me how *my* family is?" Asher asked with a smirk.

"I already know how your brothers and parents are. I see them all the time." She shook her head, smiling. "Okay, Asher. Enough. We need to make a list."

"Make a list of what?"

"I don't know? All I know is usually when you start a project, you make a list."

Lauren looked at Asher. He suddenly looked like the Asher she knew. Slightly mischievous, incredibly sweet—he had a quiet troublemaker vibe to him.

"That's true. Well, what do we need to do first? My mom said something about invitations?"

"Great. You have the date. And the venue. So now we need to invite everyone. How many people are you inviting?"

"How many people can your barn hold?"

Lauren had no idea. She'd never hosted an event there before. Well, okay, that wasn't true. She'd hosted Thanksgiving last year, but that only included twenty people, maximum—her parents, aunts, uncles, cousins, Sage, and Will. She knew she'd been to weddings in barns that held one hundred and fifty guests. Maybe she could host more? They could spill out to the land outside the barn. Easy.

"Two hundred?"

Asher widened his eyes. "Wow. That's good, though. We'll have at least two hundred for the reception. I'm sure more of the town will show up for the ceremony. Which won't be in the barn...right?"

"I don't know. What do you want?"

"No, no. It's not about what I want. It's about what Gemma wants."

Lauren nodded. "Oh. Well, sure. Whatever she wants." Lauren paused. "You think the whole town will want to see you guys get married?"

Asher almost looked offended. "Yeah, why wouldn't they?"

"Oh, no reason. I don't know. Just asking." But Lauren wondered what the town thought of Gemma. Or what they would think. Or maybe Lauren was hoping that they would oppose the marriage of Gemma and Asher, considering Gemma wasn't Lauren. *No. Don't think that way. That's mean. What do you care, anyway? You should want others to be happy, not miserable.* Lauren wasn't a competitive person, yet she felt aggressive feelings begin to rise within her.

"Where do we get invitations?"

"There's a card shop in town. Or we can order online. What are your colors?"

"My colors?" Asher looked down at his shirt, pants.

"For the wedding? Your theme?"

Asher looked up, bewildered. "I have no idea what that means."

Lauren sighed. "Okay, this is going to be harder than I thought."

"Are you serious?" Asher brought his hand to his forehead. "I don't want to do this. I mean, there are so many other things I'd rather be doing right now."

A stabbing pain seized Lauren's heart. *Ouch.* She said nothing, but she felt the sinking feeling of hurt push down on her.

"Sorry. I didn't mean that I don't want to be here with you," Asher started, but he stopped.

"No, it's fine. I get it," Lauren said. "It's okay."

She waited, hoping he'd continue. But he didn't. *Maybe he did mean that.*

Lauren started to jot a list onto the blank page. "Here, these are some things you can do on your own, without me. On your own time. Why don't you begin on those, and I'll begin on the others." Lauren handed him the list. Asher was to find out their colors, theme, the exact number of guests, and guest list from Gemma and report back to him. Her list included preparing multiple options for the dinner and dessert menus.

Asher looked at his list. "I think I can do this."

Lauren stood. "Great. So then you can go home and get started on it. You don't have to waste any more time here."

Asher looked up at her, his eyes sad. "It's not a waste, I didn't mean—"

"Okay, well, I have to go help out Sage now, so have a great rest of your day." Lauren pushed in her chair and turned around.

"Um," Asher stood, "you're having a party tonight?"

Lauren continued into the kitchen. "Yep."

"Can I come?"

"Sure. Of course," Lauren said.

"Thanks." Asher walked to the kitchen archway. "Well, then, see you later. Thanks for your help, Lauren. I appreciate it."

She looked at him, nodding.

"I honestly do," he said. Asher turned, leaving through the foyer, out the door, closing it gently behind him.

Lauren peered through the kitchen windows, holding back tears, watching him start up the Mercedes and drive away.

***

Lauren bribed Jackie and Kip, the two-year-old female goat, back to the pen with carrots. They had jumped and leaped and run their little goat hearts out, and it was time for dinner. They bleated for food, nearly knocking Lauren over as she dumped a bucket full of leftovers. Ugly vegetables and mushy fruit, grains, and pellets were fed to goats who'd eat anything.

Lauren appreciated their low-maintenance lifestyle. Goats were fun-loving, easygoing, and endlessly curious. They were able to entertain themselves. And they didn't judge her.

"You don't think I'm crazy, do you?" Lauren asked Jackie and Kip, who affectionately jumped on her between devouring the bucket of food. "I mean, you like spending time with me, right? Why would Asher say that, anyway? That's so rude."

"Say what?" Sage's voice startled Lauren. Embarrassed, she grinned as she turned to view Sage.

"What? Nothing."

Sage narrowed her eyes. "So why was Ol' Blue Eyes over anyway? That's kind of weird, don't you think?"

"Weird, how? He came over because I'm helping him."

"Helping him with what?"

"Helping him plan his wedding."

"What?" Sage brought her hands to her head. "Like today or?"

"I'm their wedding planner." Lauren grimaced, anticipating Sage's response.

"Are you nuts?" Sage closed her eyes. "Seriously, Lauren, what are you thinking?"

Lauren stood, hurrying out of the pen and locking it before the rascals could escape. She started walking away, but Sage stopped her.

"Uh, hello? Are you gonna answer that question?"

Lauren looked at Sage. "No, Sage, I'm not nuts, thanks for asking."

"Lauren, we both know how hard that breakup was for you. It's bad enough they're getting married on your farm, but now you're planning the wedding?"

"I've told you a thousand times I'm over him. That was a long time ago. I've moved on."

"So, you're friends now? Totally cool?" Sage asked, walking alongside Lauren.

"That's right."

"You're cool that the guy you were dating for, like, seven years, the guy you were gonna marry, who ghosted you when he went to grad school—"

"He didn't ghost me. Wait, what's ghosting again?" Lauren asked.

"Ghosting is when you stop talking to someone. Ignore them. Don't respond. You never call them back, they fall off the face of the earth. You know, like what Asher did to you."

"Oh," Lauren said, heading toward the barn, Sage on her heels.

"Yeah, it's ridiculous. Seven years together. He heads to New York for grad school. Says it'll be a quick two years, and then he'll be back home. Two years long distance is nothing, right? Didn't he say that?" Sage waited for Lauren to nod, then continued, "And you guys chatted a bit when he got there, then suddenly—radio silence. Nothing. Am I correctly retelling this part of history?"

"You're quite the historian, that's for sure."

Lauren unexpectedly stopped at the front entrance of the barn. Sage bumped into her.

"And have you ever talked to him about it? Ever found out what happened?"

"No."

Sage looked like she was going to burst a blood vessel in her head. "Seriously. You've never spoken to him since?"

Lauren's eyes shifted to Sage's. "I don't remember exactly what happened, Sage. I think we simply stopped talking. A distance grew between us. He stopped answering my phone calls, and when he came home for Christmas, he avoided me. After that first year, I stopped trying. I didn't want to look desperate. Then, years went on, and I never saw him in town. He moved to New York. I'd see him in church on Christmas but I avoided him. That's it—until now."

Sage brought her fist to her mouth, looking like a stooge. "How the hell did you not confront him? Say something?" She shook her head. "I'd be pounding on his door. Slashing his tires. Something— anything. Don't you want answers?"

Lauren was silent. She stared at the barn doors. A heavy sadness started to consume her, and she didn't want any part of it.

"What would he say? And what would that do? It's over. There's no turning back. He found someone new. Obviously that's why he stopped talking to me. He was in New York City, where he had access to much prettier girls. Much thinner girls. Much more interesting girls. Why would any guy stick with his country bumpkin when he had the world at his fingertips?" Lauren almost couldn't believe she said that. But she'd said it to Sage. The only person to whom she ever expressed negative emotions.

At first, Sage frowned, awash with sympathy. Then, her eyes glowed with anger.

"That is such crap, Lauren. You don't believe that, do you? You're not a country bumpkin. I mean, what is that, anyway? You're beautiful, smart, and wonderful. Please, don't say crap like that ever again."

Lauren mustered a smile, but she felt honest feelings bubbling up. "You saw Gemma. Look at me, Sage. Do I look anything like Gemma?"

"That chick's a freak." Sage looked like she could have a brain aneurysm at any moment. "Stop, would you?"

Lauren turned to the barn. "Sorry. This is stupid and a waste of time. What we need to focus on is the barn. Look at this hovel. Yuck," Lauren said, stepping into the massive space. It was dark, save for the slivers of sunlight creeping through cracks of wood, illuminating cobwebs and dust dancing throughout the air.

"I mean… it's kind of cool…" Sage said, entering the barn.

A flutter of wings spooked them, and they ran out screaming.

"What was that?" Sage ducked, looking in all directions.

Lauren looked to the sky. "A bat. It was a bat."

Reentering the barn, the two crept around its interior, surveying required repairs.

Sage sighed. "So we have to get this dump in wedding venue shape in less than six weeks?"

"Yep." Lauren sighed, too. Then she smiled. "I have an idea."

***

Nightfall arrived around seven-thirty that evening. As she pulled a rolling cooler of drinks behind her, Lauren stared up at the sky, enchanted by the bursts of fuchsia, tangerine, and amethyst that marbled the clouds above the horizon. The best sunrises and sunsets, Lauren had discovered, were when cirrus clouds streaked the sky, allowing the sun's rays to paint the white clouds like a canvas, displaying its many colors. On nights with clear skies, there wasn't much sunset to see. On nights with cloudy skies, there was the right amount of cloud cover to offer witness to a perfect display of nature's art. That night, the sun, clouds, and sky had cooperated to present Lauren with a colorful masterpiece.

She was grateful for the little things. Living on a farm, there were plenty of little things to bemoan. Inclement weather, critters and pests, endless labor, rotten plants, stubborn barnyard animals. There were also plenty of little things to celebrate. Gorgeous sunrises and sunsets, the scent of wildflowers outside her doorstep, fresh produce and dairy, peace and solitude. Lauren reveled in the melancholy retrospection of autumn as much as she welcomed the rebirth of spring.

But could she ever live this life single? Could she continue to find joy in the little things solo? Would these tiny delights become gargantuan reminders that she was alone?

"DANCING IN THE MOONLIGHT."

Lauren jumped, bass booming, reverberating against the walls of the barn she'd entered. Sage turned the button on the speakers, the music's volume lowered.

"Sorry." Sage cringed, finding a reasonable volume for the music.

"Well, at least we know the speakers work. Where'd you get those anyway?" Lauren set the cooler next to a table.

"Will let me borrow them. You know, since he's not using them." Sage rolled her eyes.

"Did his band break up?"

"His band never even got together. He spent thousands of dollars on speakers, amps, a PA system, microphones—not to mention an electric guitar—and his 'band' still hasn't gotten together once."

"Well, at least they're being used," Lauren said. "Hey—maybe he could be the wedding DJ?"

"You mean for Asher and Gemma's wedding?"

"Yeah. That's one vendor less I have to scout," Lauren said.

Sage frowned. "Yeah, I'll ask."

Lauren looked around the barn. The music was set up, the drinks, appetizers, and snacks—the easy stuff, although Lauren didn't know how Sage was able to figure out the speaker system by herself. The rest—the whole turning-the-barn-into-a-wedding-venue—Lauren hoped that would happen organically after laying some guilt trips on her guests that night.

By eight o'clock, twenty of their closest friends had shown up, including Will, Lukas, his fiancée Cora, a striking dark-haired, tan-skinned beauty, and Jacob. Lauren let Sage plan the event, which mostly included a lot of eating and drinking and dancing under the harvest moon, which happened to be big and orange that equinox night.

Lauren had other plans. By nine-thirty, as she watched everyone dance and enjoy themselves, she sauntered off to the side of the barn, grabbing brooms and dustpans, mops and buckets. Surely everyone would be happy to help, right?

"Hope I'm not too late," Lauren heard as she juggled mops and brooms and buckets in her hands. She turned to see Asher, the moonlight reflecting against his eyes.

"Oh, hi. You came."

"What are you doing?" Asher asked, instinctively grabbing stuff out of her hands to help.

"Well, I was thinking of killing two birds with one stone," she began. "The barn needs cleaning, and many hands make light work."

Asher laughed. He peeked his head into the barn, then returned his gaze to Lauren.

"You think all those people having fun dancing and drinking are going to stop everything to clean a barn?"

Lauren shrugged.

"Forever the optimist," Asher said.

"There's no harm in asking." Lauren left his side to enter the bright barn, noticing the twinkling white Christmas lights Sage had wrapped around wood beams. She could begin to feel the prickling sensation of annoyance dance down her spine. *Who does he think he is?* She made sure to stand as far away from him as possible as she waited for the current song to finish. Then, she turned the volume as low as possible, smiling as all faces turned to her. "Hey, everyone. Hope you're enjoying the autumn solstice."

"Equinox," Asher and Sage said in unison.

"Right. Equinox. So, we can continue to dance all night long, but I thought it'd be great if everyone could sort of help to sweep up some cobwebs and wash down the floors and..." Lauren trailed off, noticing the open mouths and furrowed brows on the many faces before her. She'd killed the vibe.

Sage shook her head, then looked over at a bin full of Christmas lights that hadn't been hung. "Uh, actually—I think you have the tasks out of order, Lauren. We were gonna ask everyone to help with the Christmas lights, remember?" Her grin suggested Lauren play along.

Lauren looked at the bin, then at the many wood beams and arches that could be made magical looking with white lights.

"Right. My bad," she said.

Sage nodded, turning up the music. She threw strings of lights to guests, who slowly returned to their groove, throwing strings of lights over beams while they danced and sang to the music.

Another save by Sage.

Lauren felt miserable. She had no idea what she was doing. Everything felt out of her control. How could she be a leader, a manager, when she was completely clueless?

She twisted open a bottle of pumpkin-flavored beer, guzzling it down.

"Told you." Asher sidled up to her and smirked.

Scowling, Lauren turned her back, grabbing not one, but two chocolate chip cookies. They were store-bought and not nearly as good as the cookies she baked, but she devoured them regardless. Anything to keep her from talking to Asher.

"I'm surprised Gemma said yes on the spot to this place," he said, craning his neck to get a full view of the barn. Lauren took another glug of beer. "I guess she's always been good at seeing potential. Plus, she's a visual artist, I suppose, so she sees things differently than I do." He paused. "Wait, you've had how many weddings here before? The floor is... and the walls... I ... What sort of weddings—"

Lauren had had enough. With a mouthful of cookies, she snapped, "Beautiful weddings. I'm sorry it's not up to your standards, but it's a beautiful barn. It's fully functional, too. It might not be some elite, stunning New York hotel, but it's beautiful in its own way." She took a breath.

"Everything okay over here?" Jacob approached, standing beside her.

"Yeah, of course," Asher said, miffed.

Concerned, Jacob looked to Lauren. Heat rose from her feet to her forehead. Guilt and shame immediately washed over her. Had she made a scene? Was she acting dramatic? She'd lied, and that was enough to be upset about.

"Everything's fine. I think I'm tired. I'm gonna go to bed. Jacob, tell the guests they don't have to clean. Let them enjoy the night instead. But can you make sure Sage doesn't burn down the place?" She laughed.

"You can count on me. What time would you like everyone out?" Jacob took a step closer to her, reaching over to the table to grab a cookie. His shoulder brushed hers. Lauren stepped back as he brought the cookie to his mouth, nonchalantly inching closer to her. He stood next to her and across from Asher. Immediately, Lauren sensed tension between the two. Then she realized it was coming mostly from Jacob.

Lauren looked around. "Oh, um... midnight?"

"And what about Asher? Should I throw him out now?" Jacob bit into his cookie, grinning. Asher narrowed his eyes, cocking his head, puzzled.

Laughing, Lauren smacked Jacob's bicep, hoping to stop whatever it was he was trying to start. "Oh, stop. Asher's only being Asher."

"Arrogant? Self-serving?" Jacob's grin intensified, his beard rising with it, little cookie crumbs falling off his facial hair to the ground below.

"Dude. What's up with you?" Asher stepped closer.

Jacob laughed, popping the rest of the cookie in his mouth. "Nothing. What's up with you?"

Asher was quiet. He looked around the room, then at Lauren. "I think I am going to go. I've got a lot of work to catch up on. I'll call you tomorrow." He took a long, hard look at the ever-grinning Jacob, saying, "See ya later, man." And then Asher turned on his heel and was out the door.

Jacob's grin faded and his eyes softened. "What's he up to?"

"What do you mean?"

"I don't know, Lauren. I don't trust the guy. I never have," he said.

"You don't trust Asher?" Incredulous, Lauren chuckled at the thought.

Jacob opened his mouth, about to say more, but instead, he shut it. He smiled sweetly. "I'll make sure everyone's out by midnight. Good night, Lauren."

As he walked away, Lauren wondered what he knew that she didn't. Jacob had always been so sweet to her, and she'd rejected him. Throughout high school, she'd always known Jacob had a crush on her. Over the past seven years, he'd gotten close to asking Lauren out, but had been thwarted every time, either by another guy at the bar, or by Lauren finding a way out. She knew he liked her. But she was an avoider. And she'd make sure she avoided his advances until the day she died. Although she hoped it wouldn't come to that.

She finished the rest of her beer, throwing the can in the trash, and walking away from the barn. Putting a smile on her face was easy, but dancing under the full moon with friends wasn't gonna happen that night. As she walked away from the barn and toward her house, the music faded, but her smile remained—as long as someone was enjoying her homestead, she was a happy girl.

Chapter Four

Asher

"The big fish has returned to his little pond," Duke Wolf said as he stood in the doorway of Asher's childhood bedroom. Asher sat on his bed, typing away at his laptop.

He looked up, smiling at his oldest brother who, he'd noticed, had gained a little bit of weight since he last saw him at Easter.

"But now he's a little fish in a little pond," said Tyler Wolf, arriving in the doorway.

Tyler was eighteen months younger than Duke and looked like a shorter, leaner version of his older brother. Still, Tyler was taller and stockier than Asher, which meant that as teens, when Duke and Tyler got together to roughhouse with Asher, Asher never stood a chance. The three brothers had their beautiful, sapphire eyes in common, but Tyler, unlike his older and younger brother, had sandy brown hair instead of black.

"I'm a little fish now? How do you reckon that?" Asher asked, closing his laptop and rising from the bed.

"Tyler has a habit of blurting things out," Duke said, walking into the room to pat Asher on the back.

"What? But you said—" Tyler started, but then closed his mouth. He gave Asher a head nod.

"So what's up, bro?" Duke asked. "Mom said you're planning a wedding."

"Lame," Tyler said, looking for approval from Duke, which he was not granted.

"Sorta. We hired a wedding planner to do most of it. I'm going to be making decisions. Approving things," Asher said. He faced his brothers, standing taller, his voice an octave lower than usual.

"So why're you still in town? Can't you make decisions from New York?" Duke asked.

"Yeah?" Tyler echoed.

"It's complicated," Asher said. "Anyway, what's up with you guys? How's the construction business? And your wives? Sarah hasn't realized her grave mistake yet, Ty?"

"Shut up." Tyler crossed his arms.

"Look at that," Duke said, crossing the room and heading straight to a bulletin board. He unclipped a photo, staring at it. Tyler quickened to his side. Sometimes Asher felt like they were twins, and he was an only child. He loved his brothers, but he was glad he wasn't a third copy of them. "I haven't been in here in years, and I don't remember seeing this photo. Look at how scrawny you were."

Fine, he'd give in and humor Duke. He walked to where they stood, peering over Duke's broad shoulders to see the photo he cradled. It was Asher, after his final college baseball game—state championships. He'd hit the winning run. Suddenly flooded with nostalgia, Asher couldn't help but smile as he remembered the scene. He'd felt like a hero, leading his college baseball team to win the state championships. He'd been going to graduate soon. And he had the most beautiful, loving girlfriend standing next to him, her pride to be his evident in her bright eyes and glowing smile.

But nostalgia had two parts, bitter and sweet. After his eyes lingered on Lauren's in the photo, the bitter seized him.

Tyler laughed. "I can't believe Mom hasn't turned this room into a craft room or something. She turned my room into her office the day after I moved out."

"She loves me more," Asher couldn't help but mutter. He laughed, trying to ease Tyler once he saw his brother's eyes narrow.

"Dinner's ready," Heidi called from the bottom of the stairs.

Tyler turned on his heel and was out the door, but Duke waited, his eyes lingering on the photo. Asher looked to him, wondering what he was thinking.

"Always loved Lauren Anderson," Duke finally said. He looked up, handing the photo back to Asher. His lips parted, but as quickly as they opened, he smacked them shut, turning around and lumbering out of Asher's room as he muttered, "I'm starving."

The entire bulletin board was filled with pictures like that one. Asher and Lauren on graduation day, Asher and Lauren dressed as vampires for Halloween, Asher and Lauren in front of a Christmas tree. Why hadn't he taken these down yet? Had Gemma ever noticed these, and if she had, why hadn't she said anything? Asher grabbed each photo, one by one, and hurled them onto his bed. Soon, a tall pile formed—a glossy, thin tower that eventually toppled over, splaying across his bed.

After the bulletin board was clear of photos, Asher dug his fingers into the tacks that upheld medals and ribbons—First Place, All Star, Champion. Every reminder of his big-fish, little-pond days was soon dumped onto his bed, sinking into his comforter. He spun around, his eyes scanning the blue painted walls and mahogany shelving units for more of his past he wanted to discard. Trophies and photo albums—full of pictures of him and Lauren—and yearbooks and signed baseballs all were dumped into the middle of his bed until his walls and shelves were half empty.

Whether Asher was a big fish or a little fish didn't matter. He had to get out of this pond before he drowned in it.

***

"Tyler, eat that last piece of broccoli or you won't get any apple pie," Heidi demanded as she sliced into the gooey, cinnamon-scented masterpiece she'd placed in the middle of the dining room table.

"Mom. I'm thirty-four," Tyler said, taking a swig of beer.

"So? You still need to eat vegetables. And it doesn't change the rules in this house. No dessert until your plate is clean," Heidi said.

Tyler rolled his eyes, shoving the last piece of broccoli in his mouth as Duke and Fred laughed at him. Asher was silent.

"You guys finally finish the bridge on Morningside Lane?" Fred asked Duke and Tyler.

"Last week. Finally won't have to worry about a semi cracking the old bridge in half," Duke said.

Tyler added, "This week, we started restoring the historic Jackson mansion."

Fred's eyes glistened as a slight smile crept across his face. He was proud.

"Isn't it so rewarding to look at something you created, to see your finished product—something you made with your own bare hands?" he asked his sons. His two oldest nodded, proud grins spread across their faces.

Asher looked at the slice of pie his mother had placed before him. It looked delicious. But he wasn't hungry.

"There is nothing more masculine than that," Fred nodded. "No sir."

Asher caught Heidi staring at him. She sent him a soft, warm smile, then turned to her oldest sons.

"How's the pie?" she asked.

"Delicious," Duke said.

Tyler had scarfed down his. "Great. Thanks, Mom."

Duke stood. "Yeah, thanks, but I'd better get going. Jenny has been having a horrible time putting down the boys this week. They discovered jumping on the bed," he sighed. Tyler rose, too.

"Yeah, and Sarah will be getting home soon from shopping. Thanks for dinner," he said, kissing his mother's forehead. Duke did the same.

"See ya, bro," Tyler ruffled Asher's hair, as Duke approached, placing a hand on Asher's shoulder.

"You'll be around for a while?" he asked.

Asher nodded.

"Great. Let's grab a beer this weekend."

"Sounds good," Asher said, watching them leave. Tweedledee and Tweedledum, he used to call them, but only in his mind. If he ever said that out loud he'd be missing teeth. After the door shut, Asher turned to see his father had already gotten up from the table, but his mother remained. She looked at him knowingly.

Then, without saying anything, she rose, carrying dirty dishes to the kitchen, leaving Asher alone with his thoughts.

Before he went to sleep that evening, Asher stuffed every relic he had thrown onto his bed into a rubber bin. He hauled it into his closet and closed the door. He wasn't ready to throw it in the garbage yet, but he no longer wanted those items haunting him, watching him while he slept.

***

It was Wednesday afternoon when Asher finally texted Lauren, even though Monday evening he'd said he'd call her Tuesday. He hadn't. He'd been busy with work and dinner with his siblings and hadn't thought being a day late mattered. Lauren hadn't contacted him either, so she probably wasn't put out, but Asher never could be sure. She was famous for masking her true feelings.

When Asher arrived at Lauren's farm, the sun was dipping lower into the horizon. It would set in an hour or so. Lauren was waiting for him on her porch, sitting on a rocking chair, cradling a ceramic mug, which he assumed held hot tea. Her thick mane was braided to one side, revealing her elegant collarbone, which appeared even daintier as it was dwarfed by her chunky, wool knit sweater that hung to her mid-thighs. She was wearing black yoga pants—or were they called leggings? Asher wasn't sure. Whatever they were called, they were those pants that most men found appealing. Her brown leather boots looked cute on her, too.

Come on, Asher. Stop it.

But she looked good. Cute. Sweet. A beautiful farm girl. Farm woman, rather. Could he think she was attractive without being attracted *to* her? Could he simply think she was objectively good-looking? Couldn't he believe her clothes flattered her? Come on. He could think that, right? He thought that about his mother and—ugh—he was not attracted *to* his mother. So, yes. He wasn't doing anything wrong. It was simply true. And he vowed he'd stop thinking about it.

As Asher climbed the stairs, she rose to greet him.

"Would you like a cup of tea?" she asked with a smile.

"No, I'm good, thanks."

"Okay," she said. "Should we go in?"

Asher nodded, gesturing "after you," following behind her. She led him to the couch, where she made herself comfortable as she grabbed a stack of computer paper. "So, I finally made those lists we tried writing the other day." She looked up at him. Asher was still standing. "You can sit down, you know."

Immediately, Asher sat. His arm brushed Lauren's. "Sorry," he said. She ignored him, handing him the list. There were pages and pages of to-do items, under which each item was defined in thorough detail. "Uh… this is all stuff we have to do?"

"Well, yeah. Who else is gonna do it?"

"Find tables?" Asher asked, flipping through the stack. "What does that mean?"

"We have to get tables and chairs for the barn. For the reception."

Asher nodded, then frowned. "Wait, why not use the tables you used for all the other weddings you hosted here?"

Lauren's eyes widened ever so slightly. She nodded, looking away. "Sure. But, I mean, I had to order them from somewhere. I don't own them."

"So order them again. Let's cross that off the list."

Lauren's hand swatted away Asher's after he began to cross the action item off the list. "No."

"Geez. Okay…"

"I mean," she said, shaking her head, "don't cross off any task until it's completed."

Asher stared at her. What was that about? She was acting jumpy.

"Have you decided on your colors yet? Did you talk to Gemma?"

Crap. Asher had a feeling he'd forget something. He had talked to Gemma the day before, but not for more than a few minutes, and she did most of the talking.

"Not yet. Can't we pick colors we know she'll love? There's gotta be some safe color scheme out there. Or colors that look good on us?" Asher asked.

Lauren smiled softly. "That's a good idea. It'll be an autumn wedding. Why not boysenberry and navy with some gray? Or grape and walnut?"

"Are these colors or items on the menu?"

"The menu," Lauren said, her eyes bugging out.

"Oh, so it is the menu?"

"No, no." She waved her hands. "I mean, no—these are colors. Names of colors I think would be beautiful for the wedding. I said menu because I realized I forgot to work on that." She sighed. "There's so much."

"Well, how have you handled this every other time you hosted a wedding on the farm?" Asher asked.

She opened her mouth, but nothing came out. "Well, I wasn't the wedding planner. I only had to host it. The wedding planner did everything."

"Oh." Asher nodded. "Can we look at the space again? Where the ceremony and reception will be held?"

"Sure," Lauren said, looking relieved. She returned the lists to the coffee table, leaving her mug of tea beside it.

They were quiet as they walked out of the house and down the pathway toward the barn. Goats bleated in the distance, overpowering the clucking of hens. Arriving at the barn, Asher and Lauren stopped, turning to each other.

"So, the ceremony will be on the lawn next to the barn?" Asher asked.

"That's right. Gemma wasn't specific, but I thought we could put a pergola up, wrap it in garland and flowers. Set up chairs. Maybe even set the pergola against the side of the barn. Have the old barn wood as the backdrop, rather than the fields. There are plenty of options."

"And what happens if it rains?" Asher asked, looking up at the current cloudy skies. "Or snows?" He looked to Lauren. She was so tiny compared to him. Her petite frame and her agreeable personality—palm-sized, he used to tell her.

"Then we'd have to move the ceremony into the barn."

"What would everyone do between the ceremony teardown and reception setup?"

"We could have a tent outside," Lauren said, but it almost sounded like a question. "Maybe cocktails outside under the tent while we switch over for the reception?"

"Okay," Asher said, nodding. "And you've got staff to do all that work?"

Lauren's face flushed. "I'll have to hire them."

"How many do you usually employ for a wedding of our size?"

Lauren looked like she was doing mental gymnastics. Then she replied, "Fifteen?"

Asher raised an eyebrow. "Is that a question or a statement?"

Lauren nervously laughed. "Asher, can you please stop interrogating me?"

"Interrogating? I'm asking you questions. Aren't you used to this? This is business, Lauren. You gotta toughen up," he heard himself say. Ugh. Did he truly say that? He sounded like one of his brothers. Or his dad, or someone from his office back in New York.

Lauren looked incredulous.

"I'm sorry." Asher stepped closer to her.

Lauren looked away, blinking repeatedly. Was she crying? Had Asher made her cry? He wanted to slap himself upside the head.

"Lauren?"

"No, it's fine. I get it. And you're right. I should be working on my pitches. Or have some list memorized or something." She turned away, cleared her throat, then spun around, looking up at him with a smile. "So, yeah. I'll be able to answer your questions more thoroughly soon. Any other thoughts on the barn?"

Asher looked at the barn. "It looks a little… unfinished."

"That's because it is. We're going to refinish the floors and clean it out. Hang some chandeliers. All that jazz." She smiled widely.

"Okay. Yeah. I think it'll be great," he said. "So, what's the first thing we need to do? I think my mom mentioned something about invitations?"

"That's right. We need to send out invitations. But first, we need to know your colors and theme."

Asher nodded, pulling out his phone. "Let me try to call Gemma and ask." He dialed the Japanese number, and it rang. "This costs a fortune, by the way." He smirked. Lauren smiled back. It went to voicemail. "Hey, Gem. Gimme a call back. I need to know our colors." He hung up.

Lauren nodded. "Great. While we're waiting for her to call you back, let's head to Mrs. Kelley's card and gift shop. She'll have plenty of invitations to choose from."

"Sounds good. After you," Asher said, gesturing for her to walk ahead. She rolled her eyes with a smile, heading toward the garage.

***

Lauren spent the entire ride into town marveling over Gemma's car with its slick, white leather interior and technologically savvy dashboard. Proving Asher's theory true, Lauren admitted to him she still drove the jalopy her parents gave her years ago because it was great for a farmer's market haul. She told him she felt she could never justify owning a fancy car at her age or salary. Asher wanted to inquire more about Lauren's salary, her farm life, and her overall goals with this laborious career she was pursuing, but after his "toughen up" comment, he figured he'd give his critical tongue a rest.

Mrs. Kelley's card and gift shop was located at the corner of Main Street, next to the ice cream shop owned by Lauren's mother. As he entered the shop, Asher guessed Mrs. Kelley to be almost eighty years old but he was surprised to see how young she still looked. As a child, he'd come into the shop looking for birthday and Mother's Day gifts for his mother. Stuffed bears and singing flowers lined Heidi's mantelpiece for years. As a teenager, Asher had frequently stopped at Mrs. Kelley's in search of Valentine's chocolates and sappy cards for his girlfriend, who happened to be the same woman with whom he'd entered the shop.

"It's my favorite young couple," Mrs. Kelley called from the cash register. She held a pen with a pink, feathery poof at the top, which she waved as she looked at them over her bright green, cat-eyed eyeglasses.

Lauren turned around to give Asher a look. It was one of those "Are you gonna tell her or should I?" looks.

"Hi there, Mrs. Kelley," Lauren said as she approached the glass counter Mrs. Kelley was already rounding, arms open. She embraced Lauren, looking over at Asher as she did.

"Asher Wolf, it has been ages." The tiny woman let go of Lauren and wrapped her arms around Asher's torso.

"How've you been, Mrs. Kelley? You look great," Asher said as Mrs. Kelley let go.

"Well, thank you. I credit chocolate and wine for my youthful skin." She winked at Lauren. "How can I help you two?"

"Wedding invitations," Lauren said, wincing in anticipation.

"Oh." Mrs. Kelley clasped her hands together in sheer joy. "I've been waiting for this day."

"No, it's not what you think," Asher tried to interject, but Mrs. Kelley's eyes were closed, her lips were pursed in a perpetual smile as if she were praying then and there. "It's not *our* wedding."

Lauren looked at him, smirking. "We're gonna be here all day," she said, laughing. Asher laughed back, grateful Lauren wasn't melting with embarrassment. In fact, she was almost giggling, finding it funny. Maybe it was only Asher who felt slightly embarrassed, whose body temperature was rising, and throat closing up. He confessed he didn't find it entertaining to have to explain to Mrs. Kelley that he and Lauren were not going to be wed. But why?

Asher didn't have time to wallow in his confusion. Lauren clapped her hands, waking Mrs. Kelley from her daydream.

"Now, Mrs. Kelley, we're going to need you to focus here. We have quite a few tasks we need to accomplish before you close, which is soon—" Lauren quickly checked the clock on the wall. It was almost seven o'clock, closing time.

Mrs. Kelley's eyes flung open. She looked at Lauren with an exaggerated look of surprise. Memories flashed into Asher's mind. He'd forgotten it was Mrs. Kelley who had volunteered every year to direct the high school musical. She was a dramatic woman by nature. Asher found dramatic women—dramatic people in general—exhausting.

"Asher and I are not getting married. We broke up years ago," Lauren said without much emotion. The words stung Asher's heart, but the way she so flippantly explained the facts bothered him more. "And you know that," Lauren said, sending Mrs. Kelley a serious frown.

Mrs. Kelley fluttered her eyelashes, sighing heavily. "I know, I know. But a woman can dream, can't she?"

Lauren stifled a smile as she went on. "Asher is marrying Gemma Turner, and she's wonderful. I'm helping Asher plan his wedding," Mrs. Kelley grimaced, but Lauren ignored it. "We need to purchase invitations tonight. Can you please show us your wedding invitations?"

Mrs. Kelley nodded silently, gesturing for them to follow her as she ambled over to the wedding planning section of her shop. Asher felt like his senses were being assaulted. Bright white crepe, cards, bells, silver and gold and pink and every color imaginable were flashing, hanging, bursting out of the wall at him. There was so much stuff.

"What is all of this?" Asher muttered, bringing his hand to his forehead. "It's so bright."

"Wedding decorations," Lauren said.

"Here are the different invitations I have. Formal," Mrs. Kelley pointed to a package of invitations written in calligraphy that included tissue paper, although Asher wasn't sure why tissue paper was necessary for an invitation, "modern," Mrs. Kelley pointed to a package of invitations that were written casually, "and something in between."

Lauren looked to Asher. "In between," they said in unison.

Mrs. Kelley smirked. "All right. Now, what colors would you like?"

Asher looked at the packages. There were all sorts of color combinations. How could he possibly decide?

"Yes. The navy and cranberry color would be so beautiful," Lauren exclaimed. "Navy would look great with your skin tone, and cranberry is such a beautiful harvest color." Lauren's eyes glimmered with excitement.

"Sure. I like those colors," Asher said.

"You know, I thought you could wear a navy suit. And the groomsmen, too. Then brown shoes. We'd be able to use the walnut color I mentioned before. Yes, yes, this is going to be beautiful."

"Oh, honey, I agree. Navy suits, cranberry ties. Cranberry dresses on the bridesmaids. A bouquet of yellow and orange and jewel-toned flowers." Mrs. Kelley's eyes glazed over as she envisioned this.

Were they drunk? Asher looked between the two women, who seemed to be playing out the wedding in their heads.

"And we can have hay bales and pumpkins. Oh, and mugs of hot apple cider with melting cinnamon sticks waiting for guests as they arrive. And plaid blankets and scarves as wedding favors. And—" Lauren stopped herself, catching Asher's look. He was listening intently. Her passion energized him. "Sorry." She quieted.

"No, no, don't be sorry, Lauren. This is great. I mean, it sounds like a great party to me." He smiled, catching Mrs. Kelley's mischievous gaze.

"I think it sounds like a beautiful wedding. You're lucky Lauren's planning it."

"I agree, Mrs. Kelley," Asher said.

Mrs. Kelley pulled the navy and cranberry themed invitations from the shelf. "There are two hundred invitations in this package," she said, about to hand them over. But she stopped before she let Asher grab them. "I'm invited, right?" She raised an eyebrow.

"Of course," Asher said, chuckling. But he had to admit she was slightly intimidating, and always had been. He feared the theatrics that might ensue if he didn't invite her.

Mrs. Kelley beamed, dropping the package into Asher's hands. He fumbled, not expecting that. She sauntered back to the glass counter where she punched numbers into the cash register. "Sixty-seven dollars, even."

Asher's eyes widened as he walked to the counter with Lauren. He pulled out his credit card. "Not cheap, eh?" He smiled at Mrs. Kelley.

"Pretty reasonable, actually," began Mrs. Kelley, "considering what you'd pay online. Don't forget, you still need to pay for the ink to print them."

Ink? Asher furrowed his brows. "What do you mean?"

Lauren piped up, "We have to type out the wording, then print it onto these invitations."

"What? I thought we simply mail them out?" Asher asked.

Mrs. Kelley couldn't contain herself. She began to howl in laughter. Asher looked to Lauren. *A little help, please?* His eyes pleaded to her.

"Asher, we pulled these off the shelf. Do you think they'll have all the details of your wedding magically printed on them? We'll have to design it on a computer and find a reliable printer. And, as Mrs. Kelley said, buy a whole lotta ink."

Asher shrugged. He was beginning to get a headache. "Listen, I don't know anything about weddings, so can you make sure you explain everything as we go?"

Lauren smiled sweetly at Asher. "Of course I will, Asher." Her gaze was absent of judgment or haughtiness. She looked at him like he was a sweet thing that needed nurturing. And in that moment, Asher couldn't look away.

Chapter Five

Lauren

After she'd fed the goats, the hens, secured their pens, washed the muck off her farm boots, locked up the house, dried and put away the last clean dish, turned off the lights, and stopped at the stairs, ready to march off to bed, Lauren couldn't help herself from taking one long look at the package of invitations Asher had purchased only hours prior. The full moon was nearing waning gibbous, but it still illuminated the now-clear night sky, casting light through the living room windows, and down upon the package as it sat on the coffee table.

Those were beautiful wedding invitations if she did say so herself. Deep jewel tones like cranberry, grape, sapphire, emerald, and marigold were some of Lauren's favorite combinations, and she had to admit harvest colors complemented her skin and hair tones, too. Would cranberry look good against Gemma's alabaster skin, her yellow blonde hair? Had Lauren made a grave mistake—her first task as a wedding planner—and would this upset her bride?

Gemma had never returned Asher's phone call. She'd texted him back, though. She had, in her own words, granted Asher and Lauren permission to choose whatever colors and themes they thought would look best on Gemma and against the backdrop of the farmland. But had Lauren made the right choice? There was nothing more haunting to Lauren than the worry that someone might be upset with her. That she might have caused another person pain.

But they were only invitations, right? Even if they were the wrong ones, they'd be recycled after the wedding date. She didn't take Gemma as the kind of bride who framed her wedding invitation.

The decision was made, Lauren thought as she turned away from the living room and climbed the stairs to her bedroom. She crawled into bed, pulling a fluffy comforter and soft throw blanket over her, snuggling in close to the many pillows that transformed her bed into a lush, sleepy-time haven.

If being a farmer was good for anything, it was good for ensuring a restful night's sleep. After working in the fresh air and relentless sun all day, sleep came swiftly to Lauren. There weren't too many hard decisions to make on a farm, and the decisions she found difficult came at the expense of animals, which wouldn't hold grudges against Lauren or gossip about her throughout the town. She'd been able to sleep easy the past year on the homestead, even though she had to sell a feeble goat, toil over replanting crops that weren't growing, and also euthanize diseased chickens. After making those choices, she'd drifted off to sound sleep as soon as her eyes had closed, and her head had hit the pillow.

But tonight?

The moonbeams flooded through the window curtains like a spotlight interrogation.

Am I tough enough to own a business? Is Asher on to something?

Working with people was much more difficult than working with animals and plants. Even the weather was more reasonable than most people, Lauren had discovered.

But this was what she wanted. It was her dream to own a property that celebrated every stage of life. That *gave* life.

She was pursuing her dream. She was spending her days doing what she loved. She had to remember that.

I am lucky.

***

It was Friday evening when Lauren saw Asher again. She'd finished cleaning up after dinner with Sage and was pulling a chocolate pie from the oven when she heard a knock on her front door.

Sage, cradling a glass of red wine in her hand, yelled that she'd see who it was and flew out of the kitchen to disappear into the foyer.

Placing the pie on a rack upon the counter, Lauren took a sip of her glass of red wine. This was her first time baking a goat milk chocolate pie with gooey caramel filling. The past week she'd been experimenting with all sorts of desserts. Red velvet cupcakes with cream cheese frosting, chocolate and caramel toffee bars, fudge, and now this chocolate pie. She intended to sell as many of these items as possible at the farmer's market and at her mother's confectionary. She also needed to know which items she could offer to Gemma and Asher for their wedding dessert menu.

"Wow, it smells amazing," Asher said, entering the kitchen as Sage trailed behind him.

"Yeah, that's because it is. Have you ever tasted one of Lauren's concoctions?" Sage asked.

Asher shook his head. "Not since she started doing it professionally, I guess." Asher walked up to the counter, bending over to smell the pie. "Caramel?"

"Good guess," said Lauren, pulling a third wineglass from the cabinet. "Would you like a glass? It's a cab."

"Sure. Thanks," Asher said, smiling as Lauren handed him the glass.

"So, I've been experimenting with desserts. Maybe now would be a good time to choose the dessert menu?" Lauren looked to Asher for approval.

"I am so on board with that." Sage smiled. She'd made herself comfortable at the round kitchen table, sitting on one chair, her feet propped up on another.

Lauren pulled her many masterpieces from the refrigerator, placing each dessert in a row on the countertop.

"And these are all made with goat milk?" Asher asked.

"Yep, and as many ingredients as I can find on the farm, like fresh fruit," Lauren answered.

Asher folded his arms, impressed. "So, what all can you make with goat milk?"

"Well, I make cheese, of course, and kefir, and caramel and chocolate. Goat cheese adds extra flavor to every salad, pizza, and entrée. Kefir is like yogurt, but even healthier. You'll try the caramel and chocolate and decide for yourself." Lauren thought for a moment. "Oh yeah, and I can make lotion and soap with goat milk. Super creamy and soft and good for the skin."

Yes, she could do everything. Lauren smiled as she watched the wheels turn in Asher's mind. Soaps, lotions, food, and dessert from her goats. Eggs and soon there'd be meat from her chickens. Fresh vegetables and fruit from the field and a place to enjoy it all at the barn. Lauren proudly stared at Asher, waiting for endless compliments.

"That doesn't seem like a sustainable business model," he finally said, sipping his wine.

Sage spun her head in Lauren's direction, her mouth ajar. "Um, what is that supposed to mean?" She turned back to view Asher.

Lauren's face grew hot. She took a swig of her wine.

"Well, I mean, sure it sounds great. And that's impressive that you can make all those items from scratch—from your homestead. But that's a lot of different products. And a lot of time spent making each product. When a business has its hands in too many pots, it's sure to fail. The most successful businesses focus on making one or two products, and that's it."

"Oh yeah? What about Amazon? They sell a billion products." Sage dropped her feet from the chair, sitting up straight, feet planted, ready to challenge Asher.

"Yeah," Lauren said, "what about Amazon?"

"Hey, don't get mad at me. I didn't make up the statistics. I'm only sharing my knowledge of business with you guys. I said I think it's awesome how talented you are, Lauren," he said, which made Lauren's face flush again, "but I'm telling you, if you want to make money, you should probably choose a few things to make and sell."

Lauren knew Asher wasn't trying to embarrass her, but she felt embarrassed. As if he was imparting wisdom on her, as if she were stupid and he was smart. She remembered a few times he'd behaved that way back when they were dating, but his patronizing attitude back then had focused on sports, which wasn't exactly a topic Lauren cared to know about. This—running a homestead and making money doing what she loved to do like baking and cooking and growing—this was personal. This was her passion, something Lauren knew a lot about and was proud of.

"And, for the record, Amazon is an anomaly. It's incomparable to any small business. And I'm talking about small businesses. You do realize I'm a director of business operations, right?"

Sage rose, scowling at Asher as she shuffled to the counter to refill her wineglass. "Yeah? So? What's that even mean?"

Asher smirked. "It means I help businesses run efficiently and make the most profit possible. It means I know what I'm talking about."

"I thought you worked at a nonprofit?" Lauren asked.

"I do, but that's irrelevant," Asher said. He stared at Lauren. "Listen, I'm only trying to help."

Sage nudged him as she thundered past him. "If you wanna help, get out of my way." She laughed. Asher laughed back, watching her pull three plates from the cabinet. "Can we try this dessert already? I need chocolate after that mansplaining," Sage said.

"I wasn't mansplaining—" Asher protested. He shut his mouth, probably deciding it was futile to argue with Sage. Lauren smiled at him.

"Okay. Red velvet cupcakes with cream cheese frosting. Fudge. Chocolate caramel toffee bars. And chocolate caramel pie." Lauren pointed to each dessert she'd sliced and placed on all three plates, handing the plates over to her guests.

Lauren tasted a small bite of the chocolate pie. The pie was warm and moist, the caramel gooey. It was delectable. Asher must have thought the same because he closed his eyes as he ate it.

"This is so good," he said, his mouth full of mushy pie. She watched him take a bite of a cupcake, shake his head, then taste the fudge and the bars. "Lauren, what is this witchcraft?" He smiled, his eyes sparkling as he looked at her.

"She is like a witch, isn't she?" Sage said. "You know, witches are women who know how to heal themselves and others with herbs and natural medicines. Did you know that?" Sage asked proudly.

"I did," Lauren said, grinning. "My sorcery secret is simply goat milk. And brown sugar. And butter. Lots and lots of butter, soft churned." She felt a wide smile overtake her face, scrunching to her eyes. It was such a satisfying feeling to see people express joy over something she made herself.

"Can we have all of these on the dessert menu at the wedding?" Asher asked, nearly finished with each of his slices.

"I thought that having fewer choices was better for business, eh?" Sage said, devouring the last bits on her plate, too.

Asher rolled his eyes. "Well, sure, that's for when you're trying to sell this stuff. But come on. A wedding is different."

"Well," Lauren began, "I don't want to lose money by having to prepare too much."

Asher frowned. "I'll pay extra."

Lauren laughed. She looked at Sage, who began to laugh, too.

"And can I have seconds, please? Only to, you know, be certain." Asher smiled.

Lauren giggled. "I'm glad you like it."

She watched Sage's eyes follow Asher, whose gaze followed Lauren as she returned to the counter to cut more slices. Sage's gaze shifted to Lauren, and Lauren knew what she was thinking. So Lauren cut more slices for Sage if only to keep her mouth busy.

***

An hour later, Will collected Sage for their Friday night date, sweeping her off for a late-night movie, leaving Lauren and Asher alone to finally finish the task of making the guest list and mailing out two hundred invitations.

Bellies full of dessert, Asher and Lauren sat on the living room couch, slowly sipping the rest of the wine bottle that had been emptied into their glasses. When Asher found his spot on one end of the couch, Lauren made sure to sit a full seat away from him to avoid the accidental brushing of limbs.

Thankfully, Asher had done some homework and brought with him a printed list of every guest Mr. and Mrs. Turner, Gemma's parents, and Heidi and Fred wanted to be invited to the wedding. Gemma had included her list of friends, coworkers, and acquaintances, and after looking at his parents' picks, Asher had only a few friends to add. Lauren held up the list, carefully reading, as Asher opened the invitation box, separating the invitations from the envelopes.

Lauren quickly glanced at the piles. "Wait a sec, aren't there any RSVP cards?"

Asher raised an eyebrow. "What do those look like?"

"There should be little cards that people write their name on, with who they're bringing, and which entrée they want..." Lauren shuffled through the papers. "Wow. Okay, this package is a little more casual than I thought."

"Is that bad?" Asher asked.

"Well, not necessarily. We could create a spreadsheet online, sort of like a survey form. And people can RSVP online. That would cut out a lot of the work on my end. But sometimes people find that rude," Lauren explained.

"Yeah, old people," Asher said. "You can't please everyone, Lauren."

She looked over to him, noticing his smirk. "You think you know everything, don't you?"

He feigned hurt, bringing his hand to his heart. "You're saying I don't?"

"I'm saying you think you know what I'm thinking. But you don't." Lauren narrowed her eyes. She'd about had it with Asher's smugness. He had changed over the past seven years. Who he had become, or at least who he was portraying himself to be, was not attractive to Lauren. Nope. Not at all.

"What do you think I think you're thinking?"

She rolled her eyes.

"What? I'm serious. I know you, Lauren."

"Oh, you do? Who am I?"

Asher grinned, sitting up straighter. He turned his body, facing her directly. "You are a big-hearted person. You want everyone around you to be happy—all the time. You're in constant fear of hurting other people's feelings. And you'd rather know everyone likes you than get what you want."

A boa constrictor slithered around Lauren, crawling around her chest, suffocating her. Or, at least, that's what it felt like. She knew her cheeks were red. She could feel her palms sweat. She tried to steady her breathing before she answered.

"That's not true," she said, her voice cracking.

Asher furrowed his eyebrows. "Don't be upset, Lauren. I didn't mean it as an insult."

She was breathing loudly. She blinked. "Then what did you mean it as?"

"It's only an observation. I don't know. Never mind. I guess I don't know you that well anymore, anyway. So, what *do* I know?" Asher said, giving up. He finished his glass of wine. "Anyway, I think it's fine if the RSVPs are sent through the Internet. And I don't care if a handful of Luddites think it's rude to use modern technology to make our lives easier." He chuckled to himself.

Lauren was silent. Because that's what Lauren did best. She buried whatever feelings she had deep inside her bones until she was alone and could feel the weight of them drag her down. Why couldn't she express herself in the moment? Tell Asher that he'd hurt her feelings? Tell him he was wrong? Let him know he made her angry? Lauren wasn't sure why she kept her feelings to herself. She knew that her rosy cheeks and shift in body language made it obvious she was uncomfortable. Yet, she was also good at slapping a smile on her face, wiping away sad eyes and turning to focus on something else instead. Maybe it was her Midwestern upbringing? Stoicism was expected of everyone, male and female. Life was tough in the upper Midwest with scorching summers and below-freezing winters. Farm work was grueling, back-breaking labor. And everyone had it as difficult as anyone else, so what was the point in complaining? Hearty Midwesterners expected you to grin and bear it, and to work. Always to work. That Protestant work ethic was valued more than gold.

But Lauren didn't blame her parents, or her neighbors, or her church parish for her inability to express her feelings. Sure, she grew up in a place where being proud and boastful was as unattractive as complaining, but she knew plenty of people who were comfortable expressing their anger and hurt. Sage, her best friend since first grade, wouldn't think twice before putting Asher in his place if he had upset her.

This was Lauren's issue, and she couldn't blame anyone but herself, which was a very Lauren thing to think, she realized. *Maybe I'm too hard on myself.*

"So, what should we write on the invitations?" Asher asked, staring at Lauren.

"Oh. Um, right. Let's get back to work," she said, smiling.

Back to work. The current tagline of her life.

***

Asher stood in the doorway, hands in his pockets, lips slightly purple from the cabernet. "What's next on the list?" he asked.

"Well," said Lauren, her eyelids heavy and starting to close. It was almost two a.m. and they'd finished printing the wording on the invitations.

Together with their parents, Gemma Turner and Asher Wolf request the honor of your presence at their marriage on Saturday, November third at four o'clock in the evening at Big Heart Homestead, Pine Lake, Wisconsin. Reception to follow.

The RSVP cards, which we were able to do ourselves, were also completed, which directed the invitees to a website where they could record their responses. Doing it this way had saved Lauren hours and hours of work. They'd printed mailing addresses on the envelopes, stuffed them, and slapped self-adhesive stamps on all two hundred invitations. Lauren was exhausted after such repetitive, mindless work.

"I'll drop the invitations off at the post office tomorrow," Lauren yawned, "and then we should look around town for photographers and florists. And maybe some other decorations."

"And the barn tables and chairs," Asher said. "And the menu."

Lauren nodded. "Yes. Yes, all that."

"So, tomorrow then? We can go to town and hire photographers and florists?" Asher asked.

Lauren exhaled. "Okay. Tomorrow." She began to close the door.

Asher stepped closer, stopping her. "Wait, Lauren."

She met his gaze, which was strong and sincere.

"I'm sorry about earlier. I get the feeling I hurt your feelings in some way. It's been so long and sometimes I say things without thinking. I've never been in a situation like this before," he said. "I don't know what I'm trying to say here, except I'm sorry. I would never want to hurt your feelings." Then he looked away as if flooded with memories.

"You didn't," Lauren lied. "But thanks for saying that. Good night, Asher. See you tomorrow." She smiled and closed the door, hearing his heavy footsteps down the porch steps.

He had hurt her feelings. And if he never wanted to hurt her feelings—if hurting her feelings was something he'd never wished to do—then why had he suddenly ended their relationship by pretending she didn't exist?

There was so much left unsaid, so many questions floating around the air between them, like an invisible airborne virus. If they didn't acknowledge it soon, it would be the death of their burgeoning friendship.

***

Sleeping in was not an option for a farmer. Animals needed to be fed. Plants needed to be watered. Chores waited for no one. So, on four hours of sleep, Lauren was up and at it.

By eleven a.m. she'd completed her lists of chores and tasks for the day. She stood at the open barn doors, peering in at the sorry excuse for a wedding venue.

What would she do about the floors? They were unacceptable. She'd have to hire someone to install hardwood floors. Was that practical in a barn? Yes, she decided. *For as long as I own it, the barn will be a place of celebration. Of gathering. I won't be housing animals or hay bales in here,* she thought. She'd have to remodel it, so she'd have to hire a carpenter and a flooring expert. Was there anyone who could do both?

"Ready?"

Asher's voice startled her. He waved, calling from a few yards away.

Lauren nodded, wrapping her chunky wool knit sweater tightly around her as a chilly wind breezed by. The sun was bright and warm in the sky, but the air was crisp and smelled like candy corn. Lauren, like many women who loved wearing chunky sweaters, jeans, and suede ankle boots, loved fall weather. But crunchy leaves, biting winds, and cinnamon scents meant more to Lauren than fashionable outfits. It meant that she was able to reap the bounty from the laborious summer and that she'd accomplished her goal of providing for herself. It meant that the real test was on its way— would she survive winter? Lauren knew she was humble and agreeable, not assertive. She didn't argue politics or battle intellectual ideas. She measured her strength and toughness through her self-reliance. Could she provide for herself? Could she take care of herself and other living things on a farm? Could she defend herself on her vast property, where she lived, all alone? Could she fix a leaking pipe, drill a hole through a wall? Could she deliver a baby goat? Yes, she could do all of those things. That was enough to make her feel strong. Even if that wasn't how society measured strength.

"I could use a coffee," Asher said as Lauren approached.

"Me too," she replied.

They hopped into the Mercedes, and Asher drove away from the house and onto the country road.

"Pine Lake has changed so much," Asher said as he sped down the country roads, past turning deciduous trees and steadfast coniferous trees. They were on the edge of town.

"A lot of young people want to keep this town around for a long time. I think people realize they don't want to be part of the city rat race anymore. That there's something special about living a simple life," Lauren said.

"Life isn't simple, no matter where you live and work." Asher grinned.

"Well, sure, but it can be lived simpler. Or is it more simple?" Lauren asked, unable to resist chuckling. Asher laughed, too.

"So you're telling me that waking up at the crack of dawn to milk goats makes life simpler than waking up at seven-thirty and stopping at a coffee shop on the way to work?"

Lauren rolled her eyes. "It's not about saving time. It's about enjoying the little things. Finding joy in life's simple pleasures, rather than constantly chasing happiness through status or material items."

"Being part of the rat race affords us the time and money to go on vacation to enjoy the simple things. I'm sure a lot of farmers don't have that luxury."

Lauren looked at Asher. "Why do you love to argue so much? Maybe you should have been a lawyer." She crossed her arms, turning to look out the window at the storefront buildings that were coming into view.

The town's autumn decorations were in full swing. Pumpkins of all sizes and colors were stacked upon bales of hay. Mums and marigolds overflowed in hanging planters and window boxes, and red, orange, and yellow leaves were garland-wrapped around old-fashioned lampposts. Apple cider, cinnamon and pumpkin spice drinks and food were advertised on every shop door.

Small towns and rural villages couldn't hide the seasons like big cities could. While tall, gray buildings stole the scene in cities, the surrounding flora framed squat buildings and wide roads, making it impossible not to celebrate, let alone ignore the changing seasons. Small towns forced people to live in the moment, accept the weather and its effect on rural life, whereas in the city people were always in a rush toward the future, toward the next bigger, better, farther stepping-stone. City folk could hide out in subways and in buildings, hop into cabs or seek refuge under awnings, ignoring the seasons and its weather, or at least not letting it get in the way of achieving their goals.

So, yes, life is simpler in smaller towns, in Pine Lake, thought Lauren. *No matter what Asher says.*

Asher parked the car on Main Street in front of the Lone Loon Café. Inside, the café smelled even better than nature's scent outside. Along with the wafting scent of coffee beans, cinnamon, cloves, and nutmeg danced upon the air.

Rachel Carlson, Jacob's younger sister, a slender, raven-haired beauty whose lips were painted bright red, beamed when she saw Lauren. Lauren smiled back, watching as Rachel recognized Asher, studying him.

"My brother mentioned you were in town," Rachel said. "How have you been, Asher? It's good to see you."

"Hi, Rachel," Asher said warmly, leaning up against the counter.

While Lauren had spent much of her adolescence avoiding Jacob Carlson, she'd always gotten along well with Rachel. Of course, Lauren got along well with most people, and even if she wasn't incredibly fond of someone in particular, Lauren pretended she was to avoid conflict. But Rachel had always been the quiet, artistic type, one who kept to herself and didn't get invited to many parties. She'd always been invited to Lauren's parties, though.

"So, what's the occasion for the homecoming?" asked Rachel from across the counter.

Asher stood up straighter, preparing himself to answer the many questions he knew would follow his first. "I'm getting married."

Rachel nodded with a smile, looking to Lauren as she said, "Congratulations."

Lauren shook her head. There was no way Rachel thought he was marrying Lauren, right? She opened her mouth to explain, but Rachel went on.

"But not you two, right?" She pointed at the two.

"No, no," Lauren said as Asher waved his hands.

"No, my fiancée's name is Gemma Turner. She's from New York. You'll meet her someday," he said.

"Okay..." Rachel looked confused. "So, you guys hanging out today, catching up...?"

A nervous laugh tumbled out of Lauren. "I'm their wedding planner."

Rachel's eyes widened. "You are?"

Asher shifted his weight, uncomfortable. "Yeah, but it's cool. We're cool. The wedding is on Lauren's farm."

"He's getting married on your farm?" Rachel stared at Lauren in disbelief.

"My homestead. But yeah, that's what I do," Lauren said, suddenly feeling a pang of fear shoot through her belly. *Don't mention that you've hosted multiple weddings,* she reminded herself. *Oh no, what if Asher does? I can't let him say something, otherwise Rachel will spill the beans.* Lauren knew she needed to change the subject immediately. "The place looks great. How's business?" she asked, but Rachel ignored her, turning to Asher.

"Isn't that weird?" Rachel asked.

"No, of course not," Asher said. "It's great to see you, Rachel. You look beautiful."

That was enough to shut up Rachel. It was no secret that nearly every girl their age and younger had an enormous crush on Asher throughout high school and college. Asher was handsome, talented, intelligent, and popular. He was kind, too. *Or, at least,* Lauren thought, *he used to be kind.*

"Thanks," Rachel said, pushing a stray strand of hair behind her ears. "So, what can I get you guys?"

Asher gestured for Lauren to order first. "I'll have an Americano. Double shot of espresso, please."

"I'm sure you could use it," said Rachel with a wink. Lauren stifled an eye roll.

"And I'll have a regular coffee. Thanks," Asher said.

Rachel spun around, clanking stainless steel against machinery as she whipped up their concoctions.

Asher shook his head at Lauren. She smiled back. After they paid and received their coffees, Asher and Lauren left the dimly lit, coffee-bean-scented coffee shop and reentered the brisk outdoors, walking along the sidewalk as they headed to their next destination.

"I have a feeling we're going to be hearing that all day," Asher said.

"Oh yeah."

"I mean, maybe I should mail out some pamphlets or something. Or hold a press conference," Asher said, then clearing his throat as he put on his best authoritative voice. "To the citizens of Pine Lake. I am getting married on my ex-girlfriend's farm to my new fiancée. Get over yourselves."

Lauren forced a smile, then sipped her coffee. Maybe she should have asked for three shots of espresso.

"I mean, you can't blame them," she said.

Asher raised an eyebrow. "Why not? It's none of their business."

"They're only reacting. It's an honest reaction, too. A visceral one. I'd be surprised if people didn't think it was weird."

"Really? So you think it's weird?" Asher grinned, looking at Lauren.

She couldn't read his expression. And she couldn't figure out what she was feeling in that moment, either. She only knew it didn't feel good.

"You don't?" she asked.

Asher sighed. "Of course I do, Lauren."

Lauren felt a wave of relief. "You do?" She wanted to know more. She wanted to know everything Asher was thinking.

"Listen, I don't even know how this all happened, it happened so fast. But if I had been here with Gemma when she was choosing wedding venues, I definitely would have stopped her from choosing yours."

Lauren frowned. *Ouch.*

"That didn't come out right. Man, I suck at words," Asher said.

"No, you don't, Asher. Not from what I remember," Lauren said. The most beautiful, romantic words would come out of Asher's mouth when they were young. He was no illiterate. "So why don't you tell me how you feel?"

Asher stopped walking. Lauren stopped, too, turning to look at him. He stared at her.

"Your home is beautiful. Your farm is picturesque. I bet every wedding you've ever hosted has been magical," he said, as Lauren internally cringed, "but Gemma… she doesn't know that you and I were together…"

Lauren knew that.

"I think my mom steered Gemma to your farm. And by the time she signed a contract with you, it was too late. I realized Gemma didn't know our history and I didn't know if I should tell her. Maybe that's wrong of me. Maybe she'll find out anyway considering the whole town can't keep their mouths shut." Asher sighed. "It already feels awkward for me. But I'm trying to push back those feelings. Ignore the discomfort of it all. For Gemma. So she can be happy." He stared into Lauren's eyes. "If I have to be uncomfortable for a couple of months, so be it. I'm not going to ruin her dream wedding simply because you and I used to date."

Lauren's heart crunched like the leaves beneath her feet. She swallowed, nodding. "Okay. I'll do that too," she said. Asher smiled, reaching out to squeeze her shoulder, then turned to continue down the sidewalk toward the florist's storefront.

Lauren blinked away tears, hoping Asher wouldn't look at her in that moment. The language he used—again, for someone who knew how to craft a sentence—was killing her. *Used to date? Were together?*

Lauren reminded herself she was strong. But was she strong enough to forgive her ex-boyfriend and watch him marry another woman? Sure. If he was simply her ex-boyfriend.

But Asher wasn't only Lauren's ex-boyfriend.

He was the first man she had loved.

The only man she'd ever loved.

Their relationship had been so much more than only dating.

They had been in love. They had promised forever. They had proclaimed to be soul mates.

So how strong was Lauren? Not strong enough for this.

Chapter Six

Asher

How could she be so cold? Asher thought, crunching fire-colored leaves as he walked beside Lauren. She didn't even flinch when he mentioned wanting to make Gemma happy, or casually mentioned that they used to "date." Did she feel nothing?

When Asher first learned Gemma had booked their wedding at Lauren's farm, he'd felt a swell of panic. Being home again had made him uncomfortable, but when Gemma had liked the idea of getting married in Pine Lake, he knew their path was taking a dangerous turn. When Mr. Turner told his daughter he couldn't afford her dream wedding in New York City, Asher figured Gemma would visit venues in Vermont or Connecticut. At a celebratory dinner with his parents, Heidi had raved about the natural beauty of Pine Lake and the picturesque weddings. Gemma was immediately sold. She'd never even been to his hometown in the three years they'd been dating. Asher assumed she'd see the four main streets of Pine Lake and reject the thought entirely. It wasn't hip or trendy, at least not by fashion or foodie standards, which Asher knew mattered greatly to Gemma.

Asher didn't know Lauren owned a farm—or a homestead, whatever—and he had no idea she owned a wedding venue business. He'd made it a habit to avoid all talk of Lauren whenever he visited home, ever since they officially stopped talking seven years ago.

Was it officially seven years ago? Asher couldn't exactly remember the date or the event that had caused their relationship to end. It had sort of vanished. Ever since they laid eyes on each other freshman year of high school in English class, Asher and Lauren had been passionately in love. They'd started hanging out together with mutual groups of friends, but didn't admit their feelings to each other until they were sixteen. From then, they were officially together—exclusive—throughout all of high school and college until Asher left for business school at NYU. And throughout college, they'd met plenty of attractive people they could date. Asher and Lauren talked about that often—how, despite the many fish in the vast sea, they still preferred each other. They were soul mates, Asher and Lauren declared. And Asher believed that.

Until it was no longer true.

Had Asher been only a boyfriend of convenience to Lauren?

After Asher moved to New York, he and Lauren attempted a long-distance relationship. They talked on the phone as much as possible, and Lauren visited him in New York every six weeks. Their first year was successful. Then, the fall of Asher's second year, something changed.

First, Lauren didn't always return Asher's phone calls. Then, she booked tickets to visit Asher at the end of October, but canceled them, because her mom had gotten sick and she had to manage the shop. After that, it was weeks before they spoke again, Thanksgiving to be exact. Lauren told Asher she and her parents were going to her grandparents' cabin near Lake Superior for Thanksgiving, but she didn't invite him. So they didn't see each other at Thanksgiving. They didn't speak again after that, until Christmas, when Asher went to Lauren's house, and they got into an argument about communication. They both blamed each other for their lack of contact. Still, the night ended with declarations of "I love you." But when Asher returned to New York after the New Year, Lauren went radio silent.

And that was it.

After Asher had graduated with his master's that May, he'd gotten an entry-level job at the nonprofit he currently worked at. He'd remained in New York ever since, returning home for Christmas and Easter, only spotting Lauren at church as she dipped between crowds of people to avoid making eye contact with him.

She didn't love him anymore, Asher concluded. Maybe she never had? Perhaps she was drawn to him because of his popularity or because he was one of the better-looking guys their age. Had it been "out of sight, out of mind" for Lauren? Whatever the case was, they'd never spoken of it. Yet, somehow, they'd both forgiven each other. Or, at the very least, gotten over the hurt feelings enough to carry on like mature adults.

The truth was Asher hadn't gotten over it. And it hurt him to see that Lauren had. She was hosting his wedding on her farm for crying out loud. How could she possibly stand that, unless she'd had no feelings for him?

Asher could never do it. He could never stand by and watch Lauren marry someone else, especially if it were on his property.

But you love Gemma, he reminded himself. It was true. He loved Gemma. She was fun and interesting, and gorgeous. He was excited to see her when she returned home from business trips and missed her while she was gone. They were compatible and rarely fought. He imagined a long, happy life with her. A lifelong marriage. And he knew she felt the same.

"Here we are," Lauren said as they reached the florist. He opened the door for her, and she smiled as she ducked under his arm to enter the shop. Every inch of the cinnamon-scented shop was decorated for autumn.

Lauren closed her eyes, deeply breathing in the soothing scent of flowers and spices. "The most wonderful time of year," she said, eyes still closed as she did a little twirl.

Asher felt a tug at the corners of his mouth. As much as his heart hurt every time he saw Lauren, it also warmed with love. He still truly cared about her. And seeing her smile offered him a bit of comfort.

***

After Lauren had convinced Asher to sign off on wedding flowers, they returned to Asher's car, heading to the potential photographer's house. Lauren had chosen bouquets of burgundy ranunculus, beige and cream hydrangeas, dark plum peonies, peach and coral garden roses, rust orange mini roses, wild wheat, lavender thistle, and burgundy berry sprays. That's what the form said, anyway. Asher could only identify one flower within the bouquet—roses.

"How'd you find this photographer recommendation?" Asher asked Lauren, looking ahead as he drove down the winding, forested road. The trees looked like they were aflame. Asher realized he never got sick of looking at the autumnal beauty.

"He's a friend of Jacob's."

Asher's jaw clenched at the sound of Jacob's name. "Great," he said, miffed. "Can't wait to meet this guy. Is he gonna give me grief, too?"

Lauren looked at Asher askance. "What's that supposed to mean?"

"Oh, come on. You saw the way he treated me at your party. It's like he wanted to fight or something." Asher's gaze flicked from the road to Lauren in time to see her shift uncomfortably. His eyes returned to the road.

"No, I don't think…" Lauren stopped herself. She sighed. "Yeah, I saw it. It was weird."

"Thank you." Asher grinned, feeling validated. "To be honest, I always felt like he disliked me. Ever since high school."

"Your feeling is probably true." Lauren looked to him, a sympathetic frown tugging her mouth downward.

"Do you know why?" Asher asked. "Was I ever mean to him? Or was his secret wish to be the captain of the baseball team and I stole it from him?"

"No way," Lauren said. "He's not a jock. He's a sensitive guy."

Asher furrowed his eyebrows. "Sensitive? It seems like he likes to pick fights to me."

"I think he was only protecting me. I think he saw you were teasing me, and—"

"Teasing you? I don't remember teasing you, but even if I were, teasing is not something to get worked up about."

"I don't know, Asher," Lauren said with frustration.

Asher looked at her, surprised. She crossed her arms.

"Actually, I do know."

"Okay?"

"I think Jacob has a crush on me. I think he's always had a crush on me. So it makes sense why he wouldn't like you," she said.

Asher felt his face flush. "It makes sense why he wouldn't like me in high school or college. It doesn't make sense why he wouldn't like me now."

Lauren opened her mouth and only as a little breath of air puffed out, about to be formed into a word, she snapped her mouth shut. Whatever she was going to say, she repressed it, maddening Asher.

He scowled. "So he has a crush on you and even though you and I are not together anymore," Asher felt a tightening in his stomach when he said that aloud, "he continues to dislike me because I exist?"

"I guess so," Lauren said. "Turn here."

They had passed farmland, red barns nestled between rolling emerald hills and harvested fields of corn and wheat, viewing roadside plants that had turned deep purple. As the black asphalt road split forests, Asher noted its contrast against the green grass, which looked electric—brightened by overcast skies. The forest's treetops looked like they'd been set ablaze. White birch trunks centered between fiery orange and rich saffron leaves. He turned onto a narrow dirt road, leading to a lakeside log cabin. Birch, red maple, and aspen trees surrounded the enormous lake, where mist danced upon the waters.

Asher parked outside of the quaint home. Smoke writhed out of the brick chimney. As he exited the car, Asher reveled in the comforting scent of a roaring fire.

"He said to come the back way," Lauren said, gesturing for Asher to follow her around the cabin to the back lawn, which faced the lake.

"Wow." Asher took in the view of beautiful Pine Lake, the lake the town was named after. It was massive, surrounded by forest and cabins, docks leading to boats bobbing upon the waters. Asher walked up to the wooden dock on the property, Lauren following behind him.

"I'm not comfortable with trespassing," Lauren said nervously. Asher turned around, smiling at her.

"It's not trespassing when someone invites you over, silly," he said.

Lauren smiled coquettishly. She stood next to him at the end of the dock, wrapping her arms around herself, bracing against the chilly waterfront winds. The waves were choppy, and a lake mist sprayed them.

"Something so calming about water, even when it's this wild." Asher breathed in the air, then looked at Lauren. She looked up at him, her cheeks and tip of her nose rosy.

"I couldn't agree more."

They stood like that, their arms brushing against each other as the winds whipped them for a few minutes. They stood in silence, watching the waves knock against the dock.

Asher turned to Lauren, who looked so fragile against the white sky and white-capped waters. He wanted to reach out and hold her. It was an intense feeling, one that scared him, but he couldn't drive it from his mind. He wanted to wrap his arms around her, nuzzle his face into her neck, breathe in her scent, and kiss her cold cheek. When she looked up at him, her eyes bright like honey against the white light, he felt himself smile. Then, abruptly, he looked away, turning on his heel and marching down the dock, back toward land and the rear entrance. He was ashamed of himself in that moment, embarrassed by his thoughts, disappointed in his wandering desires.

Lauren joined him at the back door. saying nothing. Asher noticed the door was ajar. He knocked. The door crept open.

A tall, older man with thinning gray-brown hair arrived at the door, a soft, warm smile stretching across his face. He had to be at least seventy-five years old, Asher guessed. He wore a dark, wool sweater and his jeans were baggy on his lean body. Round glasses framed his marble gray eyes.

"You must be the lucky groom," the man said, welcoming them inside. "Come in, come in." He opened the door wide, allowing Lauren and Asher to enter.

The cabin was warm and smelled like burning logs and leather. A few lamps glowed in corners, lighting the room along with the fire. Cozy couches and reclining chairs faced the fireplace. Asher's attention was drawn to many framed photos that lined the log cabin walls. They were all smiling faces of children, the man, and a beautiful older woman who Asher guessed was his wife.

"Thank you so much for meeting with us, Mr. Carlson," Lauren said.

Asher shot her a look. Carlson? So he was Jacob's grandfather. Artistic talent must have been hereditary. He hoped temperament wasn't.

A framed photograph of Jacob and Rachel sat on the mantel above the fireplace. Lauren smiled at Asher and shrugged.

"I'm Don Carlson," the old man said, extending his hand to shake Asher's. Asher shook it. "Thank you for coming all the way out here to meet with me," he said, mostly as a reply to Lauren's comment.

"Not far at all," Asher said. "It's nice to see Pine Lake on a day like today."

"Isn't it beautiful?" Don asked. He walked over to the enormous window viewing the lake. "Cold, choppy waters, but that loon is still out there... a brave soul." He looked up at the pine trees right outside the cabin. "I saw a bald eagle this morning catch a fish and fly into that tree." He pointed.

"You must love living on the lake," Asher said. He wondered if he would like it. Or would it get boring?

"I do. I loved it more when my wife was here with me. But I still love it," he said.

Asher felt a sting of sadness. Could he ever live alone on the lake after his wife passed away? The thought saddened him. When he imagined his "wife," he saw Lauren. An image of Lauren and him, wrinkly and gray, snuggling by the fireplace, flashed in his mind. Once it dissolved, he felt ashamed.

"So, you're looking for a wedding photographer, is it?"

"Yes, Mr. Carlson. My fiancée and I are getting married on November third. I know it's short notice, but we're hoping to hire an experienced photographer to capture our special day." Asher's father had taught him well when it came to respecting his elders. Somehow, Asher's voice would change its tone and his vocabulary expanded to converse with the elderly. He was always surprised by it. Never say "yeah," Fred had taught him, always speak in complete sentences, look the person in the eye, and be more formal than informal. So, Asher tried the best he could.

"Experience is certainly one thing I have. Talent is something I'll let you decide for yourself." He smiled wryly, carrying two thick photo albums over to the coffee table in front of the comfortable couch where Lauren and Asher sat.

As Lauren opened the photo album, Asher observed each photo while she slowly turned the pages. Neutral colors, poufy hair, bell sleeves. The first few pages of the photo album was full of weddings from the 1970s. He certainly had years of experience. Surprisingly, even the cheesy photos (which Asher knew was trendy at that time) were clear and captured emotion. They flipped page after page, the 1980s, 1990s, 2000s, 2010s, and even his latest wedding was beautifully captured. He had talent—that was true.

Don crossed his legs. "Another way I can help you decide is by letting you see if you feel comfortable with me as your photographer. So we can do some test shots. I'll take photos of you and you can see if you like my style. Some people might like my work, but not like the way I work."

Asher was puzzled. "Are you unique in your style?"

Don laughed. "No. I'm honest and I like to capture candid photos better than I like styled photos. Some brides don't like that. They like to have the control. If you're okay with me making the artistic decision, then it shouldn't be a problem."

Asher couldn't imagine Gemma rejecting Don's style. She valued artistic license and although he could see her wanting certain photos staged, he figured she'd given up so much control over this wedding that she wouldn't have a problem with Don's photography style.

One of the last photos caught his attention. It was a summer wedding, probably from this past summer. A bridesmaid stood in front of a mirror, fixing her hair, staring into her own eyes. In the reflection of the mirror, a groomsman stood off to the side, watching. He was almost unnoticeable—hidden in the corner of the photograph. But the look in his eyes was unmistakable. He looked at that bridesmaid with adoration. Asher pointed to the photograph.

"What's the story behind this photo?"

Don's face lit up. He leaned forward, taking a long look before he began. "Those two had been friends their entire lives, so the bride told me. I had witnessed that look all morning, and finally captured it in that photo. He loved her—I could see that. I'm not sure anyone else could, especially the bridesmaid. When I showed the bridesmaid that photo later that day, she covered her mouth, and a few tears fell from her eyes. She said she had loved him since she was a young girl, but never thought he felt the same. That night, she asked him to dance, and he finally declared his feelings for her. The two are engaged, and I'll be shooting their wedding next spring."

Asher felt goosebumps seize him. He looked at Lauren, whose face was bright and rosy. Her smile was soft, almost melancholy. Asher cleared his throat to avoid a crack in his voice. He couldn't help it. He was sentimental, and that story got to him.

"Well," he said, "I think I like your style."

Don grinned. "Great."

Lauren perked up. "Mr. Carlson, may I please use your restroom?"

"Sure, darling. It's down the hall there." He pointed. Lauren smiled, getting up to leave the two alone.

Asher looked at Don, who was smiling sheepishly.

"Can I show you something?" he asked Asher.

"Sure," he said, leaning forward as Don grabbed his professional camera. Asher waited as Don clicked through, then, when he seemed satisfied, he handed the camera off to Asher.

"Have a look." Don nodded.

Asher held the sleek, heavy camera in his hands, viewing the LCD screen. The image was of a stunning bald eagle, wings spread, legs reaching into the rough waves, a fish caught in his talons. Its dark brown feathers stood out against the white backdrop. Its eyes were fierce.

"That's amazing," Asher said, chuckling. "Wow. One beautiful bird."

Don nodded. "Go ahead, click to the next one."

Asher did. His eyes widened. It was another photo of the lake, but this time, the focus wasn't a bald eagle and a fish. Rather, it was Asher and Lauren, who stood at the end of the dock. Asher felt his cheeks flush. He looked up at Don. "I'm sorry if we went out there without your permission—"

But Don fervently shook his head. "Not a problem. That's not why I took the photo. Look closer," he said.

Asher stared at the photo, hoping to see what Don saw.

Although Asher knew he and Lauren weren't touching when they had stood at the edge of the dock, it looked like it in the photo. They were so close. And it looked like they fit together.

"Go to the next one," Don said.

Asher clicked to the next photo, which showed him and Lauren facing each other, the waves crashing behind them, the mist surrounding them. Their eyes were locked. Their smiles reflected in the other.

Asher felt nervous. He looked up at Don. "What do you see here?"

Don only smiled. "You tell me."

Asher's heartbeat pounded in his ears. He was afraid to admit what he saw—what he had felt—in that moment.

Don rose. "Whatever you see, I see it too and more."

Asher looked up, and after a pause, rose, too. He took a deep breath, taking in the photo one last time before handing over the camera to Don.

The bathroom door squeaked open and Lauren walked down the hall, arriving beside Asher.

"Well, thank you so much for your time, Mr. Carlson. I'll discuss this with Asher and Gemma and get back to you."

"My pleasure," Don said, walking them to the front door, near where they parked.

Asher looked at Don. "Thanks, Mr. Carlson. It was a pleasure meeting you."

Don nodded, closing the door behind them.

"Hungry?" Lauren asked with a chipper smile, opening the car door and ducking inside.

"Starved," Asher said, closing the car door behind him and pulling out of the driveway, his eyes taking one last look at that wise man's cabin before he returned to the road.

***

Don Carlson's cabin was located between two roads that were equidistant from town. Asher could either return to the road he took there—Country Highway E—or take the one to the left of the cabin—Country Highway F—which would bring him back into town. He'd been on Highway E several times since his return to Pine Lake. And there was something along Highway F he had been itching to revisit.

"Do you remember the diner on Highway F we used to go to all the time?" Asher asked Lauren, delighted when he witnessed her eyes widen and a smile spread across her face.

"I haven't thought about that place in years." She turned to him, giddy. "Let's go. Now that I'm thinking about their pancakes, I won't be able to get them out of my mind until I have one."

Asher laughed. "Remember the hot ham and cheese sandwiches? Those were so good. Why?" He crinkled his nose. "Think about it. Only white bread, honey ham, and American cheese."

"Cheddar cheese," Lauren corrected him. "And I think you should lose the attitude before we get there."

He smiled at her, the white sky and backdrop of dark pine trees revealed specks of green in her brown eyes.

"Oh man," she started, "we're gonna show up to that little dinner in these rustic woods in... *this*." Lauren ran her hand along her smooth, white leather seat. "I don't want to draw attention to us, you know?"

Asher shook his head. Only Lauren would eschew good attention. Most people would want to be seen in a flashy car, a symbol of status and wealth, no matter where they were. Most people wouldn't care about anyone else's feelings about that car, either. A lot of people drove flashy cars to make people feel bad—to make people feel jealous. That's not why Gemma drove this car, or at least, Asher hoped she didn't, but he knew some people did have the goal of evoking envy in others.

"What else would we do?" Asher asked. "Walk there?"

Lauren began twirling her hair. Asher smiled to himself.

"Can we park it somewhere and then walk to the diner?"

"Lauren, come on," Asher said.

"No, Asher. I don't want people to look at us like we think we're better than them. You know everyone who lives this far from town doesn't have much, and they work honest, backbreaking jobs. A Mercedes doesn't belong out here."

Asher sighed, looking over to her. Her eyes were pleading.

"All right. But I don't want someone breaking into the car, either." Asher slowed the car as he approached a dirt road off the highway. It ran along a forested pond. He turned onto the dirt road and parked. "Think it'll be safe here?"

"I'm sure it will be," Lauren said. "It's only a car, you know." She smirked. She was cute.

"I know. Do *you* know it's only a car? Maybe you shouldn't put so much meaning behind it."

She shrugged, a coy smile playing at her lips as she got out of the car. Asher hopped out and clicked the remote twice to lock the car. The air felt crisper in the forest than it had at the lake. Less moisture, less wind. It was pleasant weather enough to walk a quarter mile down the highway.

Giant pine trees shot toward the sky, their lower branches bare, allowing shorter birch trees to pop up between them, bright yellow leaves against the olive-colored pine needles. Asher looked to Lauren, whose eyes were soaking in the view.

"Nothing like a brisk walk in nature to wake you up, hmm?" she said. Asher nodded.

In the distance, a ranch-style log cabin appeared. A green awning above the wide windows read "The Diner." It was a small, cozy restaurant in the middle of the woods, and had been where Lauren and Asher spent many Sunday afternoons drinking coffee and eating buttermilk pancakes. The tradition was to go there the day after an important high school sports game. During college, it was their go-to breakfast joint to relax after a late night out with friends. And sometimes, Lauren and Asher had gone there only to be alone amongst the ancient pine trees after a romantic walk in nature. There were so many memories returning to Asher's mind, images flashing before him. Why was he torturing himself by returning here with her?

***

"Yum," giggled Lauren, eyes wide, as an oblong plate full of enormous buttermilk pancakes was placed before her. "Thank you," she said to the waitress, who had placed Asher's plate of bacon, eggs, sausage, and silver dollar pancakes before him. The waitress smiled and walked away.

"Have you ever come here and ordered anything different?" Asher asked with a smile.

Lauren shook her head. "Nope. Buttermilk pancakes, every time." She slathered butter on top of each thick flapjack, dumping a generous amount of syrup on the stack. "You always got that dish, didn't you?"

"Or the ham and cheese. Once I tried the French toast. It was delicious. But I need meat." Asher took a bite out of a sausage, making Lauren laugh.

"The coffee has gotten worse," she said, taking a sip and sticking out her tongue.

"Or your tastes have become more sophisticated." Asher took a sip of his coffee. "Or maybe both." Yuck. It was more like coffee-flavored water.

"Do you ever go to places like this in New York?" asked Lauren with a mouthful of pancakes.

"Not really. I either eat a lot of street food or we go out to restaurants that cost half a paycheck. Doesn't necessarily mean the food's any better than here, though." It was true. Sure, the tastes were different, and Asher was always amazed by what flavors chefs could invent by putting two seemingly opposite foods together. Yet, that food was never as satisfying as a couple of greasy meats and pancakes.

"Do you like your job?"

Asher looked at Lauren. She suddenly seemed so curious. Lauren had always been good at asking questions, listening, and putting on a cheerful attitude, but she seemed genuinely happy to talk about Asher's life. Why? Asher could only think she'd completely moved on from him. That's why she was able to talk to him as if he were an old friend.

"Well, yeah, I guess. It was my first job out of grad school, and I don't have much to compare it to. I mean, I enjoy the work I do. And my coworkers are nice people. So, yeah."

Lauren nodded. She looked like she wanted to say something but wasn't sure if she should.

"What?" Asher asked. "You can say it, Lauren."

Her face flushed pink. "Well, I was only going to ask if you felt like your job was meaningful? Like you were doing meaningful work?"

Asher chuckled. "What's that even mean?"

Lauren shrugged, sheepish. "Do you think your work matters? Makes the lives of others better?"

"I don't know. Do you?" Asher felt himself getting defensive. Heat rose to his forehead.

Lauren blinked. "Yes, I do think it matters. And I do think, in some small ways, I make the lives of others better."

"I work for a nonprofit," Asher began, "we do a lot of good things for people. We help make food more available for homeless people and people who are food-deprived. I'd say that matters. As much as you think selling goat milk matters."

Why was he getting so defensive? Lauren wasn't attacking him. She was simply asking a question. Did Asher feel judged by her? Maybe.

"I think it's great that you've worked at that company for so long, doing good work. I was only curious, that's all," Lauren said, her voice meek.

Asher sighed. "I'm sorry. I didn't mean to get defensive."

She sat up straighter, "I've recently read a lot about this. People feel happiest in life when they feel that their work has meaning, and that their lives have purpose. A lot of people find that through the work they do, whether it's at a big company or taking care of a family. I suppose I wanted to make sure you were happy."

You are a huge *jerk.* Asher wanted to slap himself. She only wanted to make sure he was happy. She was only being big-hearted Lauren. Another voice inside him asked why then did she end our relationship long ago?

The waitress stopped by, leaving a receipt at the table.

"Whenever you're ready," she said, then shuffling away.

Asher grabbed the receipt. "It's on me. It's the least I can do."

Chapter Seven

Lauren

Lauren felt uncomfortable from the moment Asher went on the defensive until they exited the diner, returning to the crisp outdoor air. She felt horrible that she'd offended Asher. She hadn't meant to suggest his work wasn't meaningful—quite the opposite. She was proud of him for sticking to work that probably didn't make paying New York City rent any easier. What she wanted to ask was did he truly enjoy living in New York City? Did he love Gemma? What did he think about *Lauren's* work? And what had made him so unhappy that he stopped talking to her years ago?

Asher had changed. He would never have snapped at her years ago. He was always calm, cool, and in control of his anger. He defended the weak, stood up to bullies, and cheered for the underdog. Maybe the traffic and crowded city streets had gotten to him.

They walked in silence down the highway toward the car. Crows squawked overhead as if they were gossiping about the two ex-lovers.

"I don't think selling goat milk is stupid, by the way," Asher broke the silence. "I hope I didn't come across that way."

"No, that's okay," Lauren lied. Maybe she lied as much as Sage did. Lying to avoid hurting people's feelings was different from lying to get what you wanted, wasn't it?

Asher stopped abruptly, turning to face her. "No, it's not okay, Lauren. I shouldn't have talked to you with that tone of voice. And I shouldn't have implied that your work doesn't matter," he said, stepping closer to her. "Because I think it does."

"Well, thank you. I think it matters, too." She stared up at him. She could see he wanted to say more the way his eyebrows furrowed, the way his eyes searched hers. "And, honestly, I'd be more than happy to take any business advice you have. You know, to make it more profitable." Lauren shook her head. "I mean, I'm not trying to get rich but to live a comfortable life. And I know you mentioned something before about selling too many things, and I've been thinking about that, and I thought that maybe you're right..." She was rambling. Asher's gaze had shifted beyond her, looking toward the trees. They had reached the pond.

"Is this... it couldn't be... could it?" Asher stepped away from her, looking up and down, walking near the pond, which reflected the turned leaves, the gray skies. The water was still, showcasing a perfect mirror reflection.

"What? Could be what?" Lauren walked up to him where he stood at the water's edge.

He put one foot in front of the other, counting, "One, two, three, four..." He walked off, Lauren following behind.

"Asher, what are you doing?"

He stopped when he arrived at an old pine tree. Its trunk was thick at the bottom, but a few feet from the ground the trunk split into two pine trees, shooting up toward the heavens. Lauren studied it. At the top of the tree, one tree was slightly taller than the other. It was two pine trees with one trunk, one foundation.

And then she remembered.

"Oh my gosh... it's our tree," she said, stepping beside Asher as he placed his hand on the rough bark. "I'd forgotten about this tree."

Nostalgia seized her. She felt the bitter, the sweet.

This was *their* tree. They'd fallen in love at this pond, under this tree. They'd been together a year—only seventeen—when Asher took Lauren on a picnic date. He'd packed an entire picnic basket full of delicious food, brought a blanket, and candles. Lauren suspected Heidi had helped in some way. She most certainly baked the cranberry-apple pie he'd brought.

Under that tree, Asher had first told her that he loved her. But it was more than love, he said. Like the tree, he felt connected to Lauren at his roots. He thought they were one—soul mates, meant to be. Individuals who would grow together, not apart, for the rest of their lives. They'd reach for the sky together, encouraging each other to pursue their dreams. But they'd remain planted firmly, stable in their love for each other, the foundation of their lives. He'd called her his soul mate. He'd said they were meant to be. It was more than love. It was destiny. It was forever.

A sneaky tear slid down Lauren's face, and she quickly wiped it away. Was it all a joke? A line? Why had he told her such beautiful things, only to forget about her years later? Was his poetry a sham?

She believed it in the moment. She wanted to believe it now.

"It's so beautiful," Asher said, craning his neck to view the top of the trees. "I'm so glad it's still here."

Me too, thought Lauren, but words couldn't escape from her trembling chin. She had to pull herself together or she'd sob right there. But how? How could she push the thoughts from her mind, the memories of Asher and her under that tree, wrapped in each other's arms, his sweet kisses promising her forever? How could she forget the crushing disappointment when he stopped returning her calls? When she saw him in town, and he'd do everything in his power to avoid her? It was too much. She walked away, biting the inside of her cheeks, blinking rapidly to drive away the tears, to avoid breaking down.

She waited at the car, watching Asher look up and smile at the tree. She watched him take a deep breath as he looked at the trunk. He felt the tree again, moving his hand across it, lost in the moment.

Then, he looked up to see Lauren, arms crossed, waiting. He smiled weakly and headed her way.

***

Somehow Lauren survived the drive home from the diner. Asher was quiet, turning on the radio to drown out the deafening silence. He dropped Lauren off, thanking her for her help that day, and was on his way. She didn't ask what he was doing that Saturday night—she didn't want to know. She wanted to release the tears that were rising inside her.

Alone, she let it all out. It felt cathartic to cry like that. She hadn't cried about Asher for years. When it was clear they were done with, Lauren had spent months—many months—in a state of melancholy. Naturally, in public Lauren walked around with a perpetual smile pasted on her face and acted like her chipper self. No one besides Sage and her parents knew how devastated Lauren was about the breakup. Lauren threw herself into work, picking up as many hours as possible at her parents' businesses. She worked six days a week for years. That's how she was able to save up enough money for a down payment on the farm. It helped that she lived with her parents, became manager at both of their businesses, and earned managerial salaries. Lauren was frugal, and not incredibly materialistic. Maybe she wasn't born that way, but she'd trained herself to want not. Of course she got through the austere days by dreaming of cute throw pillows and stoneware she'd purchase to make her future house a home. And yes, she had to walk quickly past boutiques so she wouldn't stop to covet gorgeous dresses and trendy shoes. So, no. Lauren wasn't a saint. She did like nice things, like cute clothes. But she wanted a homestead more than anything, and she practiced discipline to get there.

Setting a goal like the homestead was the perfect distraction from wallowing in self-pity. She felt in control of herself, her emotions, her actions, and even her future. She wanted to live a life that was independent and self-reliant. She wanted to live simply and enjoy the little things in life. And she would find love again. But this time, she wouldn't wait around for it, or wonder where it'd gone. She'd pursue it as passionately and intentionally as she had the homestead.

This time she would cry once, let it all out, and be done with it.

She'd be strong.

She had to be.

**

On Sunday, after church, where Lauren hadn't seen Asher but only his parents, she spent the afternoon making goat milk caramels and chocolates. It was relaxing, despite the hours-long process— the extremely detailed recipe that had to be followed carefully, and the meticulous measuring required to produce the perfect candies. Since she spent most of her days performing manual labor outside, it was a luxury to bake inside. It was dainty and feminine and always resulted in a sweet reward.

She thought about the wedding, a little more than three weeks away. If Asher agreed to Don Carlson, they'd have their photographer and florist booked. Asher had approved her desserts for the wedding, and she'd cook him a few meals next weekend to help him decide on the menu. The invitations had been sent out, and Lauren was already receiving notifications that guests were replying online. There was still much to do, though, when it came to her property. She had to refinish the floors, fix the issues with the barn itself, buy (or build) tables, find chairs, hang chandeliers (which would probably require an electrician), and harvest or buy all of the produce for the menu.

How will I cook it all?

Lauren looked around her cozy kitchen. It was beautifully updated, had a large farmhouse sink and a six-burner stove, but it was nothing like an industrial-size kitchen. She had to cook two hundred meals. *How?*

She licked caramel off her fingers, a crease forming in between her eyebrows. What had she signed up for? Was she out of her mind? It all seemed so simple. She grew all the food she needed. She didn't have the chickens yet to slaughter, but she knew plenty of farmers who would sell theirs for an affordable price. And what about insurance? She hadn't even thought of that. Did her property insurance cover hosting weddings?

She reached for her hair, about to twirl, when she remembered her sticky fingers. At least she had plenty of candy to eat tonight while she worried about the details.

***

Wednesday, October first, Lauren and Sage drove twenty miles north of Pine Lake to Blackstone Lumber, Lukas Blackstone's lumber company. Lukas showed Lauren and Sage several options when it came to installing flooring in the barn, and Lauren trusted him entirely. He suggested reclaimed wood—but not the expensive flooring that was trendy in chic homes and condos. It was piles of scrap wood bundles, all different stains and sizes. It was wood flooring Lukas couldn't sell and didn't want to discard. Much cheaper than installing brand-new floors that could get damaged easily, this reclaimed mishmash of wood would still look chic and sophisticated for a wedding or event. It cost the same to purchase as vinyl or pouring cement, and it would show much better in photos, and feel much nicer to dance on. Installing the floors would cost more than the other options, but Lukas assured her his price was the lowest she'd find anywhere. She trusted him.

After meeting with Lukas, Sage and Lauren returned to town to peruse antiques shops for chandeliers.

"What about this?" Sage asked, holding up a faux crystal chandelier.

"Um, a little too flashy, don't you think? For a farmhouse?" Lauren replied.

Sage looked at it, shrugging. "It could look cool *because* it's too flashy." She playfully raised and lowered her eyebrows to entice Lauren.

"Or not." Lauren smiled politely.

"I might buy it for me then," Sage said. "Even though I have nowhere to put it. But I could stare at it and be happy," she said, laughing. Lauren rolled her eyes with a smile.

"I was thinking white, French-looking vintage-inspired chandeliers. You know?" Lauren rummaged through light fixtures, not finding what she'd described. "Think farmhouse, Sage. If that wasn't obvious."

"Uh-huh." Sage looked at Lauren and asked casually, "So how was Saturday with Asher? Get much done?"

Lauren shrugged. "It was fine. We booked the florist and I'm pretty sure he'll go with Don Carlson for photography. Although I haven't heard from him since then."

"And how was it—spending the day together?"

"It wasn't the first time we've been alone since he returned."

"I know. But you spent the whole day together."

Lauren looked at Sage. "It was a long, emotional day."

"Spill." Sage dropped whatever was in her hands—luckily, it only made a small crashing noise without breaking—and stared straight into Lauren's eyes, crossing her arms. "Tell me everything."

Lauren sighed, looking around the shop. It was an endless room filled with junk. Some of it was useful, beautiful junk, while some of it was useless, hideous junk. There was enough in that room to absorb her words, no room for echo, so Lauren wasn't worried about expressing her private thoughts to Sage.

"Well, the first thing that bothered me was he referred to our relationship as us 'dating.'"

Sage's eyes bugged out and her lip curled. "Dating? Dating is when you go on dates with people and decide if you like them or not. You guys were engaged to be married. You were, like, what's the word? Betrothed."

"I know," Lauren said. "Then, he said he had no idea Heidi had shown Gemma my homestead, otherwise he'd have made sure she didn't choose it for their wedding."

"What a jerk." Sage shook her head.

"I know. So clearly, he's wanted to avoid me altogether. It gets better—er, I mean worse." Lauren thought. "We stopped at The Diner, you know *the* diner in the woods?" Sage nodded. Lauren continued, "Which was probably a stupid idea considering that's where we would go for everything. It was *our* place. Anyway, I asked if he liked his job and did he think it was meaningful, did he think it mattered, and he sort of snapped at me."

Sage gritted her teeth. "I'm going to murder him."

"He apologized later, telling me that he thought my work mattered a ton, and that my job was important." Lauren sighed. "That's not all."

Sage's eyes bugged out again.

"We realized that we'd parked near our tree. It's this old pine tree that is two trees in one. It meant a lot to us when we were together. He recognized it first. We didn't talk about it, and I couldn't compose myself, so after that, he dropped me off."

Sage rubbed her temples. "Call it off."

"What?"

"Call it off, Lauren. This isn't healthy. You're torturing yourself. For what? To prove something to yourself? To prove something to Asher?"

"I'm not doing it to prove anything. I need their business. I need the money and the reference. I can't reject my first client."

"You should." Sage looked hard at Lauren. "And if you can't, then at least you should not spend any time alone with him. He's messing with your head like he did when you guys broke up. You don't deserve this."

Lauren nodded. She knew that. She also knew that she was more sensitive than most people and that her heart was more easily wounded than others. Maybe this wasn't a big deal. It'd been seven years. And she was healed. Right?

"I love you, Lauren. You know that, right? You're like the sister I never had."

"Sage, you have *two* sisters," Lauren said.

"Yeah, but I don't like either of them," Sage said, and Lauren laughed. Sage came from a huge family. Two sisters and three brothers. Raised on a dairy farm. That was enough to understand Sage. "Anyway, I only say this because I don't want you to feel sad. And how could you not feel sad? It's emotional turmoil. It's one thing when something happens that you can't control. But this. *This* you can choose not to go along with. You don't have to allow Asher to play mind games with you like this."

"Do you think he's playing mind games with me?" Lauren wondered. She simply couldn't imagine Asher doing that.

"How would you describe what he did to you at the end of your relationship? He ghosted you. And still hasn't brought it up?"

"Why does he hate me?" Lauren asked without thinking, without realizing tears had welled up in her eyes and were pushing themselves, one by one, off the edge of her eyelid, falling from her eyes like off a cliff, to their deaths on the cold floor below. "No, no," she said, angrily smacking away the tears. "I'm done crying. I'm done crying over him."

Sage kicked aside the heaps of stuff between her and Lauren and threw her arms around her, hugging tightly. "You will never be done until you find out what happened. Until you have closure. You have to ask him why he stopped talking to you. How he could discard you. You have to be brave and ask, Lauren, even if that means he won't like you. What do you have to lose, anyway?"

Lauren nodded, her head still buried in her friend's shoulder. Sage was right. She had already lost Asher. There was nothing worse than losing him.

***

The rest of the week went quickly, every waking hour filled with tasks like harvesting, milking, cleaning, feeding, watering, and repairing. Next week, Blackstone Lumber would deliver and install the new floors. The following day, an electrician would install the four chandeliers Lauren had found. They weren't exact replicas of each other, but each chandelier was white, with a French country-farmhouse vibe to it. They'd add much-needed lighting and ambiance in the barn. The additions to the barn were necessary for its general aesthetic and function as a venue, but it didn't mean they wouldn't cost a pretty penny. Whatever Lauren would earn from this first event, most of it would go to bills like the mortgage, utilities, insurance, and repairs, not to mention whatever ingredients and products she'd have to purchase that she hadn't grown. Whatever profit was left over would go straight to funding the next event or the next month's mortgage.

What if there isn't a profit? Lauren worried that Friday night, as she pulled up to Lone Loon Brewery in her rusted minivan. Should she be spending any money on beer tonight? Maybe it would be best to return to her days of penny-pinching.

I'll only have one, she told herself, dashing from the van to the front door of the bar. Drizzle fell from the heavens, and the air was the chilliest it had been all season. It was fall, all right. *The perfect night for a fire.*

Inside the warm bar, the clinking of glasses and knocking of pool balls mingled with a crackling fire and soothing indie rock. One half of the building was the bar with the fireplace and seating where musicians would sometimes play live music, and the other half had a pool table, air hockey, ping-pong, darts, and a few arcade games. It was possible to spend all night in either of the rooms.

Tonight, Lauren noticed a stool set up near the fireplace and a guitar sitting lonely in a stand. She wondered who was singing that evening.

"I'm so glad you decided to come," Sage said, squeezing Lauren as she pulled her up to the bar counter.

Will turned around, his dark blonde hair shaggy, a slight stubble across his face. He was a farmer, too, and had recently taken over his father's corn and soybean farm. Will and Sage had too much in common to not be together. They were extremely competitive people, which helped keep their relationship passionate rather than complacent. They were perfect for each other, even though they fought all the time. The difference, Lauren noticed, was what they fought about. How to plant seeds, which fertilizer was the best, when not to plant, what the sunset might reveal about the coming day's weather, who should be drafted in the NFL. Ridiculous things in Lauren's opinion. They had never, ever fought about big values—

their belief in marriage, their desire for children, their faith, their goals in life. They would get married soon when Will had felt confident in his first harvest without his father's help. Lauren was happy for her friend, and only a little jealous.

"Lauren, Sage tells me you are quite the slave driver," he said, smirking as he sipped his beer.

"Nothing compared to the way she orders you around," Lauren quipped. She and Will had gotten along like brother and sister since they met. He was one of the few people she felt comfortable being sassy around.

Will laughed. "Hey, I'm the boss in this relationship." He lightly smacked Sage's butt. She narrowed her eyes, smacking his butt in return.

"No, *I* am."

Lauren chuckled. "Okay, kids, let's not start this argument again."

Jacob appeared behind the bar. "Lauren." He was beaming. "I'm so glad you came. Oktoberfest?"

"Please," she said, surprised by his chipper greeting. He was always warm, but it was rare to see a smile that wide cross Jacob's face.

After Jacob handed Lauren her pint, he motioned toward the fireplace. "The booth next to the fireplace recently opened up. You should grab it."

"Okay," Lauren said, smiling as she left the bar to sit at the booth. Will and Sage followed, joining her there to the left of the fireplace. The stool and guitar stood to its right. Whoever was singing tonight, Lauren would get the best seat in the house.

As Will and Sage began arguing about who was the greatest songwriter of all time (Will said Tom Waits, Sage said Van Morrison), Lauren peered around the bar, counting all the faces she recognized. She saw Lukas and Cora. Rachel was there with her husband. Friends from town, friends from high school, and a few middle-aged churchgoers. She even spotted Tyler Wolf and his wife, Sarah. Soon, they were joined by Duke and Jenny Wolf. Lauren made eye contact with the families and smiled, waving. They spoke often, but never about what happened between Asher and her. The brothers had always been sweet to Lauren, ever since she first met them. They had never changed.

She always found it interesting, however, how similar they were. Maybe it was more that Tyler idolized Duke and seemed to live his life in a mirror image of his brother's. Duke went into the construction business and married a beautiful blonde elementary school teacher, Jenny, settling down not too far from his parents. Tyler then went into the construction business and married a beautiful blonde elementary school teacher, Sarah, also settling down in a house near his parents, and, consequently, near his brother. But maybe they were both following in the footsteps of their father Fred, who built a business on fixing things, working with his hands, and married a beautiful blonde high school teacher. Asher was marrying a sexy blonde, but that was all he had in common with his father and brothers. He had always felt inadequate compared to them, he'd told her, when he was younger. Even though Asher was athletic and handsome, his father and brothers were ruggedly masculine and competitive. They worked with their hands—they built and destroyed things for a living—and lacked the sensitivity Asher was born with. Asher was better with ideas than with things. He'd learned from his father and brothers how to fix a leak and build a deck, but that was the extent of his ruggedness. Lauren could never understand why that affected him so much—why he felt so worthless compared to them—and she supposed she never would. But she knew it had always driven Asher to shoot for the moon, to compete and win in any way that came naturally to him. Perhaps that was why he worked so hard to get into a top business school. Maybe that's why he had broken up with Lauren and was now marrying Gemma. Because she was the cream of the crop. She proved that Asher had "made it." Gemma was the ultimate trophy. And Lauren? Lauren…was only simple country girl.

Suddenly the music stopped, and Jacob walked from the bar counter toward the guitar stand. He swung the guitar over his shoulder and sat on the stool.

"Good evening, everyone," he said loudly, getting the room's attention. "How's everyone doing tonight?" People hooted and hollered, clapped and whistled. "I figured I'd play a set tonight considering tomorrow's Cran Fest and we've probably got some out-of-towners. Anyone here for the first time?" A few people raised their hands. "Welcome to Pine Lake, heaven on earth." Jacob smiled widely. "Well, I hope you enjoy yourselves. Tonight, I'll be playing some covers and some originals. I hope you all like Neil Young." Of course they did. The crowd grew quiet, listening and sipping beer as Jacob began "Heart of Gold."

Lauren looked around the bar, sipping her beer. Maybe this wasn't so bad after all. It was a beautiful evening, the fire felt warm and cozy, and listening to Jacob's voice while a slight beer buzz enveloped her made her feel happy and relaxed. As Jacob finished, the crowd applauded, and he went onto his next song, a cover of The Rolling Stones.

A puff of cold air got Lauren's attention. She looked toward the front of the bar where the door opened and Asher walked in, straight to the booth where his brothers and their wives sat. He sat down and looked up in her direction. Lauren immediately looked away.

Why would you do that? That's weird.

So Lauren returned her gaze to where Asher sat, but he was focused on his brothers. *Well, you can't stare at him all night—that would be creepy.* She returned her gaze to Jacob, who caught it, smiled back, and winked at her. She returned the smile.

A waitress set three full glasses of beer before Sage, Will, and Lauren, and collected the empty glasses at the table. Slightly annoyed, Lauren looked toward Sage, who mouthed "on me."

Fine. One more beer, but then I'll drink three glasses of water and stop for a burger, Lauren told herself. She decided to try one more time looking in Asher's direction, catching his gaze in time. His eyes met hers and he smiled. She smiled back, a little too eagerly maybe, and her hand darted up with a quick wave, knocking her glass of beer and sloshing a bit of it over the rim, spilling onto the table. Quickly, she grabbed napkins and wiped it up, hoping no one saw. At least she didn't knock over the entire beer glass, which she'd done many times before, even when completely sober. She looked up to see Asher chuckling and shaking his head. She smiled and shrugged.

She took a glug of her beer.

Jacob finished his song. "Thank you," Jacob said to the crowd as they clapped. "This next one is an original I wrote about a special woman."

Anxiety froze Lauren. She had a terrible feeling this song was going to be about her, but she hoped she was wrong.

Jacob strummed his guitar, the melody soft and soothing like a lullaby. His voice was deep and gravelly, soulful and complex. If she imagined this song was about another woman, it could be pleasing to listen to. But Jacob stared at Lauren as he sang, his stare intense. It was almost like he was gazing into her rather than at her. As if he were looking straight into her soul.

Lauren didn't know what to do. She was sitting front and center, and everyone was witnessing this happen. Her eyes remained glued onto Jacob, a polite smile plastered onto her face, the sound of her heart thumping in her ears. She reached out and took another big gulp of her beer.

His song started out generic. It could have been about any woman. How could she think it was about her, anyway? That was pretty arrogant to assume, she told herself. As he sang, certain lyrics stuck out to Lauren, although she tried to wave them off as vague and trite. "Sweet like honey," he sang. "I know you see me watching you from afar." When he sang, "Twirling your chocolate hair," Lauren felt her chest tighten. *No, please don't. Please don't sing about me, Jacob.* Even if the song wasn't about her, Jacob was singing *to* her. His eyes flicked down to his guitar as he switched chords, and sometimes he closed his eyes passionately, but when he looked upon the audience, his gaze remained focused on Lauren.

"He didn't deserve you," he sang, "and I know I do."

Lauren sat there, not even blinking for fear that she might have a heart attack or spontaneously combust. She wished she could disappear. Her palms were sweating. Her neck was sweating—she could feel her hair sticking to the back of it. Sitting in front of the fire, across from Jacob, was enough to make her feel like she was lying on the sun. Yet she was frozen.

"I wanna wrap myself around you, tangled up beside you, like your finger in your hair," he sang. "You're sweet like honey, and I love you, I love you, and I know you know I do."

After those lyrics, Lauren felt like her spirit had left her body. Everything in her peripheral vision had blurred, and the only thing she could see were Jacob's glowing eyes. Was he sucking the life out of her? All she could think of was Asher. He was witnessing this—the whole town was witnessing this—and she was mortified.

As Jacob strummed the last chord, there was a deafening silence in the room. Tension throbbed against the walls.

"Woo," Sage called out, clapping, and Will clapped along with her. Seconds later, the room erupted, cheering and applauding. Jacob smiled. And after that, everything went black.

***

"Lauren. Lauren." Lauren heard Sage's voice as the ringing in her ears had stopped.

"What? What happened?" Lauren asked, looking up to see Sage and Will standing over her.

"I think you fainted," Sage said. "How do you feel? Are you okay?"

Lauren looked around the room. Music had returned to the overhead speakers, and bar patrons were talking amongst themselves, laughing and drinking.

"Yeah, I'm okay. Did anyone see?"

"I don't think so," Will said. "Everyone was focused on Jacob as he got up, and your eyes sort of rolled back into your head and you slumped over. It looked like you'd fallen asleep."

Lauren hoped no one had seen that. As if she needed another reason to feel embarrassed.

"Where's Jacob?"

"He's taking a break. He'll be back with more originals, though, don't you worry." Will grinned.

A waitress placed a glass of water in front of Lauren, and she chugged it.

"Did you eat today?" Sage asked.

Lauren nodded. "I had my usual breakfast and made myself a sandwich for lunch, but I never got a chance to eat it, I was so busy. So I brought it with me but forgot to eat it in the car." It was true. It'd been an incredibly busy day, and Lauren didn't have much in her belly when she arrived at the bar.

"You probably had low blood sugar," Sage said, searching her purse. "Maybe I have some candy. We should get you a burger."

"You probably were reacting to that 'performance,'" Will said, using air quotes and raising his eyebrows with a grin.

Lauren groaned. "Why me?"

Sage sighed.

Lauren looked around the room. "So no one saw? What about during that song? How were people reacting?"

"Well, Asher looked a bit concerned," Will said, and Sage shot him daggers. "What? It's true."

Lauren sat up straight. "Asher was concerned about the song or me fainting?"

"I think both," Will said. "It almost looked like he wanted to come over here, but he didn't. I think he's afraid of you," he said to Sage.

"Me?" Sage asked. She scowled. "Good. He should be."

Lauren drank the rest of the water. "I should go home."

"You're not driving yourself home," Sage said.

"I'll drive her."

Lauren looked up to see Asher standing next to their table, hands in his pockets, looking cool and casual.

Sage narrowed her eyes, opening her mouth, but Will placed his hand on her forearm, sending her a look indicating she should cool it.

"Are you sure?" Lauren asked. "Don't you want to stay longer and hang out with your brothers?"

"I'm ready to go home."

Lauren looked to Sage and Will. Sage rolled her eyes and shrugged, and Will nodded with a smile.

"Okay," Lauren said, rising.

Asher extended his hand to help her, and she accepted.

Chapter Eight

Asher

"So, are you okay? That was a little scary," Asher said as he and Lauren walked from the bar toward the Mercedes. The night air was chilly. Watching Lauren hug herself made Asher want to wrap his arms around her, but he pushed the thought out of his mind.

"Yeah, I think I'm exhausted and stressed. I'm a fainter," Lauren said.

Asher knew that was true. Lauren had fainted on stage during their senior year of high school while making a speech to the student body. She'd fainted during cheerleading tryouts in college. She was a sweet, timid one. And he thought that was precious. It'd only made him love her more—back then, of course.

"Tomorrow's Cran Fest," Asher said. "Are you going?"

She looked at him and smiled as she nodded. "I would never miss Cran Fest. What about you?"

Asher shrugged. "I plan on it. I suppose I'll see you there?"

Lauren smiled. "Sure, I mean, if you want we can—"

"Lauren. Lauren."

Asher heard heavy footsteps run down the street behind them. They turned around. Jacob, out of breath, approached them. He wasn't wearing a jacket and he looked confused.

"Where are you going?"

"I'm going home. I don't feel well," Lauren said.

Jacob frowned. "But I'm in the middle of my set."

"I know—I'm so sorry."

"Did you hear my last song?" Jacob's eyes were hopeful. He didn't even acknowledge Asher's presence. Asher's jealousy rose to the surface.

"I did. It was so good. You're so talented, Jacob. It was a beautiful song." Lauren's tone was sincere. She meant what she said.

"But you're leaving with him?" Jacob pointed to Asher as if he were a monster.

What was up with this pompous dude? Asher couldn't help but look at him with disdain. It was bad enough Asher had to sit there and listen to this guy's song proclaiming his love for Lauren and his disdain for Asher, but now he had to stand here and watch him pursue Lauren further. Didn't he get it? She wasn't interested.

"Asher offered to drive me home. I shouldn't drive myself," she said.

Jacob sighed. "Promise me you'll come listen to me play again, another time. I have more songs I want you to hear."

Lauren smiled sweetly. "Absolutely, Jacob. I promise."

Jacob grinned, then waved, turning on his heel and trotting back to the bar.

Asher wanted to rail against him, call him every name in the book, but he didn't. Instead, he drove Lauren home, chatting with her about mundane topics, never broaching the topic of Jacob's love song, or their complicated history. He dropped her off and went home, falling asleep with her on his mind.

***

"I miss you, babe," Asher said into his iPhone the next morning. He was FaceTiming with Gemma in Tokyo, where it was near midnight.

"Aww, I miss you too, babe. How's the wedding planning going?"

"Good. Lauren's good at this. We're getting a lot done."

"That's good. It must be nice to hang out with her and all your old friends again."

Asher nodded, feeling guilty. "Yeah, it is. How's the launch going?"

Gemma frowned. "It's slow but steady. Honestly…" She paused, looking around her empty hotel room. Her chin trembled. "I feel a little incompetent."

"What?" Asher had only seen Gemma insecure a few times before, and usually about inconsequential things, or unrealistic issues, like a couple of extra pounds on the scale or saying the wrong thing in front of clients. She looked like she was about to cry, and Asher felt hurt for her. "Why would you feel that way?"

"I don't know," she said. "This is a lot harder than I imagined."

"Of course, babe. This is a huge deal. It's gonna be hard. But you can do it." Asher smiled at Gemma. If anyone could do it, Gemma could. She truly was amazing.

"Thanks. It's only... sometimes I have no idea what I'm doing. I'm usually so decisive, but I've been feeling so much self-doubt lately."

"That's hard," Asher sympathized.

"And I miss you," Gemma said. "I miss you a ton."

"I miss you, too," Asher said. "When will I see you next?"

"Not until this is done... so, our wedding." Gemma brightened. "Unless you come visit me in Japan."

Asher didn't want to do that. As much as he missed Gemma, he had no desire to travel to Japan.

"I don't think that's a good idea," he said.

Gemma frowned. "I know. It's dumb. But we'll get through this."

Asher wondered what that meant. Of course they would, wouldn't they?

"Anyway, I love you so much. And I want to say, I appreciate you more than ever," Gemma said, smiling.

Asher felt moved. He smiled. "I love you, Gem."

She blew him a kiss, then hung up.

He did love Gemma. But more, he respected her. He admired her. So whatever old feelings about Lauren he had felt rising to the surface, he needed to squash. Immediately.

***

After he'd showered and dressed for the day, making sure to wear his heaviest flannel and warmest boots, Asher headed downstairs, ready to spend the day at Pine Lake's annual Cranberry Festival.

"Off to Cran Fest?" Heidi asked from the kitchen, where she poured herself a cup of coffee.

The sunlight shone in through the kitchen window, illuminating her blonde hair, which was neatly wrapped in a bun at the top of her head.

"Yeah. Are you going?"

"I'm meeting my girlfriends later." She smiled. "Are you going with anyone?"

Asher crossed his arms. He still hadn't confronted his mother.

"I might see Lauren there. Why?"

She shrugged. "Only a question, dear."

He took a breath. "Mom, tell me the truth." Heidi's eyes widened, but she remained calm, standing across from him, holding her mug, waiting for his question. Asher asked, "Why did send Gemma to Lauren's farm? Why did you think it'd be okay to tell her we were only friends? And why on earth did you think it would be fine to have our wedding at Lauren's farm?"

Heidi didn't flinch. She stood there thinking while her gaze remained steady upon her son's.

"Honestly? It was an accident. Of course I would want my son to get married close to home. What mother wouldn't? But when I pulled up a list of wedding venues in town, I didn't realize until after I mentioned Lauren's homestead that it was Lauren who owned it. I had never heard of Big Heart Homestead before. I didn't want to cause a big scene by telling her that Lauren happened to be the love of your life—"

"Gemma's the love of my life," Asher interjected with a frown.

Heidi closed her eyes, bringing her hand to her pendant necklace, clutching it. She opened her eyes. "I'm sorry."

Asher huffed. "I'm sorry—it's only… This is an uncomfortable situation."

"I understand." Heidi looked away, biting her lip. When her gaze shifted back to Asher, she said, "I'm not sure there's much we can do now other than accept it."

"I think I should tell Gemma about Lauren. That we were together for a long time."

"Darling, some things are better left alone."

Asher frowned. "You think I should lie to my soon-to-be wife?"

Heidi shrugged. "You already have."

That shot Asher straight through the heart. She was right. His mother's hand rested on his shoulder. "Honey," she said. "It'll all be okay." He looked at her. "Do what you think is right and ignore everything else."

He wasn't sure what she meant by that, but he didn't want to be home any longer. Nodding, he walked out of the kitchen and out of the house, into the brisk outside.

***

For seventy-five years, Pine Lake had been celebrating its most treasured export—cranberries—at the town's annual Cranberry Festival, located in the center of town on Main Street and Cedar Street. Local police officers would park their cars perpendicular to the street, blocking any cars from entering. Vendors erected white tents under which they displayed their products. Honey and maple syrup derived from local beehives and trees were bestsellers, along with local cranberries, which were made into jams, jellies, sauces, pies, breads, lotions, candles, and about a hundred more products. Asher was always amazed by the creative ways people were able to use cranberries. Artisans sold their hand-knitted and woven clothing, hand-carved woodworks, handcrafted pottery, jewelry, and art. Farmers got in on the action, too, selling fresh produce and dairy. And who could resist the Amish stands where gooey cinnamon rolls and pies with buttery, famous flaky crusts were sold? Asher always stopped there first, emptying his pockets for monkey bread, pecan pie, and cranberry-apple cider.

Having already devoured a cinnamon roll and a slice of pumpkin pie, Asher slowly sipped his steaming hot cranberry-apple cider as he meandered through the festival crowds. A country-folk band played music on a stage at the end of the street, where people danced and swayed, Asher guessed not only because the music was good but also because they wanted to warm up.

By the time of the Cranberry Festival, which was always the first weekend of October, the leaves in the northern woods had almost all changed or begun changing. Asher knew that in two to three weeks' time, every single tree would have turned orange, yellow, or red and started shedding, leaving completely bare trees by early to mid-November. Would Gemma get her dream autumn wedding? Most likely not, fretted Asher. He warned her "up north" really was far up north, even showing her a map, but Gemma could often will her way, even when it came to weather. With the turning leaves came nose-reddening air, crisp breezes, and a damp drizzle that soaked the bones. Although the sun shone brightly in the sky, it was chilly enough for scarves and hats on this early October weekend.

Dancing wasn't the only way people warmed up after a brisk breeze. A local winery sold its popular cranberry wine. Local restaurants and taverns sold hard cranberry cider. And, of course, Asher's favorite person, Jacob, sold his craft brews at the tent near his bar. Asher made sure to walk right past Jacob and his smug beard-covered face. He felt a pang of loss, too. When he'd first interacted with Jacob upon his arrival, Asher had been under the impression Jacob wanted to become friends. It was now clear he did not. It was also painfully clear he wanted to be with Lauren. Asher had to give him a little credit, although Asher had felt embarrassed *for* him, Asher also had to admit it took guts to proclaim love to someone in a song before a crowded room. Jacob must have loved Lauren enough to put it all out there and get rejected in front of not only a crowd of people but a crowd of his customers.

Yet, Asher realized, Lauren hadn't explicitly rejected him. But she would. There was no way Lauren would ever be with Jacob. They simply weren't right for each other.

Who could Asher see Lauren with?

He stopped at a tent where vendors were serving whiskey-infused cider. He'd need a shot of that in his cider if he were to continue his thought.

"You're here," a sweet voice interrupted his thoughts. Asher turned to see Lauren, cute as a button in her cranberry-colored hat, scarf, and gloves. Her hat had a little faux fur poof at the top. She looked adorable.

"Well, you're certainly prepared in case there's a blizzard," Asher said with a laugh.

She shrugged. "Can never be too prepared up north. Didn't it blizzard that one year?"

"Oh yeah, freshman year of college. That was horrible."

"Yet they still didn't cancel Cran Fest," Lauren remembered.

"Ah, come on. Pine Lake people are too tough for that nonsense," Asher said.

Lauren smiled. "How's the cider?"

"Delicious. Want a sip?" Asher extended the hot mug of cider.

Lauren leaned forward, about to try, but then stopped short. "Maybe I shouldn't." She smiled politely. *That's right,* Asher thought. *It would be weird to share drinks with someone who's not your girlfriend.* Internally, he sighed. Things had gotten so complicated.

"Here alone?" Lauren asked.

"Lukas said he'd meet me a little bit later, but otherwise, yeah. What about you? Will Jacob be arriving to sweep you off your feet?" Asher couldn't help but smirk. Lauren swatted him.

"Stop. I'm trying to pretend that never happened. The only problem is half the town witnessed it."

"I hear he's the headliner for tonight," he said, watching Lauren flinch, "all original songs about a 'special woman.'" She rolled her eyes, shaking her head.

"Har, har, har," she feigned laughter. "I wouldn't be surprised. That's why we have to avoid him at all costs." Her eyes were sparkling with playfulness. Asher couldn't stop smiling. "Has the Amish bakery stand sold out yet? I got here and I'm in desperate need of a cinnamon roll."

"Let's go check," Asher said, and off they went, ambling through the crowds, stopping along the way to peer into tents.

At the Amish bakery stand, Lauren eyed the many pastries. She asked for a cinnamon roll, looked at the pumpkin cupcakes, then looked away.

"Did you want that cupcake, too?" Asher asked.

Lauren looked at him, grimacing. "Of course I want it, but I probably shouldn't."

"Why not?"

Lauren frowned, looking at Asher as if he should know.

"What? Is it a woman thing?"

"I don't need to gain any more weight," she finally said, avoiding eye contact with him. But Asher let an incredulous guffaw leave his mouth, and her eyes shifted back to his.

"Why would you worry about that? You look great, and you've always looked great." Asher wanted to use a different adjective, but he was not a single man. As an afterthought, he added, "More than great," hoping that she'd catch his drift. *I probably shouldn't say anything to get me in trouble,* he thought, but he couldn't stand the thought of Lauren criticizing her own body when she looked so incredibly—well, he'd leave it at "great."

"Only the cinnamon roll?" the young Amish girl asked at the register.

"That's it," Lauren said with such discipline Asher knew it wasn't her first time practicing composure.

Asher had already eaten two pastries and was now buying himself two more. It was a shame that Lauren felt the need to deprive herself of that second pastry when she looked...*great.*

They walked down the streets as they nibbled on their pastries. A group of children clustered around a table where an old man sat, painting a child's face. With a spindly paintbrush, the man flicked quick brush strokes against the young girl's soft cheeks, creating beautiful twirls and bursts of glittery paint. When he was finished, he handed her a mirror. As she saw her reflection, her eyes lit up, shimmering like the sparkly paint that framed her sweet little face. The children surrounding her stared at the masterpiece, and then rushed the older man, begging him to work his magic on them.

"That's so sweet," Lauren said, watching the old man throw his head back in laughter as the children bombarded him.

Asher looked at Lauren. "Do you still want six of them?" He remembered how much Lauren wanted to have children and be a mother. She'd always told him that they'd have six kids. She'd hated being an only child. Six? Really? Asher would ask her. She'd reply that she'd have as many as her body would allow and their bank account could afford.

Lauren laughed. "I don't know about six... but more than two." She shook her head. "I can't believe I wanted six kids. But that's what you think when you're young. The world is your oyster and your body is invincible." Asher listened, wanting to know more. She went on, "The moment I turned thirty, I swear, it felt like my energy drained by half."

Asher chuckled. "I hear you. Seriously, the moment I turned thirty I started getting backaches. And my knees—they make this cracking noise when I do squats."

Lauren giggled. "I suppose it's better to have kids when you're younger, then. I don't know how some women farmers do it. Farming and chasing after kids all day? Plus, they're probably sleep deprived. At least I get eight hours a night," she said.

Asher nodded.

"Do you and Gemma talk about having kids?" she asked. It sounded more like she was only trying to be polite rather than curious.

"Well, not in too much detail. In general, I know Gemma wants kids. We're on the same page with that, but I don't think having kids is something she's been thinking about much. It's more of like, yeah, sure, in the future... one day."

Lauren nodded. She was quiet after that. They stood for a bit, watching the old man paint another child's face. Then, Lauren pointed at the table next to him.

"Looks like you can paint your own face if you'd like," she said.

Asher saw a sign reading "Paint Your Own Face $5" on the table next to the old man, where an old woman sat, arms crossed to keep warm.

"Should we?" Lauren asked, her eyes dancing playfully.

"I'm the worst artist ever," Asher said.

"Oh, come on." She tugged at his jacket, and he followed her to where the older woman gestured for them to sit down.

"Five dollars each. Two dollars extra for the glitter paint," the old woman said gruffly. Clearly her husband was the charmer and she was the business operator.

"Well, we have to do the glitter paint." Lauren dished out fourteen dollars cash, handing it over to the eager woman.

"No, Lauren, please. Let me get this—"

But Lauren shook her head at Asher. "It was my idea."

He submitted, plopping down on the hard, plastic chair, which also happened to be freezing cold.

"How about I paint your face and you paint mine?"

Asher looked at Lauren. "Really? You *want* me to paint your face?" He watched as she laughed and shrugged. She was so cheery. How? How could she be so happy when he'd talked to her about having children with another woman? His entire adolescence, Asher had pictured having children with the petite woman who was now sitting across from him—who was no longer his girlfriend.

Lauren grabbed a skinny paintbrush, swirling it around dark blue, glittery paint. "I'll paint your face first, and then you can paint mine." She smiled as Asher shrugged in compliance. "How do you feel about the color blue?"

"It's better than the color pink," Asher said. "Wait a sec. I realized I'm going to have to walk around Cran Fest with glittery paint on my face. I don't want to get beat up by a gang of local farmers."

"Oh, don't worry. After a few whiskey ciders, you'll forget all about the face paint." And with that, Lauren brushed the paint across Asher's forehead while he frowned.

As she brushed his face with cold, wet paint, Lauren's expression remained focused and thoughtful. He stared into her eyes, those big, beautiful brown eyes, and tried to imagine what she was thinking.

They used to do things like this all the time. Lauren loved seasonal festivals, county fairs, and summer carnivals. She was drawn to childish games and activities like a moth to a flame. Her natural sunny disposition thrived in such an energetic, lively environment. Asher had always been the opposite. He preferred to compete at sports or watch others compete. He'd always worried he'd be judged if he behaved like a child, like a boy. Mostly, he was afraid of being judged by his brothers and father. They never let him forget that he was the baby.

Hopefully, he wouldn't run into his brothers at the festival, although it was almost impossible not to. Everyone in town went to Cran Fest. Maybe he'd ought to start drinking that whiskey cider sooner rather than later.

Lauren suddenly laughed. Asher looked at her. "What?"

"No, don't move your face," she said. She continued to paint. He looked down at her lips. She had Cupid's bow lips, so beautiful and feminine. Her kisses had always been tender and loving.

He closed his eyes, trying to shake away the thoughts. This was wrong, so very wrong.

"Done." She giggled, grabbing the mirror to show him.

Asher stared at his reflection. He looked like a blue alien, but it was beautiful. Black and blue and dark green glittery paint was creatively swirled and splattered along his temple, cheekbones, and brow. He didn't look too silly.

"Now me," she said, sitting up straight and closing her eyes.

"You don't have to close your eyes," he said.

"Oh yeah." She smiled.

Asher dipped the paintbrush into a glittery purple color. That would look great with her skin tone. He twirled the brush on the apples of her cheeks. Then, dipping it into a passionate berry red, he swept it across her eyelids. He had no idea what he was doing, but he became lost in the curves and lines of her face. Her high cheekbones, button nose, bushy brow—he loved having a reason to remember those features. The features he'd memorized so many years ago.

Lauren's eyes flickered from the ground up to him, meeting his gaze. She stared at him while he lightly dabbed pink glittery paint around her temple. What was she thinking? Did she find him attractive? Was he still handsome to her? Suddenly self-conscious, Asher finished, lowering his hand, his gaze still upon Lauren's, her eyes focused on his.

In a breathless whisper, Asher said, "Done." It was all he could muster. Lauren's eyes remained upon his for a few seemingly endless seconds. Then she grabbed the mirror.

"Beautiful. I look like a fairy," she said, looking back at Asher with a smile.

He smiled. "You are a fairy." But she didn't hear. She placed the mirror back upon the table, rising.

"Now, how about that whiskey cider?"

Asher rose, agreeing that he needed that whiskey now more than ever.

***

A few hours later, and several whiskey ciders in, Asher and Lauren had stopped at the high striker, Asher winning Lauren a stuffed animal, placed their guess on the weight of the largest pumpkin at the fair (the closest guess receiving $100 prize), and eaten all the fried cheese curds, grilled corn on the cob, and pulled pork they could.

Darkness was settling in after a crimson and amethyst sunset, the stars and sliver of the moon beginning to appear. Lauren and Asher made their way to the stage where a full band set up. Asher recognized a few of the members from high school. He had seen almost a hundred familiar faces that day. Between every tent and activity, old friends and neighbors stopped Asher to say hello. He hadn't been forgotten. He hated to admit that to himself, but he had begun to worry that his memory had been erased from the people who meant so much to him, who had helped shape his character.

A chill descended upon the crowd. The sun no longer warming them, the brisk night air forced the audience to huddle close together as the band began to play. Lukas and Cora had joined Asher and Lauren, along with Sage and Will. Even Tyler and Sarah and Duke and Jenny arrived, leaving their kids with Heidi and Fred, who sat farther back from the stage, dancing with their grandsons.

The band played hits from the 1980s and 1990s. Country hits, rock hits, and even some pop hits, the audience in heaven, singing and dancing along, childhood and adolescent memories flooding them with happiness.

Asher felt the slight buzz of whiskey warm him as he sang Journey's "Don't Stop Believing" at the top of his lungs, belting it out with Lauren, turning to sing into Sage's imaginary microphone. A thought looped through his mind: he rarely had this much fun in New York. Sure, nightclubs were swankier, more comfortable, and less crowded. And he could get quality whiskey at the bars in New York. And of course, he'd been to bars that still play classic hits. But there was a feeling of belonging that he felt that night, dancing in that tight clump of friends and relatives, which he rarely felt in New York. In the city, he often felt like an insignificant blip among massive buildings and mobs of people. In Pine Lake, he was known and loved. He belonged.

He was a big fish in a small pond.

And maybe that was the problem.

Maybe, even after all these years, Asher was afraid of being a nobody. Without any genius or talent, model good looks or Wall Street wealth, Asher didn't stand out in the Big Apple. Here, even if he didn't stand out like he used to, he was still brought in like a collective, warm embrace. Was he a coward? Was he weak for wanting to feel like a star and knowing that he'd failed in New York, but could always succeed in Pine Lake? Was he giving in to his insecurities, his ego, and his desire for attention? It was easy in Pine Lake. It was difficult in New York. Maybe this was all about his fear of failure, his phobia of being ignored, and had nothing to do with truly loving Pine Lake and its residents.

Asher wasn't sure. But he did know that he was dancing too close to Lauren. He should stop dipping her and spinning her, singing old favorites with her. He was having too much fun with her. And someone was getting it on camera. After a few flashes, Asher looked up, searching until he spotted Don Carlson, snapping photos on the sidelines. He must have been the official photographer of Cranberry Fest. And Asher was sure he'd documented plenty of damning evidence.

You're not doing anything wrong, Asher reassured himself. And he wasn't. His hands were not creepily touching Lauren's hips or anything like that. He was only dancing with her as any friend would do. The problem was his feelings, not his actions. He felt like he wanted to bring her close, slow dance with her. He looked at her with tenderness. He wanted to kiss her. And that was wrong. *Think of Gemma. You love Gemma.*

The whiskey doesn't help, he decided and made a note not to purchase another.

He'd forgotten all about the glittery paint splattered across his face. Lauren's spirit had energized him, and for the first time in a long time, Asher felt accepted for who he was. There were no airs he had to put on, no important people's egos he had to stroke. Even Jacob Carlson was too busy at his bar's tent to bother Asher and Lauren. It turned out to be a perfect day and a magical night.

For the rest of the evening, Asher danced and sang with his friends, but he kept his mind on Gemma until he fell asleep that night, dreaming of her.

Chapter Nine

Lauren

On her way back from Blackstone Lumber to collect salvaged wood that she would eventually use to build tables, Lauren couldn't help but stop at the tree in the woods.

It was Wednesday, October eleventh, a little more than two weeks until the wedding. Lauren had to construct twenty tables that seated ten people if she wanted to be able to host two hundred people in the barn. Purchasing that many large, solid wood tables would cost a fortune. Thankfully, Lukas Blackstone was donating massive planks of wood—a mishmash of barn wood, driftwood, and scrap from torn-up, red oak wooden floors. Sage had shown Lauren the website of a nearby antiques-slash-retail shop that sold old-fashioned metal bistro chairs for practically nothing. Practically nothing multiplied by two hundred came out to something, however. Still, Lauren estimated she'd spend a fraction of the price by shopping this way.

As she slowed down along the highway, her old van rattled, the planks of wood making clunking noises. She pulled onto the pebble clearing between the pond and the trees, turning off the car.

This is silly, she told herself. *Why are you doing this?*

But she silenced her conscience and strode up to the tree, placing a bare hand upon it. Craning her neck, Lauren looked toward the top of the pine tree, where one trunk split into two.

Soul mates.

Two words repeated themselves in Lauren's mind.

Would she ever love a man as much as she'd loved Asher? Did she still love him? Was it possible to love someone who had shredded your heart, or who'd made you doubt your worth?

Seven years ago, when Lauren had finally realized it was over, she likened the feeling to having the rug pulled out from under her. Falling on her rear, completely shocked and confused, unexpected. It was abrupt and unexplained. *Why?* The question throbbed in her mind. Why did he stop talking to her? Why was he such a coward that he couldn't even break up with her like a normal person? Why had he so cruelly ignored her, pretended as if she didn't even—or ever—exist?

She had to ask him. She had to confront him. Lauren couldn't even confront a person who so obviously cut in front of her in line at the grocery store. How could she confront the person who'd shattered her world? But she had to.

A crow squawked repetitively in the branch above her, an irritating cry. It shrieked and then flew away, frightened by something. Lauren squinted, looking up to the top of the tree. A massive bird perched on the tallest branch. Looking closer, she realized it was a bald eagle. It was majestic. A silence fell upon the woods as the great bird surveyed its kingdom. Suddenly, the tree branches shook as another bald eagle appeared, clasping onto the tallest branch on the shorter tree. Each bird claimed one of the split trees.

Soul mates, Lauren thought. And that was enough for that day.

***

"Does that look wrong?" Lauren turned to Sage, who stood there scratching her chin.

"Well, it doesn't look right," Sage said, squatting down to study the poorly erected table.

It was Thursday evening, and Lauren had spent all day trying to drill legs on a single table, doing her best to repeat what she'd viewed on YouTube videos and website tutorials.

"Maybe we should call somebody. Asher's brothers are carpenters. Why not get them over here?" Sage asked.

"Why not? You can't think of a single reason why I would want to get Asher's brothers involved in this?" Lauren sighed. "Not to mention, I want to avoid the question of how we managed to seat people at other weddings. It's going to come out, Sage. All those lies," Lauren said, twirling her hair.

"No one will ever find out as long as this wedding goes off without a hitch. And look at this barn." Sage stood, marching around the barn. "Look at those gorgeous lights." Lauren had to admit the chandeliers gave off a beautiful glow. "These floors." Sage tried her best to tap dance, making Lauren laugh. "All we need are tables and bada-bing-bada-boom."

"This is going to take forever." Lauren looked at the heaps of tabletops, the boxes of legs. "I'm way over my head."

"Listen, we can do this. It all happened faster than we expected, but that's life. Sometimes trial by fire is the best way to do things." Sage looked hard at Lauren. "You should ask Asher to help you. What else has he got to do? Stare at his old trophies? Put him to work."

"I don't think that's a good idea. Honestly, the less time we spend together, the better."

Sage looked askance at Lauren. "And why would that be?"

Lauren frowned. "Because. Just because."

"Because you're starting to develop feelings for him?" Sage asked. Lauren twirled her hair. "Or you realized you've never stopped loving him?"

Lauren felt like she would throw up. "I should have dated around more these past seven years."

"You never had time. Always working."

"Maybe I should be with Jacob? He's, like, in love with me."

"I bet he'd treat you like a princess," Sage said. "He'd worship you, write you songs and serenade you all night long." Sage smirked, waiting for Lauren's response.

Those images stuck with Lauren. She was silent as she imagined.

"Wouldn't it be nice to be worshiped by a man? To be his muse?" Sage walked up and down the barn, twirling her scarf in the air. "He would call you every night, I'm sure. Though it might be hard with your schedules. You're an early bird and he's a night owl. I'm sure you could make it work. He'd do anything for you." Sage paused. "I think that was a lyric in his song?"

"Stop." Lauren felt ill. "I've thought about it. I have. I'm sure Jacob would be a great boyfriend. I'm sure he'd be the best boyfriend. He'd be a good husband, too. Maybe even a good father, I'm not sure."

"But?"

Lauren looked to Sage, whose expression was knowing. Why even bother asking?

"But I'm not attracted to him. And I don't mean he's not an attractive guy. He's handsome. But I don't feel it. I don't feel the pull to Jacob like…"

Lauren stopped talking, but she knew Sage understood.

"I don't know what to tell you, Lauren, except what you already know. You shouldn't have agreed to this wedding. You should have canceled long ago. And you most certainly should confront Asher."

Another twisting knot formed in the pit of Lauren's belly. A high-pitched jingle startled her. Lauren pulled her ringing phone out of her pocket, the knot in her belly twisting even tighter.

"It's Gemma," Lauren said, an expression of terror seizing her features. "She's FaceTiming me."

"Answer it," Sage said, backing away. "I'll be eavesdropping outside but pretend I'm not here." She slipped out of the barn, disappearing from view.

Lauren cleared her throat. Her heart was racing. *It's only Gemma*, she reminded herself. *No one to be afraid of.* Nervousness seized her as she pushed the "accept" button. Gemma's beautiful face came into view. Her skin appeared to be glowing.

"Hi, Gemma," said Lauren with a smile.

"Hi. Oh my gosh, are you in the barn?"

"Yep," Lauren said, swiveling the phone around so Gemma could get a better view. "I don't know if you can see, but—"

"I *love* those chandeliers. Gorg. And the floor?"

Lauren shifted the phone to the floor.

"Beeeeautiful."

Lauren returned the phone facing her, trying to avoid looking at herself in the mini rectangle at the bottom of the screen. Her hair was tied into a bun at the top of her head and she wasn't wearing any makeup. Gemma, on the other hand, looked like she was going to be photographed for *Vogue*.

"So how's the opening going?" Lauren asked.

Gemma rolled her eyes. "It's going. We've had some hiccups, but I'm getting the hang of it now, and I have to admit—I love this leadership role."

"That's great."

"Yeah, I mean, if this goes well, there might be more opportunities to expand the company in the future, and they've implied I'd be the lead again." Gemma beamed, proud.

"Congrats."

"Well, it's not official, of course. And this is all boring, I'm sure, so tell me how things are going with the wedding." She pursed her lips, ready to listen as if Lauren were one of her subordinates. *I suppose I am.*

"Well, as you can see, the barn is remodeled, and we're setting up tables and chairs." Lauren quickly showed Gemma the tables and chairs. Gemma made a noise of approval. "Oh, and Asher and I ordered the flowers, some pretty autumn flowers. Deep jewel tones like plums and—"

"Jewel tones?" Gemma frowned.

Lauren's heart started racing again. "Um, yeah, is that okay—"

"Would they go well with hot pink bridesmaid dresses?"

Lauren swallowed hard, but her voice cracked anyway. "Hot pink? I didn't know you wanted hot pink."

"I mean, I told Asher to choose the color theme, but I figured he knew me well enough to know I liked hot pink."

Lauren blinked. She didn't know what to say except her go-to phrase. "I'm sorry. I should have consulted with you first. But we can cancel the order—"

"No, don't. That's a waste of time. Everything looks great with hot pink, so forget it. Okay, so what else?"

"We sent the invitations to your guest list. I've received a lot of RSVPs online so far."

"Online?" Gemma narrowed her eyes.

"Yes, instead of traditional mailed RSVPs, the invitation sent guests to a website where they could—"

"Got it. That's efficient. Next?"

Wow. She is damn good at this boss stuff.

"I'm pretty sure we have a photographer, I only need Asher to confirm."

"Why hasn't he confirmed yet?"

"Um, actually, I don't know." Lauren grimaced. "I'm sorry."

"Okay, what else?" Gemma looked away, bored, causing Lauren to feel self-conscious.

"Oh, um, desserts. We are going to do fudge, red velvet cupcakes, chocolate and caramel toffee bars, and a chocolate caramel pie—"

"That's a lot of chocolate."

"We don't have to do that—"

Gemma started talking to someone else in the room that was out of view, and then her eyes returned to the camera. She looked at Lauren. "I have to go. It all sounds fine, Lauren. I trust you," she said. She smiled, waved, and then the screen went black.

Lauren stared at her phone, trying to digest the conversation.

"Wow," Sage said, returning to the barn. "She's a force to be reckoned with."

SLAM. The table Lauren had assembled crashed to the floor, causing Sage to jump, clinging onto Lauren. They looked at each other, frazzled. And because they could do nothing else, they burst into laughter.

***

"Wow," Asher said, surveying the barn full of tabletops, unattached legs, and stacked chairs. "I thought the groom wasn't expected to do any work…"

Lauren flashed him a charming smile to win him over. "Everyone is expected to do work in Pine Lake."

He chuckled, nodding. "That's true." Asher bent down, popping open his toolbox to grab his power drill. "But I'm no carpenter, Lauren."

"Oh, come on. Your brothers have taught you something, right?"

Asher guffawed. "I guess. All right. Let's get to work."

With that, they were off. Asher spent that Saturday morning and afternoon constructing twenty tables, ordering Lauren around as if she were his assistant. They stopped to take a lunch break—a quick sandwich—but remained focused on the task. Only a bit of bickering ensued, surprising Lauren. Trusting his knowledge and abilities, Lauren let Asher lead, which she guessed helped them avoid any arguments. With their Midwestern perseverance, they were able to erect all twenty tables by five o'clock.

***

"How's that for working an eight-hour day?" Asher wiped the sweat from his brow, returning his hands to his hips.

Lauren checked her phone. "Wow. That *was* eight hours."

"Time flies when you're having fun." Asher began un-stacking chairs to surround the table. "Ten chairs per table, I'm assuming?"

"Right," Lauren said, watching him. "But that can wait. Aren't you exhausted?"

He looked exhausted. And, Lauren figured, so did she. She had, however, made an effort to avoid looking exhausted today. She sported a little caffeine-infused under-eye concealer, bronzer, and lipstick—she'd even curled her hair before she put it up into a ponytail. Asher wouldn't notice Lauren had primped before he arrived that morning, but he *would* notice she looked great.

"I figure I'm on a roll. Why stop?" Asher had already finished placing chairs around one table, and then he was off to the next.

Lauren stood back, observing the barn. She had to admit those tables looked good. They looked like they had been purchased from Restoration Hardware. They looked like they'd cost her a fortune, but they hadn't. And the white chairs surrounding the tables were a perfect touch. Everything was coming together.

A thought crossed Lauren's mind. "Would you be upset if I made you dinner?"

Asher looked at her sideways. "Upset? I'm starving."

She smiled. "Great. I think I'll make a few different meals. I have a bunch of fresh ingredients, so I thought I could make some sample meals for the wedding menu."

"Sounds perfect," Asher said. "Once I get all these chairs in order, I'll meet you in your kitchen."

Lauren nodded, trotting out of the barn and toward the house. Exhilaration buzzed through her. It was like they were playing house, she realized. Asher working outside, finishing up chores while Lauren got started on dinner. This was always what she'd imagined their future would look like, even though she knew it was wrong of her to think this way. It was dangerous to enjoy this feeling, to get wrapped up in this moment, lost in fantasy, pretending it was something more than it was.

But she didn't care. She didn't want to stop, and she wasn't going to force herself to shut down these feelings. She felt *good*. Why should she snap back into reality when pretending felt so good? She knew she'd pay for it later. But for now, it felt right.

***

A beautiful tossed Tuscan garden salad of romaine and Bibb lettuce, tomatoes, radishes, and balsamic vinaigrette looked crisp and fresh in a large wooden bowl. Next to the salad, a plate of goat cheese-stuffed dates, speckled with bacon bits cooled down, fresh from the oven. And a platter of colorful roasted vegetables—carrots, cauliflower, and asparagus—sat in between.

Lauren pulled three separate pans from the oven. One with three double cuts of a rack of lamb coated in an aromatic blend of fresh herbs and spices, one with salmon, broiled and seasoned with bread crumbs, garlic, lemon, and butter. The final pan displayed buttermilk marinated chicken breasts with oregano and garlic.

"What on God's green earth is that delicious smell?" Asher asked, stepping into the kitchen, peeling off his scarf and jacket.

Lauren beamed. "Chicken? Lamb? Salmon? Or maybe the goat cheese dates with bacon?"

Asher stared in wonder at the array of food on the kitchen island.

"You made all this, right now?" He was incredulous. "How long was I gone?"

She smiled. "I've been marinating this meat for the last two days, planning to make it on separate nights. And all these vegetables, well, those are from the garden. I harvested them last week. All I had to do was preheat the oven, drizzle them with olive oil and spices and toss them in. The salad is easy. And the dates—I made those yesterday. Thank God for the invention of refrigerators."

"This is all from your farm?"

Lauren nodded. "Not the dates. Those I bought. And the meat I purchased from the local butcher. I had planned on slaughtering my chickens," she said, feeling an involuntary shudder, "but I haven't bought any yet."

"Sorry, but I don't see that happening." He smiled as she frowned, explaining, "You couldn't hurt a fly, Lauren."

She sighed. "You're right. Who am I kidding? I'll never be able to slaughter them."

"That's okay," Asher said, stepping closer to her. "Why should you? First of all, you have plenty of chores already. Secondly, I don't think selling chicken meat is your dream job, is it?"

Lauren couldn't conceal her smile. "No, it's not."

"Well, then, there you go."

Asher's eyes glowed soft and tender as he gazed at her. Reflexively, Lauren backed up, bumping into a stove burner. "Ouch," she said, turning around. "Looks like the meat is ready." She felt a rush of hot air as she opened the oven, grabbing the pans with her oven-mitt-covered hands. Were her sweaty neck and palms a result of the blast of oven heat, or because of the look on Asher's face?

This is not real, Lauren told herself. She wasn't Asher's wife, as much as she was pretending to be.

Placing the pans of meat on a cooling rack, Lauren turned off the oven and slipped off her mitts, heading toward the wine rack to grab a bottle of Pinot Noir.

"This will go great with the lamb." She reached for two wineglasses from the cabinets, rising on her tiptoes. They were out of reach and after her frustrated groan, Lauren heard Asher shuffle over to her. He placed his hands at her hips—ever so gently and for only a split second—to squeeze by. She lowered her heels, turning to see his mischievous smile.

"Having trouble?" He grinned, effortlessly swiping two glasses from the tall cabinet, placing them on the countertop.

"Thanks," Lauren said, feeling warmth rise to her cheeks.

Without being asked, Asher uncorked the wine bottle, pouring generously into the wineglasses.

This is probably a very bad idea. What was the difference between this and a date?

Asher handed her a glass, clinking his against it. "Cheers," he said, and winked.

"Cheers." She clinked hers against his, sipping the light, spicy Pinot. After she dished a little bit of everything onto a plate, she handed it to him, then doing the same for herself as they sat at the round kitchen table.

Lauren smiled at Asher, permitting him to dig in. He began cutting the meat and vegetables, genteelly raising the fork to his mouth to savor each bite. Closing his eyes in delight, Asher made noises that caused Lauren to believe he liked her cooking. But she knew that already. She'd made lamb for a reason—it was his favorite. She knew he'd love the combination of goat cheese and dates, and that the only vegetables he'd eat were carrots, asparagus, and cauliflower using her secret ingredients: garlic and sea salt.

She knew him. She knew his favorite dessert was anything that combined caramel and chocolate. She knew his favorite cheese was Wisconsin aged cheddar—best if it was fried cheese curds. His favorite beer was Indian Pale Ale. His favorite wine was Pinot Noir, even though he didn't know it, she'd taken note every time he'd taste a Pinot and say, "I like this wine. Why do I like this wine?" She knew he'd work tirelessly until he finished all twenty tables that day, and that he wouldn't stop until the chairs were in their places. She knew that he would beat himself up over any mistake he made today, whether it was that touch on her hips or staring into her eyes for too long. He was a man of integrity. She knew his favorite scent on her was amber oil, which was why she wore it that day, even though she knew it was completely unfair that she did.

But she didn't know why he'd stopped talking to her, or why he'd broken up with her. So maybe she didn't know him at all.

"That is simply divine," he said, playfully raising his voice a few octaves and dragging it out into a Southern twang. She knew he'd do that, too, at some point or another. He loved putting on an old Southern woman's voice when he tasted something truly delectable.

"I'm glad you like it," she said.

"The lamb is my favorite," he said, devouring the last cut. "But I know it'd be way too expensive to offer everyone lamb, right?"

"It's totally doable, but yes. It would be expensive." She knew that eventually Asher would decide on the chicken. But she couldn't resist cooking lamb for him this one last time.

Something had come over her. Was she possessed? Were the lies Sage told transforming her into an evil home-wrecker?

"Salmon is good, but not everyone likes fish," Asher reasoned, finishing up the salmon. A few roasted vegetables remained.

"You should finish those vegetables before you claim to be full," Lauren said with a smile. Asher would do anything to get out of eating vegetables.

"I will, jeez," he said. He took a bite of the chicken. "That's some creamy, juicy chicken. Let's go with the chicken, then."

"Great choice," Lauren said. "And the roasted vegetables and salad will be sides. The goat cheese-filled dates will be an appetizer along with maybe some bruschetta and cheese and crackers."

"You got it." Asher forced down the last of the roasted vegetables before finishing off the chicken. He gulped his wine. "This is good wine. I don't usually like wine," he said, only proving what Lauren already knew.

Lauren finished the food on her plate, which were significantly smaller portions than what she'd dished onto Asher's plate. She took a sip of her wine.

"Is it bad that I'm hoping you made dessert?" Asher grinned.

"I didn't make any fresh dessert. But I do have a few week-old slices of chocolate pie left. It might be a little bit mushy," she said.

"Hey, I'll risk it."

Lauren smiled and rose, heading to the refrigerator. She could feel Asher's eyes watching her, and she suddenly felt self-conscious. She was glad she wore her most flattering jeans and a loose-fitting top, especially after eating such a filling meal. His eyes followed her as she plopped the slices on a plate, placing it before him.

"Are these both for me?"

"I might have a few bites," Lauren said, returning to her seat. She reached her fork over the table, stealing a bite of the pie on his plate. He smirked.

"This is good," he said after a bite. "Not too mushy."

She agreed, her fork dipping back into the pie on his place. As she pulled the fork back toward her, the blob of pie dropped from her fork, onto the edge of his plate. Asher stabbed at it with his fork, picking it up and extending his own fork toward her mouth.

"Here," he said without thinking, his fork diving into her open mouth.

She ate it, trying to avoid brushing her lips against his fork, but it was near impossible. The moment was tense with heat. He stared at her, mouth ajar. Lauren could only think that he'd realized how inappropriate that move could have seemed. How close they were teetering to the edge... the precipice of danger.

But the buzz of wine had so quickly warmed her, and Lauren didn't care. Something had switched inside of her. She wasn't afraid of him anymore. She wasn't afraid to love him still. And she did. She loved him still.

His electric blue eyes lingered on hers. "Lauren." His voice was soft, delicate.

She felt as if she was on the edge of her seat.

"I think we should..." His gaze shifted to his wineglass. His large, masculine fingers strangled the dainty neck of the glass.

"What?" she asked, almost begging.

Ask him. Ask him what happened. We should talk about it, that's what we should do.

"I think we need to," he began again, but his voice was even quieter this time. Quickly, he raised the glass to his lips and gulped down the rest of his wine until the glass was empty.

"We need to...?" Lauren's voice was as quiet.

Asher was struggling. He was being tormented by something— she could tell. *He must be thinking of Gemma. Maybe he's going to admit he doesn't love her. That we should cancel the wedding. That we should be together.*

"We should call it a night," he finally said, looking up, his eyes finding hers. Then, as quickly, he looked away and rose, almost knocking the chair out from under him.

Lauren stood up too, feeling suddenly frazzled and lost. It felt like something was being stolen from her. "No, it's early." She looked at the clock on the microwave. Eight-thirty. "So early for a Saturday night."

Ask him now.

But he was scurrying away, placing his plates and glasses on the counter near the sink, reaching for his coat on the hook by the kitchen door. Lauren was on his heels, frantic.

"I mean, I doubt you're going to church tomorrow, right?" Lauren laughed, trying to lighten the mood. But Asher's emotions were heavy, sinking in the air around them.

"I probably should," he said, stuffing his arms through his coat, throwing his scarf on, and indicating he had no time to get it right.

He turned the doorknob and the kitchen door opened, and a sharp wind blew in.

"You had a glass of wine. Maybe you shouldn't drive. Do you want to wait a bit while it wears off—before you drive?"

He was halfway out the door. "All that food will soak it up." After saying that, he snapped to, as if his mind was suddenly clear. "Thank you, by the way. That was delicious. I think the wedding menu will go over well. You're a talented cook, that's for sure." A smile flashed across his face and he turned around, calling, "Good night."

Within minutes, he was gone.

Lauren stood at the open kitchen door, the cold air slicing against her, but she didn't care. She watched until the red glow of his taillights disappeared.

***

It was hard not to watch Asher the entire seventy-minute church service the following day. It wasn't because old Pastor Heinz was boring, or that the heat was on full blast and lulling everyone in the building to sleep. No, it was because Lauren was trying to decipher what it was she still loved about Asher.

Asher went to church, but only when he was nagged. That had always been the case. Although Lauren liked to think of her faith as a more personal, private relationship with God, she acknowledged the benefits of regularly attending worship services. She'd tried to convince Asher of said benefits in the past to no avail. Still, he'd drag himself to church when one of the women in his life badgered him enough. Usually, it was Heidi. Who had persuaded him to go today? Lauren couldn't be certain, but she did wonder if he felt the need to show up after using it as his excuse last night.

Asher was handsome. *That is objectively true*, Lauren thought as she watched him mouth the words to the eighteenth-century hymn the parish sang in unison. Lauren knew Asher wasn't singing. He hated his singing voice, so all these years, he simply opened his mouth and lip-synched, hoping no one around him ever noticed. She watched his lips open and close. Oh yes, he was lip-synching now. Totally.

Regardless, his lips were beautiful—kiss worthy. Asher wasn't only empirically good-looking, but also he was attractive *to* Lauren. Much different from him simply being objectively good-looking, like Jacob Carlson. Jacob Carlson had pretty eyes, a great smile, good bone structure, a fit body. He was technically handsome. But Lauren wasn't attracted to him. Asher, on the other hand, also had good bone structure—well, model bone structure—and a thick head of hair, gorgeous eyes, beautiful lips, and a strong, muscular body. But he also had a scar that cut into his top lip, a slight unibrow, a chipped front tooth, and short legs. He had imperfections, in other words, but those imperfections made him so incredibly attractive to Lauren. Best of all, Lauren knew all of his physical flaws. She'd memorized them. And his personality flaws? Sadly, she'd learned those, too.

They'd simply fit. One of their favorite things to do when they were together was watch a movie. Together on the couch, under mountains of blankets, Lauren and Asher would snuggle, fitting together like two spoons. His arms wrapped around her, making her feel safe from any danger that could befall them. Every few minutes he'd kiss her shoulder, or her neck, or her cheek, without having to say anything at all, and for no reason at all. They fitted together like jigsaw puzzle pieces, snapping into grooves, locking together for eternity. They were meant to be, body and soul.

Yes, that was what she remembered she loved about Asher. They connected beyond the physical. Maybe they'd even been together before.

She also loved that Asher remembered everyone's names. That Asher would meet someone, whether they were a band geek or his grandfather's ninety-year-old roommate at the nursing home, and he'd remember their name, their story, their value. He made people feel special and welcomed. She'd witnessed him shake hands or hug dozens of people last week at Cran Fest. He'd remembered every single person—even asking how their family members were or if they were still doing whatever they had been doing in college. He took the time to genuinely get to know people, to listen. Ironically, he was a good communicator.

That's why Lauren was certain he'd chosen to cut off communication with her. She knew he had a knack for schmoozing.

He was talented at asking questions and conveying feelings. He was a leader, a manager, a captain. No shrinking violet was Asher Wolf.

She remembered the pain he caused her years ago. She still felt it.

And she remembered how much he'd loved her. How well he'd loved her for seven full years. Yes, she'd mentioned to Sage that perhaps Jacob Carlson would worship her, love her madly. And she believed he would. But not the way Asher had loved her. He loved her with otherworldly magic. That's why she loved Asher.

But the real reason Lauren still loved Asher was for no reason at all. Because when you loved someone, your lists were futile, your excuses worthless.

Lauren loved Asher, but it didn't matter why.

And it was with that realization that Lauren decided she was going to fight for him, one way or another.

Chapter Ten

Asher

New York City smelled.

Had it always smelled, Asher wondered as he glided down the bustling streets, his dress shoes clopping along the sidewalk. *Maybe it had always smelled, but not this bad? It couldn't have. How could I have stood this stink?*

The garbage bins were overflowing with garbage bags, which leaked onto the sidewalk... How long had Asher been gone?

It was Monday, October twenty-second, and Asher had been in Pine Lake for four weeks. In less than two weeks, he'd be married to Gemma on Lauren's farm. Now, he walked down the grimy streets of New York City, the sunrise only a sliver of orange hidden in the sky between skyscrapers. There were no roosters or singing birds— unless you counted pigeons—to naturally wake him from his slumber.

As he arrived at the large glass doors of his office building, Asher suddenly felt out of place. He was fumbling and awkward, unsure of who should go through the doors first, him or the three ladies waiting behind him? He smiled and pushed through, holding the door for them, his smile fading as they ignored him. Seven years in New York, but it only took four weeks for him to forget how to be a New Yorker.

Everyone was in a hurry, scrambling down the wide hallways, their heels and dress shoes click-clacking against the freshly waxed floors. At the elevator, Asher had to squeeze between people or risk waiting for the next elevator. No one said anything to anyone.

When he entered the office, the hipster college intern at the front desk glanced at him but said nothing, despite Asher's cheery wave and overdone smile. He found his way to his tiny office—and it was nothing more than a closet with a desk, no windows—surprised to see stacks upon stacks of papers on his desk. Folder and files and spreadsheets.

"Long time no see, eh?" Asher's boss Tim, only a decade older than him, fit and handsome and fashionably dressed, asked, standing in the doorway.

"Yeah, feels like forever," Asher said.

Tim nodded. "I'm sure it does when you're in the middle of nowhere." He walked up to Asher's desk and pulled out a few files. "So, we spoke about these on the phone last week. Gonna need you to reconcile these numbers and get back with us on the monthly report."

"You got it. And the meeting's at eleven?" Asher asked.

"Same time every day," Tim said, patting Asher's chest and heading out the door.

Taking a long look at the work before him, and the lack of natural light in that room, Asher felt the walls closing in. He took a deep breath and got started anyway.

***

The meeting could have been half as long, in Asher's opinion. There were so many non-issues that had been made into issues and so many topics of conversation that didn't need to be talked about. If Asher were completely in charge, he could have made that meeting much more efficient. It also made him realize that he'd been incredibly productive the past month in Pine Lake. He'd been able to get so much work done during business hours and had time to spare at the end of the day. Wake up with the sunrise, go for a run and lift weights, return home for breakfast—all of that could be done before nine a.m., *and* he'd still be highly productive until five o'clock. He'd even have time to make a big, delicious lunch while working from his parents' home. And most weeknights, he had been spending time with Lukas and Cora, his parents, Lauren, or simply alone. Life was slower paced, yet more productive. It was only now that Asher realized he valued that lifestyle.

Maybe Lauren was right, Asher thought. Life *is* simpler in a small town like Pine Lake. But did that mean it was less exciting?

"Hey, buddy." Elias was at the door, the buzzing fluorescent lights shining down on his shiny, bald head. "We're going out for drinks. You coming?"

Asher glanced at his work, then back at Elias. Colleagues had been interrupting him all day to ask him questions or request feedback, resulting in less work finished than Asher had hoped. Elias was a colleague whom Asher considered a friend. "Friend" was a relative term in New York. Asher would go to a basketball game, a concert, or a bar with a friend in New York, but he would never confide his feelings in any of his friends there.

"Well, I suppose I should finish working on this stuff," Asher said.

"Ah, come on. I bet you've been bored out of your mind in Wisconsin. Your work can wait until tomorrow." Elias grinned like he wasn't going to take no for an answer, or maybe he'd insult Asher until he gave in.

"Yeah, you're right," Asher said, grabbing his jacket and leaving his briefcase in the swivel chair behind the desk. He marched right out of the closet-office with Elias, pulling on his jacket along the way.

"How's the whole wedding thing going?" Elias asked, raising an eyebrow.

"Not too bad. I think we've got a lot of the planning done. I'm guessing there's a lot of little things to take care of now."

They pushed through the tall, glass doors. It was six o'clock, and they were one of the last few still in the office. For a nonprofit, Asher's company still attracted a lot of ambitious employees. Six o'clock wasn't staying late for most companies, especially law firms or investment firms. But for the nonprofit world, his colleagues still valued climbing the ladder, and whatever that entailed.

"And Gemma's going to take care of them, right?"

Asher looked at Elias as they entered the elevator. "No, I am."

Elias shook his head. "Oh, that's right. You mentioned something about her in Japan. So, what, you're like at home with your ma, going over the flowers and stuff?" Elias guffawed.

"Uh, no, actually, I am not going over flowers with my 'ma,'" Asher said, rolling his eyes. "We got a wedding planner."

"Is she cute?" As Elias smirked, desire to punch him swelled up inside of Asher.

"She's my ex-girlfriend," he said through his teeth. Already knowing where this conversation would lead, Asher felt instant regret.

"Your ex-girlfriend is planning your wedding? Wow. That's a new one. So is Gemma through the roof?"

"She doesn't know she's my ex-girlfriend," Asher said, spinning to look at Elias square in the eyes. "And you're not going to tell her."

Elias raised his hands in surrender. "No way I'd ever, buddy." He laughed and shook his head. "But I gotta say, that seems unlike you, to keep a secret like that from Gemma. I mean, if she was a high school sweetheart, what's the big deal? Gemma seems pretty confident to me. I don't see her flipping out over this."

Asher considered that. "Yeah, I don't see it, either. But I've already gone so long without telling her, and Lauren and I have called ourselves 'old friends' so many times in Gemma's presence, I can't go back now."

The elevator dinged and they exited, walking down the now empty, wide halls with floors that would be waxed yet again that evening.

"Well, how serious were you? I mean, could you pull off having been 'old friends'?" Elias's expression was serious now. Asher could tell he genuinely cared, which caused Asher to feel compelled to tell Elias everything.

"We were serious. We were going to get married."

Elias's eyebrows rose toward his hairline. He scrubbed his hand with his face. If he had hair, Asher felt like he'd have run his hands through it already. He was a dramatic New Yorker, nothing like the stoic Wisconsinites.

"Wow, and she doesn't know?" Asher shook his head. Elias continued, "Why didn't you get married?"

A long exhale left Asher's mouth as they entered the crisp air outside. The sky was dark and cloudy, not a single star visible. Neon lights flashed outside of buildings while bright florescent buzzed inside. They walked down the street, holding conversation despite the honks and screams and thuds and rattles of people and automobiles.

"She stopped talking to me," Asher said. "When I moved to New York. We decided we'd be long-distance while I was in grad school, and see where we wanted to live after that, but it never worked out."

Elias shook his head. "She stopped talking to you?"

Asher nodded. "Cancelled her flights, didn't return my phone calls. I didn't even bother with email. We weren't big on that. Neither of us had smartphones at the time. So, yeah. That was it. It sort of faded, I guess."

"How long had you been together?"

"Seven years."

Cigarette smoke clouded the air in front of the swanky bar where Asher and Elias were headed. Women dressed in stilettos and lots of black, either miniskirts or pantsuits. They all looked sleek, rich, and important. Asher knew they were probably none. False advertising was everything in the city. As Elias and Asher slipped past them, Elias flashed the ladies a flirtatious smile.

"Seven years and she ghosted you?" Elias was incredulous.

Inside, the bar was dark, almost too dark for Asher's liking, and smelled like a mix of cologne and whiskey. The ratio of men to women was staggering, and every man wore a business suit, their jackets and ties slung over the backs of chairs, their shirts wrinkled from a long day of work. A few women dotted the place, eyed by the men who sipped their brandy Manhattans.

Elias and Asher found a tiny, round table and two empty chairs. They made a beeline straight for the table before anyone else could claim it. A twenty-something waitress appeared. Her russet hair hung to her hips, and her eyeliner was smoky. She was beautiful. But her hair made Asher think of Lauren, if only for a moment.

"What can I get you two?" Even her voice was attractive.

"I'll have an old fashioned," Elias said.

Asher thought for a second, then asked, "Do you have any seasonal beers?"

"Seasonal?" the waitress asked.

"Yeah, like an Oktoberfest?"

Elias raised an eyebrow at that. The waitress shook her head.

"No, we don't, I'm sorry."

"Oh," Asher said. "That's okay. I'll have an old fashioned, too."

She smiled and walked away. Elias looked to Asher. "Oh man, did you see her?"

Asher almost laughed. *What kind of question was that?*

"Get her number," Asher said, leaning back into the chair, undoing his tie. He'd gotten used to not dressing up for work. And he'd gotten used to liking it.

"I think I will," Elias said with confidence. "So what's Lauren like?"

Asher frowned. "What do you mean?"

"What's she look like? How's her personality? Has she changed since you've seen her? Is she married now with three kids?"

Asher sighed. He didn't want to talk about Lauren. Or maybe he did. A jolt of excitement ran through his veins. There was so much to say about Lauren, so much Asher wanted to discuss, but he didn't want to indulge in those feelings. They were wrong. Weren't they?

"Lauren is petite. Long, dark hair. Big, beautiful brown eyes. She's adorable." Asher saw Elias grimace. "What?"

"You're still attracted to her."

"Look, I'm only describing her. You asked me to. It's a fact. I mean, it's objectively true. She's pretty. Very pretty."

"As pretty as Gemma?"

"Dude. Can you not?"

Elias raised his hands in surrender. "I'm sorry, don't be mad at me. Can I be honest with you?"

Asher groaned. "I have a feeling you will be anyway."

Elias nodded, smiling. "You know me too well." He looked around the room, shaking his head. "I look around, and I don't see much promise. All these old guys, doing the same thing over and over. Work, drink, sleep. A lot of miserable people in this so-called elite bar. But you, you have this amazing fiancée. Don't screw it up, Asher."

Asher furrowed his eyebrows, offended, as the waitress placed their two drinks on the table before them and traipsed off. Within seconds, the strong whiskey was hot in Asher's throat, crawling down like some potent creature. *That's terrible stuff,* he thought.

"What does that even mean? You think I'm going to cheat on Gemma? Because I'm not. I would never do something like that. Never."

"I never said you would, and I don't think you would either," Elias said. "And, hey, I'm no saint."

Noticing his face was flushing and his breathing steadily increasing, Asher tried calming himself. "Then what are you saying?"

Elias took a long sip of his drink, shrugged his shoulders, and said, "I am getting the sense that you're wrestling with something. And all I can tell you is any man would kill to be in your shoes marrying Gemma."

A heavy silence fell upon Asher, as the whiskey started to buzz. Elias was right, and Asher knew it.

***

Closure. That's all I need. Getting ready for work the next morning, Asher took note of his and Gemma's tiny Manhattan apartment. Small, but it was also sleek, like a new piece of technology. It had clean lines, smooth surfaces, and was minimalist. The furniture, paintings, and paint colors all in hues of black, white, and red made it look like a magazine ad for Swedish furniture, but not in the same way Lauren's home looked like a magazine ad. Asher suddenly hated everything in his apartment, especially the emptiness. The truth was he missed Gemma.

So, he called her. Running late for work, Asher decided to multitask, shaving and video chatting Gemma simultaneously. After a few rings, she answered.

"Babe. I miss you," she said first, sending a wave of relief through Asher.

"I miss you too," he said.

She laughed. "Are you shaving?"

"I had trouble getting up this morning. Had a few whiskeys with Elias last night."

"Nice. Did you have fun? I bet it's nice to be back in the city."

Asher shrugged. "It's noisy. I guess I've gotten used to the rural silence."

Gemma smiled. "I can't wait to see you. Being here has only made me love you more."

Asher's ego swelled. "Same here." He looked down at the phone as he washed off his razor. Man, she was stunning, and he was so completely attracted to her. "I forget how beautiful you are sometimes."

She smirked. "Forget? Is that a good thing or a bad thing?"

"It's a good thing. It means you get more stunning every day."

"Well, thank you. You're pretty darn handsome yourself... You're going back to Pine Lake, right?"

"At the end of the week," Asher said. "Though Lauren has a good handle on things. Don't you think she can do it without me?"

Gemma frowned. "No. I mean, yeah, probably. But I want you to be there. She'll need your help, but also, I have a long list of things you need to be there for physically. Unless you want to fly back every weekend." Gemma knew how he'd answer that. Asher hated flying, which is why he appreciated that his job didn't require business trips.

"Fine," Asher submitted. "Are things any better?"

Gemma perked up. "Yes. I've got this new company working like a well-oiled machine. I will be receiving a big raise and an even bigger bonus." She flashed a smile at Asher.

"You impress me every day, sweetie."

"I love you. I'll talk to you later." She blew him a kiss and hung up.

Asher looked at himself in the mirror. Shaving cream inconsistently dotted his face. After splashing his face with cold water, Asher returned to his reflection, trying to find answers in the looking glass. He saw nothing—nothing but a man conflicted, sparring with his past and his future.

***

Wednesday, Asher was beginning to feel claustrophobic. He squeezed into a flimsy rolling chair at the long mahogany conference table, his shoulders nestled up next to Elias, with another colleague next to him. The table was full of Asher's colleagues, stuffing stale doughnuts down their throats, and sipping bitter, black coffee. While his boss Tim boasted he only ordered coffee and pastries from the best bakery in Manhattan, Asher begged to differ. There were no flaky, buttery crusts on these pastries, no gooey middles. Amish pastries were in a class of their own. And Lauren's baked goods came a close second. Yet the sugar-laden, mass-produced food and drinks were trendy amongst the elite businesspeople and, Asher guessed, cost nearly ten times as much as what he could find in Pine Lake.

Disdain. That was the emotion Asher was beginning to recognize as it first brushed against him. It didn't take long to feel that emotion dig into his skin, penetrating his bones. Why was he feeling this way? Months ago, he'd have believed Tim when he touted some restaurant or bakery. He'd give in to the peer pressure of waiting in blocks-long lines for the new latte concoction at some overpriced, hipster café. But he was beginning to smell the phoniness and starting to taste the difference.

"Okay, everybody. Listen up," Tim said, standing at the head of the table. "We need to work on rebranding. Based on Asher's recent calculations and input, we're losing out on massive amounts of charitable donations because our brand is no longer speaking to our donors."

The men and women around the table groaned. Who didn't groan when the word "brand" was used?

"What does that even mean?" Elias asked petulantly.

"Asher?" Tim zeroed in on Asher, who felt sleepy. *Must be all the sugar.*

"Um, yeah, so it means that for some reason, our wealthy donors are not connecting with our message thus donation checks are smaller or infrequent."

Elias rolled his eyes. "They don't connect to the message of feeding the hungry?"

Tim crossed his arms. "Elias, you know that we serve our donors."

"Yeah, I know that, but I think it's ridiculous. We're supposed to be serving our neediest people, the homeless, the food-deprived."

"We all know that's not how charities work." Tim was irritated.

Asher looked to Elias next to him, making eye contact. He completely understood where Elias was coming from. It was ridiculous, wasn't it? Trying to appeal to wealthy people so that they'd choose to give to your charity? Picking color schemes and logos to catch their attention? Creating pithy taglines to interest them? Wasn't helping the helpless enough? But that was life, and Asher was no fool.

"Asher, I think it'd be wise to have you put together a game plan for us all, and spend the next week working on it with your colleagues... *some* people need a refresher course in Nonprofit one-oh-one." Tim shot dagger eyes to Elias, who looked away, shifting uncomfortably in his seat.

"Spend the next week? Um." Asher sat up in his chair. "I have to go back home next week," he said quietly, almost a mumble.

Tim shook his head, letting out a sigh. "Is that necessary?"

"Well, I can still work on the plan at home and communicate via Internet video calls, but I need to be back to work on the wedding..." as soon as the words came out of his mouth, Asher witnessed several colleagues snicker, turning to whisper to each other or mumble to themselves. It was pathetic, wasn't it, Asher having to be holed up in his hometown to plan a wedding.

"Let's talk about this privately," Tim said. "Moving on, Kirkwood, let's go over marketing strategy."

As Kirkwood spoke, Asher tuned out, only able to hear his rapidly increasing heartbeat and feeling the sweat form on the back of his neck. *Everyone thinks I'm a fool.*

After he accepted this fact, Asher was faced with his feelings. The truth was, Asher had been excited to return to Pine Lake, though simultaneously worried about spending more time with Lauren. He had to admit it. He was still attracted to her—very much so. Shame engulfed him as he confessed this truth to himself, but he felt relief from suppressing it. More importantly, he cared about her. And he enjoyed spending time with her. But Gemma was the love of his life. And he was going to marry her.

All he needed from Lauren was closure. He needed to know what happened so many years ago. He needed to understand why. Once he received that information, he could move on and be at peace.

"Asher," Tim said, interrupting his thoughts. Asher looked around, watching as his colleagues rose from the conference table, shuffling out of the room to leave Tim and him alone. "Let's talk about next week."

"Oh, yeah, I'm sorry Tim," Asher said. "That was a dumb reason I gave."

Tim waved his hand. "No, that's all right. I appreciate your devotion to your fiancée. I think that's wonderful and not to sound tasteless, but it's good for our brand."

Asher's eyes widened. "Really? How?"

"Well, it shows that this company is made up of people who have values, strong foundations. I know you pretty well, don't I?" Asher nodded. "You're salt of the earth. You're who I want this company to model itself after. A man who cares. A man who has morals. A man who helps others. A man with dignity." As Tim went on, Asher felt his stomach twist. "So, I think it's only right you go back home to commit to your fiancée and your declaration of love. I think that's beautiful. We're not a religious company, but I think your dedication to your family and your community is as close as we might come to faith."

If he only knew, Asher thought, feeling self-loathing. *I'm a man of integrity? More like a man who's spending his time thinking about kissing his ex-girlfriend as he plans to wed another woman.*

"Wow, um, thank you. That's one of the nicest things anyone's ever said to me." Asher smiled. "What about training my coworkers?"

Tim grinned. "That's the catch. You'll have to put in some heavy-duty hours tonight and tomorrow to bring them all up to speed if you want to make it home next week." He winked, turned on his heel, and walked out.

Of course. There's always a catch in this town.

Asher grabbed a frosted doughnut, its icing melting down its dry, doughy sides.

Disgusting, he thought and reached for a second.

***

It was midnight when he left work after finally finishing his report and presentation that he'd spend the entire next day presenting to every individual coworker.

Asher's frustration rose to the surface as he strolled down the sticky sidewalks, dodging not-so-friendly-looking people, and dropping dollar bills in beggars' plastic cups. He felt himself gritting his teeth, furrowing his brows. It was midnight, yet the streets were speckled with people. Smells and sounds became overstimulating. The juxtaposition of Jaguars and Bentleys, real fur coats and jewelry stores against the steaming manholes and scurrying rats irritated him. He thought about the company and its rebranding to appeal to the wealthy, simply so they felt like the charity they were donating to had a hip enough image. It sickened him. He thought about the fifteen-hour day he worked, and the poor diet he'd already grown accustomed to the past three days alone in the city. He thought about all the coworkers he'd spend hours with tomorrow, anticipating their eye rolls, groans, and blank stares. No one cared. No one had a passion for their jobs. No one found their work to be meaningful.

He stopped in his tracks, watching a cockroach climb up the curb. Another beggar mumbled incoherently in his peripheral view.

Did his work matter? *Was* it meaningful?

Lauren's questioned bounced around his brain. She'd only asked because she was curious and cared, not because she was accusing Asher of leading a superficial life, of wasting his day fretting over meaningless work.

What was his answer to her question? On the surface, Asher's work looked meaningful. He spent his days finding ways to bring in more money from donors that would eventually help the needy. But did those donations truly help? Did they solve the fundamental problem?

Asher wasn't sure. His gut, some instinctive voice buried deep down inside of him, a voice without language, told him *no*.

My work is not meaningful. Not to me. And I'm not sure if it matters.

Instead of relief, Asher felt anger. Had he wasted seven years in New York? Had he been lying to himself? Was it all for nothing?

He emptied his pockets of cash, stuffing it in the beggar's bucket, turned to walk a few yards down the sidewalk, and then let out a frustrated yell.

No one flinched. It was New York, after all. And he'd had about enough of it.

***

On Friday, October twenty-third, Asher got on a flight back to the Midwest, landing at Duluth Airport. After a long, bumpy bus ride to a larger Wisconsin city, he then took an expensive cab ride back to Pine Lake. Traveling for hours was the last thing Asher would ever choose to do, but he knew asking Lauren to pick him up would feel even worse.

With Heidi chaperoning a PLHS dance that evening, and Fred already snoozing on his recliner, Asher decided to satisfy his hunger by driving to The Diner in the woods. A week of New York hot dogs, pizza, and too-bitter coffee was enough to send him on a made-from-scratch food mission.

The sun had long set by six o'clock, casting a bluish glow throughout the forest. When Asher opened the driver's side door after parking in The Diner's lot, he smelled the familiar scent of cedar and pine wafting through fresh air. What a difference.

A slight drizzle fell from the heavens as he entered, taking refuge in the warm, muggy restaurant, smells of bacon and coffee still prominent even at evening time. Alone, he sat at the counter, next to a line of truck drivers. He ordered meatloaf and mashed potatoes, which he knew were made with local butter from grass-fed cows, the meat in the meatloaf from a farm nearby. Though tiny and off the beaten path, The Diner was way ahead of the curve—serving local and healthy produce, meat, and dairy decades before it was trendy, allowing them to keep their prices low.

Asher ate his meal slowly, savoring each flavorful bite.

Was it absurd to prefer a meal cooked in a tube-shaped diner in the middle of the Wisconsin woods to an upscale, New York steakhouse? Asher felt ridiculous at the moment, but when he looked around to get a better look at the place, his self-judgment eased up. Maybe it was absurd to others, but not to him. This was home.

***

There was no way he could leave the woods without stopping at their tree. It was raining now, and Asher had forgotten an umbrella. He pulled his wool pea coat over his head, placing a hand on the rough bark.

He needed something. An answer. A direction. A guide. He hoped the tree would give it to him. He hoped the answers Lauren would eventually offer would quell his restless soul.

A flash illuminated the forest as thunder boomed in the distance. *Probably not the safest place to be right now*, Asher thought, taking one last look at its enormous trunk, its towering branches. He nodded to himself, returning to the car, sliding onto the leather seat.

The rain fell harder now. Lightning flashed, and thunder roared every few minutes. Soon, it was pouring.

He started up the car, flipping the wipers to their highest speed. The winding, forested highway was not his favorite place to be in the middle of a thunderstorm, but at least he wasn't on a boat in the middle of the lake. Pulling onto the highway, he focused on the yellow painted line along the road, letting it guide him through every curve and twist. Water sloshed against the windshield and it was impossible to see for more than a second. Normally, Asher considered himself to be brave, not often set off by tense situations. He remembered many occasions Lauren would sit next to him in a car worrying about the weather, afraid of the lightning, quietly praying as her hands gripped the edge of her seat. During those moments, Asher would comfort her. He'd remind her he wasn't scared, and he knew what he was doing. He'd remind her if ever she were caught in a blizzard or a torrential downpour, to focus on the yellow lines or the car's lights in front of her. To not get distracted or look too far ahead. Focus on the moment, on the few feet ahead of you. Like any distraction in life, the moment you look away, you'll crash.

He came to an intersection, knowing he had to turn left. Squinting as he peered through the windshield, Asher concluded no cars were turning in either direction. He accelerated, tugging the wheel to head left. That's when he felt a jolt, heard a crack, and everything went black.

Chapter Eleven

Lauren

"Are you okay?" Lauren felt an icy sensation against her cheeks. She opened her eyes, reaching for her throbbing head. She saw Jacob, leaning over her, his cold hands holding her face. "Lauren, are you all right?" He looked terrified.

"Yes," Lauren said, although she wasn't sure. Nausea, a stiff neck, sore ribs. She looked at her hands. No blood. That was a good sign, wasn't it? "What happened?"

"I think we hit a car," Jacob said. "I'm going to go check on them. Can you call nine-one-one?" He reached for the latch to open the car door, but waited for Lauren to respond. She nodded, slowly reaching for her purse, where her phone was located. "I'll be right back," Jacob said, slamming the door behind him.

Lauren looked out the car window, but could only see pouring rain, so she dialed the police and asked for an ambulance. All she knew was that they were on Highway F traveling north toward the national forest. She looked at her smartphone's GPS, able to pinpoint an exact location for the dispatcher. When she got off the phone, Lauren closed her eyes. Placing her hands at her temples, she tried to ease the severity of her headache as she pieced together the night.

The past week had been a productive week where Lauren had focused on the homestead. Asher's absence allowed her to ignore the upcoming wedding for a bit and tend to the many daily chores and tasks that had been put on the back burner since his arrival.

Thursday, she'd been surprised by a text from Jacob asking if he could take her to dinner. How much longer could she dodge Jacob? How much longer could she pretend she didn't know about his feelings for her? She had to work up the courage to reject him once and for all. It was wrong to lead him on, she decided. So she said yes.

At six o'clock, Jacob arrived at Lauren's homestead to pick her up in his large, sturdy pickup truck. It wasn't only farmers up north who had large vehicles designed for hauling. Everyone owned a pickup or a van or an SUV, including sensitive songwriter Jacob. Although Jacob was no jock, he couldn't help but boast about his new pickup's masculine look. Most important, he had assured her, was its safety rating. Deer didn't stand a chance.

He was taking her to a new steakhouse near Pine Lake, which was slightly past the forest—and The Diner—on Highway F. They weren't more than a half-hour into their date when they crashed. And Lauren was nowhere near rejecting him yet. She worried that this accident had derailed her plan, literally. *What about the other car?* Lauren hadn't even thought about that yet. She felt fear, guilt, and urgency. She wanted to rip off her seatbelt (which had probably saved her from going through the window) and jump out of the car to check on the other driver.

Wait. The paramedics always say stay put, don't they? Lauren worried over her next move. *Should I wait? Stay? What if I have an injury I'm not aware of? Perhaps I should wait for a paramedic to take me out safely. What if the car blows up? Should I get away from the scene of the accident as soon as possible?* With all this spiraling crazily through her mind, it was only then that she saw a glimpse of the other car, between the frantic windshield wipers and complete darkness. When lightning flashed, she saw the other car was a white Mercedes, and her heart nearly stopped.

"Oh my gosh. Asher."

She didn't think twice, knowing it was Asher, and ripped off her seatbelt, pulling open the truck door, running toward the driver's side, where Jacob was leaning over, talking through the window.

"Lauren, what are you doing? Stay in the truck," Jacob said. With the booming thunder and the heavy rain, Jacob was yelling. But she could sense a tone of anger behind his words.

"Asher?" Lauren peered into the window, seeing Asher, lethargic sitting there. His eyes were open, but she didn't see any blood. Slowly, without turning his neck, Asher's eyes shifted to the corners, and he looked at her.

"I'm okay," he said.

"Are you sure?"

"Lauren, stop, you'll make things worse," Jacob said.

"Worse? What does that mean? Are things bad? What happened? Is he hurt?" Lauren's heart was racing. She was on the verge of tears. *Be strong*, she told herself.

"We don't know yet," Jacob said. "Did you call the ambulance?"

"Yes, they're on their way," she said, returning her gaze to Asher.

He stared ahead, blinking slowly. Scanning his body for any signs of injury, Lauren felt slightly relieved. But his eyes—they looked cloudy, as if he were slipping between dreams and reality.

"Asher?" Lauren asked, stepping closer. Cold rain was seeping through her wool coat, and her hair was drenched. She ignored the discomfort. "You don't feel like you're going to pass out, do you?"

Asher shook his head then winced. A "no" fell softly from his lips.

"Don't move your neck," Jacob said with urgency. "Lauren, stop talking to him."

"But this is what you're supposed to do so that people don't slip into unconsciousness," Lauren said.

Jacob glared at her. She'd never seen his eyes on fire like that. She knew something was bubbling to the surface, jealousy and hurt that had been buried deep below.

Lauren looked away, noticing blood on Asher's right hand. "Asher, your hand—" she said, leaning over, reaching for the door handle.

"No," Jacob said, grabbing her hand and pushing it away. "Don't touch him." He stepped closer to her. "You could hurt him worse."

And that was enough to set Lauren over the edge. Tears began rolling down her cheeks, merging with raindrops, as her chin trembled, and heat rose from her belly to her ears. She was angry and scared. Angry at Jacob for standing in her way, and scared that Asher could be seriously hurt. Angry that she'd not known what happened between her and Asher for so many years, and scared of her intense love for him still.

Jacob embraced her. "I'm sorry, Lauren. I'm sorry for being a jerk, but this is serious, and we don't know what we're doing. We have to wait for the professionals." He held her tightly, although in his arms was the last place Lauren wanted to be, and kissed her head. The high-pitched call of an ambulance and fire truck softly wailed in the distance, growing louder as it neared.

Warmed by Jacob's strong arms, Lauren stood back and watched as paramedics pulled Asher from his car, lifting him onto a stretcher, placing a neck brace around him, and sliding him into the ambulance.

A muscular paramedic pulled Lauren gently away from Jacob, leading her to a second stretcher.

"What are you doing? I'm not hurt," Lauren said.

"It's protocol," the paramedic said, firmly holding Lauren's arm and guiding her down onto a stretcher. Looking over, Lauren saw that the same was happening to Jacob. A police car and then a tow truck arrived at the scene, scoping out the cars and the accident site. A second ambulance arrived, and Lauren and Jacob were ushered into it. She stayed silent the entire ride, listening to the beeping machines and rain pounding upon the ambulance's tin roof, trapped inside her thoughts.

***

"Sign here," said the nurse at the front desk, her long, red acrylic nail pointing to the signature line on the release form. Lauren obeyed her instructions, handing the paper over to her.

"Is it possible for me to see a patient here before I leave?"

The nurse stared at her blankly. "Patient name?"

"Asher Wolf."

As the nurse clicked around in her computer, Jacob arrived at Lauren's side.

"How are you feeling?" he asked, his eyes soft. He smiled warmly, looking like a changed person.

"Oh, um, I feel fine. What about you?" Lauren looked him up and down. He looked unscathed.

"I'm fine. Reeling."

"Looks like Wolf comma Asher is in recovery."

Jacob's ears perked up, and his eyes followed Lauren as she stepped closer to the counter, attempting to peer over it at Asher's file, which the nurse flipped over, Lauren assumed because of HIPPA violations.

"What does that mean? Did he have to have surgery?" Lauren's voice cracked, full of emotion. A cloud descended upon Jacob. Lauren could feel his energy shift.

The nurse stared at Lauren. "All I can tell you is that he's okay and recovering. He is not accepting visitors at this hour, however." The nurse pointed to a sign that clearly stated visiting hours were only until eight o'clock p.m. Lauren glanced at the clock directly above the sign. It was nine-thirty p.m. "There's always tomorrow."

Lauren smiled. "Thanks." She turned to Jacob. His eyes were steely gray.

"Rachel is here to pick us up. She can drive you home."

"Thanks, Jacob," Lauren said, about to say more, but she stopped. What else was there to say? What, was she going to run down the hall and burst into Asher's room, despite what the nurse said? Lauren followed the rules. Knowing Asher was okay would have to suffice.

She let Jacob place his hand on her back, gently guiding her toward the sliding doors, exiting into the dark parking lot. The rain had stopped, but puddles of water pooled every few feet.

"The truck is okay," Jacob said. "Wasn't totaled. But I'll have to do some work to repair the grill. We're lucky that the truck is so safe and sturdy. And thank goodness we were wearing our seatbelts. A pretty amazing invention, huh?"

Lauren forced a smile, nodding.

Jacob continued. "It was a classic T-bone. That rain was so crazy, I don't think anyone could see anything. I definitely didn't see Asher turning. I mean, I don't think he'll do anything stupid, but I have good insurance, so I'm not too worried."

Lauren scowled. Good insurance? Sturdy truck? *Who cares about your stupid truck?* Anger—a feeling Lauren rarely felt, and never expressed. She'd been feeling it more often than usual the past month, and she didn't like it. She didn't like the heat rising inside of her, the furrowing of eyebrows, the clenching of her jaw. But it was happening.

"I'm starving. Are you? We can go back to the Lone Loon and order some takeout. Relax by the fire. I think we both need to rest." Jacob was looking at her, Lauren could feel it, but she avoided making eye contact. She was busy calming herself. If she opened her mouth, she might say something she regretted. Now was not the time to let Jacob know how she felt about him.

"I forgot something," Lauren said, turning on her heel and facing the sliding doors. "I'll be back," she said as she rushed through the doors and ran down the hall. She ignored the glares from nurses and patients as she made her way toward the ER rooms. Panicking, Lauren hurried from door to door, gazing into every door's little square window, squinting to see the patient, hoping to recognize Asher. As she got to the door to Asher's room—she could see his black hair, his bright eyes staring at the TV ahead of him—something dug into her bicep.

The nurse from earlier glared at her, her acrylic nails digging into her skin.

"Ouch." Lauren looked at her.

"I said visiting hours are over. Do that again, and I'll call the police." Her eyes widened as she released Lauren from her grip.

It was all right. Lauren had gotten what she needed—the proof that Asher was okay. She apologized and rushed back out of the hospital, meeting Jacob in the parking lot as he was closing the passenger's side door of Rachel's car.

"Get in," he called, and Lauren did, panting as she closed the door behind her, hurriedly securing her seatbelt.

**

After relaxing in a hot lavender-infused bath and resting in bed to heal her sore neck and aching head the next morning, Lauren dressed for the day and fixed herself a plate of cooked veggies every color of the rainbow. Although the doctors told her she was fine, Lauren decided to take extra precautions by eating and drinking nourishing foods and beverages to comfort her body and speed up any necessary recovery.

Looking out at her farm, Lauren felt a desire to leave it. There was much to be done, but all Lauren could think about was Asher. But before she visited him, she had to get something out of her system.

So she hopped in her van, turning onto the country road, and headed toward Highway F. Driving past the accident scene, Lauren felt a shiver up her spine. Broken glass, skid marks, and bits of plastic splayed across the black asphalt. She swerved to avoid any glass, and kept driving, soon entering the national forest.

When she arrived at the tree, she pulled onto the pebble pathway, putting the car in park and pulling the keys from the ignition. Once her boots hit the muddy ground, Lauren felt grounded—safe. She marched up to the tree—their tree—and placed her hand on the rough bark.

Damp, chilly, misty—the forest felt enchanted. Only the sound of a few squawking crows and rustling leaves could be heard. The nearby pond's surface was glass.

Lauren closed her eyes, placing a second hand on the tree trunk.

Tell me what to do. Should I tell him how I feel? Should I swallow my feelings, and keep planning his wedding? Who was she asking? Uncertain, Lauren opened her eyes, staring up at the towering branches above her, feeling drips of rain from earlier fall onto her head.

BUZZ. BUZZ.

Startled, Lauren realized her phone was vibrating in her pocket. One new text message, and it was from—her eyes widened—Asher. Hastily, she clicked onto the message.

Hey. They're releasing me and my parents aren't available to pick me up. I'm sorry to bother you, but if you're available, would you mind?

Like lightning, her fingers dashed across her smartphone's screen, replying, **Yes, I'll be there soon**. As soon as she hit the "send" button, Lauren regretted her haste. She was such a people pleaser, always at everyone's beck and call. *You have to stop, Lauren. You have to start standing up for yourself. Oh, right, as if that's easy.* Dueling voices inside Lauren's head set off her headache again. With one last look at the tree, Lauren returned to her car and back onto the forested highways.

***

Asher was already sitting in the waiting room when Lauren arrived at the hospital. He had a few butterfly bandages on his head, a bandage around his wrist, and a small paper baggie, which he held up to show Lauren.

"Drugs," Asher told Lauren, followed by a laugh. "Though I don't think I'll need them. It's not too bad." He walked slowly with Lauren through the glass sliding doors, into the crowded parking lot. Clouds overhead moved quickly, allowing glimmers of sunshine to warm them.

"So you're not in a lot of pain?"

"Only a little sore all over. I have a pretty bad cut on my forehead. No concussion, no breaks. Lots of bruising, though."

"That's amazing," Lauren said, reaching the van, and hopping in. Taking it easy, Asher slowly climbed onto the passenger's seat, and Lauren waited until he fastened his seatbelt in before she drove off. "I mean, it's a miracle almost. Right? Jacob T-boned you with his monster truck."

Asher rolled his eyes. "It's no monster truck. But yeah, it would have been worse if I had a passenger." Asher looked out the window as Lauren cruised down the Highway E, ever more careful of her speed. "He probably did it on purpose."

She quickly turned her head to see Asher, sending him a frown, and as quickly returned her eyes to the road. "Oh my gosh, no way. You're joking, right? I mean, there's no way Jacob would do that on purpose. That would be, like, attempted murder."

Asher laughed. She was probably wrong—what did she know about legal jargon, especially criminal acts? Lauren scowled. "Well, I don't know what you'd call it, but whatever it is, Jacob didn't do it on purpose. We couldn't even see ahead of us. You know that."

Asher sighed. "Calm down, Lauren, I'm only kidding."

Lauren took a deep breath. "Oh."

"It was an accident. And a coincidence that it happened to be Jacob driving... with you in the car."

Or was it fate? Lauren wondered. *And if it was fate, what was the purpose?*

Lauren cleared her throat. Did she owe it to Asher to explain herself? She felt compelled to tell him. "We were on a date." Immediately, Lauren felt a shift in Asher's energy, like she had felt with Jacob. Tension seized his body. Her eyes flickered to his, which stayed steady upon the road.

"So, you'll be leading him on for the rest of your life, I guess."

That made Lauren angry. She was tired of feeling angry and of suppressing her true feelings.

"No, I won't." Her voice was strong, steady, calm. "I'm going to tell him that I'm not interested in him, and never will be. I'm going to let him down—kindly. It's only, well, I wanted to make sure. I've never let him take me out, so I wanted to make sure I knew what he was like and that he knew I wasn't interested." She nodded. "But I was going to be kind about it. No matter what it is, there's always a way to be kind about it."

"And it's always good to be honest, no matter what." Asher leaned over, turning up the heat.

Lauren looked at him. Her heart was racing. Now was the time to ask. Now or never. *Not while driving. You don't want to get into another accident, do you?*.

No, she didn't. With white knuckles clutching the steering wheel, and her heartbeat loud in her ears, Lauren glanced at the rearview mirror, making sure no cars were close behind her, as she jerked the car to the side of the road.

"What are you doing?" Asher asked, reaching out to hold on to the dashboard as the van jumbled around against the bumpy grass off the road. Lauren put the car in park, sharply turning to view Asher.

"You're right, Asher. It's always good being honest. So let's do that. For once, let's finally be honest."

Asher stared at her, surprised. His eyes wide, mouth ajar, he blinked, and began to shake his head.

"About what?"

Lauren swallowed. Her heart was racing so fast it was painful. She felt like she was floating outside of her body, staring down at herself. No, she felt like she was shrinking inside of herself, like a Russian stacking doll. And the smallest doll was her voice, which was a muffled cry calling from a far distance when she said, "About *us*."

Asher let a puff of air out of his mouth, stunned. He nodded slowly, then got comfortable in his seat, facing her. "I think that's a good idea."

"So," Lauren began. She swallowed, thirsty. Her mouth was dry. Her tongue felt like a swollen blob in her mouth—like a beached whale. "So, what happened?" She was breathing heavily while trying to control it. She hoped she didn't look like as big of a mess as she felt.

"You tell me," Asher said, resolute.

Lauren sighed. "Come on, Asher. We can't keep doing this. We've spent four weeks together, and not once talked about the elephant in the room."

"Which is?"

Anger bubbled inside of Lauren. *I can't feel this way anymore.*

"Why you broke up with me. Why? Why did you stop talking to me, Asher? Why did you pretend I never existed? Why did you suddenly put a distance between us? You cut me off. Like I was nothing to you. All without an explanation." Lauren's eyes had already welled up with tears, and her chin had begun to tremble. As soon as teardrops fell, she pushed them away, biting her lip to stop her weeping.

Asher looked astonished. For a moment, he was speechless, reeling over her words. Then, he shook his head. "I didn't stop talking to you... *you* stopped talking to me."

"What?" Lauren chuckled incredulously. "That's not true at all. Don't spin this around on me, Asher."

"Are you kidding me? Seriously? You're joking?"

"No, I would never joke about this."

Asher ran his non-bandaged hand through his hair. "Lauren, I called you endlessly, you never returned my phone calls. You canceled your flight to see me—"

"Because my mother was sick. You knew that. I asked you for another date to reschedule the flight, but you never got back to me."

"What are you talking about? Yes, I did. I said two weeks later would be fine. We talked about it."

"No, we didn't. We absolutely did not. I kept waiting to hear from you, to book another flight, but you were radio silence."

"Not true at all. I always returned your phone calls when I missed them."

Lauren felt dizzy. Her hands shot to her temples, massaging them. "Well, I don't think you're right. I know I tried every possible way to get in contact with you, and you stopped talking to me suddenly. Then, at Christmas..." Lauren watched as Asher's eyes widened.

He interrupted her. "We fought about this exact issue. You blamed me, but it was obvious you wanted nothing to do with me. You didn't invite me to Lake Superior for Thanksgiving—"

"What? Of course I did. You were invited. That was implied. I had to ask you?" Lauren's brows furrowed, tears of hurt turning to tears of anger. Rage wasn't an emotion Lauren was capable of, at least she didn't think she was. But angry tears? They were flowing.

"Well, I didn't assume that, especially since things had been so rocky."

Lauren guffawed. "Well, that's your fault."

Asher grew angry. "What about the next Christmas? Remember at Christmas you hid from me? You avoided me, like you've been avoiding Jacob all your life."

Lauren frowned. "No, that's not true. You didn't even look at me. You rushed out of that church like it was on fire." Her body was warm with the memories, the hurt, the pain from her past.

"You're right. I rushed out of there because I was so exhausted from coping with my feelings. You... you hurt me, Lauren." Asher's words were quiet. It was hard for him to admit.

"You hurt *me*," Lauren said.

Asher looked away, through the windshield at the trees ahead of them. A few trucks and cars zoomed by them, shaking the van each time one passed.

"I don't get it," Asher said. "What does this mean?"

Lauren shrugged. "I don't know. All I know is that I never intended to lose contact with you. I never intended to break up with you. Asher, I intended to... to marry you." She was scared of his reaction. But pride swelled inside her. *You did it. You told him your truth.*

Asher's hands covered his face as he shook his head. "No, no. Don't say that, Lauren."

"What do you mean? You knew that. We talked about it. I mean, we planned on getting married. We were going to get married when you graduated from grad school." And then the thought hit her. Maybe this wasn't as innocent as she thought. "But you met someone else. You met Gemma. So that's why you were able to move on, be okay with our breakup. You found the girl you wanted to marry. I'm not your dream girl, am I, Asher?" Once the words left her mouth, grief engulfed her, like she'd lost something, as if something had died within her.

His hands dropped to his side, his neck turned, slowly, so his eyes could meet hers. "My dream girl?"

Lauren's chin trembled. She bit her lip, looking away. She'd dug up an entirely different fear. The fear that she wasn't beautiful enough, thin enough, sexy enough for Asher. That even if he loved her then, there was no way he could still love her now. Not after he could call Gemma his.

She felt so naked, so vulnerable. The worst feelings she'd ever felt—the devastation of their breakup, the realization the love of her life was no longer hers, the affirmation that she was nothing special and, possibly, unlovable—those feelings reentered her body, sinking deep within her soul.

"Lauren, I..." Asher thought for a moment, his eyes searching the wilderness before him. He sighed. "I intended to marry you, too. You..." He stopped himself from saying whatever it was he wanted to say. "I never purposefully ignored your phone calls or chose not to call you back. I never avoided you in town, except that last Christmas, but that was only because I thought you hated me. I thought you were done with me, and I couldn't bear looking at you... seeing you... seeing you and not being able to kiss you, and hold you, and love you. I couldn't bear it. So I didn't."

Lauren let a cry escape. Tears streamed down her cheeks, faster than she could wipe them away. "So... so neither of us wanted to break up?" Asher shook his head sadly. "And we both thought the other one broke it off?" Asher nodded. "And for seven years we've been wrong?" Asher blinked, understanding the gravity of the situation. It was almost funny, except it wasn't. If Asher weren't engaged to be married two weeks from that day, Lauren would laugh. Call it unfortunate and see where they could go from there. But where *could* they go from there?

"This sucks," Asher yelled, slamming his fist onto the seat cushion, causing Lauren to jolt.

"Asher..."

"I'm marrying Gemma. That's it, Lauren. I love Gemma," he said forcefully, only causing Lauren's chin to tremble more. "And I can't do this to her."

"We're not doing anything, Asher. Only talking," Lauren said.

"I ... I can't believe this. I can't believe this." It was as if Asher's "on" button had been flipped. "You loved me? You didn't want to break up?"

"We agreed…" Lauren said, nervously watching Asher's energy increase. He sat up straight, his leg quivered, his foot tapping against the van's floor.

"You loved me. You didn't hate me. You didn't want to break up. You didn't want to be with Jacob." He turned to her. "You don't want to be with Jacob?"

"No, definitely not." Lauren watched him, on edge.

And all at once, as quickly as he'd heated up, he cooled down. He was silent. Turning to her, his eyes were soft, pleading. "Do you love me still?"

A sharp pain shot through Lauren's heart. She was afraid to answer. *Be strong. Be honest. Share your truth. Stand up for yourself.*

"Asher, I…" She took a deep breath. "Yes, I still love you, as much as I've tried not to." Asher closed his eyes tightly. "Asher, I still believe we're…" but Lauren stopped herself as a tear pushed itself from Asher's eye, sliding down his cheek. He turned, viewing the road, eyes open, but tired, heavy.

"I'm sorry that all of this happened, Lauren. Hurting you is the last thing I'd ever want to do in my life. I hate that you've been in pain for so many years. I've felt it, too. But it was seven years ago. We were in the past. We can't go back, even if we want to."

Lauren stopped herself from gasping. She clutched her heart, feeling her lips invert, stifling a cry. She nodded, reaching for the gear, shifting it to drive.

"Okay," she said, pulling off the grass and back onto the road. Through bleary eyes, she drove down the winding roads, passing forests and farmland, in silence, Asher by her side. When she dropped him off at his house, he said nothing but "thanks" as he exited the van.

She wept the rest of the drive home, on her walk up to her house, and until she reached her bed, where she sobbed until she fell asleep.

Chapter Twelve

Asher

How could this have happened? How could they have gone seven years without knowing how the other felt? If there was anything Asher and Lauren had a knack for failing at, it was communication. They'd figured that out when Asher went to graduate school, through the first semester.

What had Lauren meant by his "dream girl"? Who did she think he was? Asher was a man, and any man's head would turn if he were to see Gemma. Did Lauren believe Asher loved Gemma and not Lauren because of the way Gemma looked? Didn't Lauren know Asher well enough to know he was not a superficial chump and Lauren was undeniably beautiful? There was so much he didn't understand about Lauren, so much he didn't understand about Gemma for that matter, but what puzzled him most was that Lauren had been able to repress all of her long-ago feelings, only now telling him how she felt years later.

On the other hand, Asher had done the same. Instead of swallowing his pride and asking Lauren years ago if she was no longer interested in him, Asher had been passive. He'd been lazy. Maybe he'd expected Lauren to do too much of the work, like flying out to see him, inviting him to her parents' for holidays, making a huge deal when he returned to town at Christmas break. Maybe Asher had been selfish. Egotistical. And when Lauren didn't continually make plans to see him, or get excited about his homecoming, Asher had retreated from their relationship. If there was any reason for that, it was to protect his already fragile ego.

Painful to admit, but Asher had to sift through the details of the past decade of his life to figure out where they had taken a wrong turn.

Wherever they had taken it, there was no going back.

If it was Asher who had failed at their relationship—and Asher believed it'd been both of their faults—he couldn't possibly fail at another.

The truth was he loved Gemma. And he knew she would be a good wife and mother. They could—no, they would—have a happy life together.

Sitting on his old bed in his old bedroom, Asher stared at the closet door. Behind it, the bin full of photographs was stored. Should he burn those memories? His entire high school and college years were spent with Lauren by his side. They shared history together. Why would he burn those photos, those memories, unless there was something sinister, something shameful about those memories? *Don't be an idiot,* he told himself.

Lauren would always be a part of his life. He would always love her. That's simply the life he would have to live. It was an unfortunate part of their story that they weren't able to end up together, but at least they had their memories. That's all they could hope for.

Asher looked around his room and its empty shelves, empty walls. He'd taken down everything that had reminded him of his past—his trophies, certificates, diplomas, photos, posters. Now, this room was truly a guest room with indigo-painted walls and mocha-colored bed sheets. It wasn't Asher's old room. It wasn't a time capsule any longer. All of his memories were stored in a large rubber bin, pushed to the back of his closet. And that's where they'd stay until Asher no longer existed on earth. But the thing about memories is that they last a whole lot longer than people do. And no matter how far you push them back, there's no way to truly forget them.

***

Sunday, October twenty-eighth, less than a week until the wedding, Gemma called Asher.

After explaining the car crash to Gemma, and how her car was practically totaled, he finally got Gemma to calm down enough to discuss the wedding. The car situation was unfortunate, but Gemma felt confident her premium insurance would cover it. She was also on a power trip about her promotion and raise and said she could buy an even bigger, better, flashier car. *I can afford it,* she'd bragged.

"So, that's it then. Everything is finished. Right?"

Asher looked at Gemma through FaceTime. "I think so. The venue is ready, Lauren only has to put up the decorations on the day. And the RSVPs are all in. The food is set. We have our photographer. Florist. All my groomsmen have their suits tailored. Mine is tailored. You have your dress?"

Gemma's eyes were wide. "Oh my god, Asher. You're so on top of it."

Asher furrowed his brows. "You say that like it's a bad thing."

"It's not. I'm simply amazed you have the list down."

"Well, yeah, because you've forced me to plan our wedding, Gemma. Of course I know the list of to-dos."

"It's sweet," she said. "Yes, babe. I have my dress. And my bridesmaids have theirs."

"Okay, then. I guess we only have to write vows?" Asher's eyes widened. "Wait a second, do we even have a preacher?"

"You mean an officiant?" Gemma smiled.

"Yeah? My mom will probably want Pastor Heinz from our church to marry us. But it's such short notice."

Gemma rolled her eyes. "Um, no. First of all, it's not your mom's wedding. So, that's a negative on the boring pastor. Secondly, I have a friend who will marry us."

"A friend? You have a friend who's a pastor?" Asher was skeptical.

"No, I have a friend who is a shaman."

"A what?"

Gemma sighed. "A shaman. He's a spiritual leader. He is going to marry us and it's going to be amazing."

"Can he do that?"

"Of course. You don't need an actual priest. A wedding ceremony doesn't have to be religious at all. It's whatever you want it to be."

Asher shrugged. "Okay, then, I guess."

"What? You don't like that idea?"

Asher considered. Did he? He had always imagined a pastor officiating his marriage. Not a witch doctor. "Is he going to cast spells or something?"

"Wow, Asher. That's offensive."

"What? I wasn't trying to be offensive. I'm curious. I have no idea what a shaman is."

"Time to get educated." Gemma shook her head.

Asher laughed. "Okay, I'll look it up. So I'm assuming that means you've got that part of the wedding covered? We don't have to worry about all that technical marriage stuff then?"

"Don't worry. I've got that covered. For sure." Gemma grinned. "So, babe, my parents are coming in on Thursday. They're going to stay at your parents' house."

"Are you serious? I thought they were staying at the inn?"

"Well, your mother invited them, and my parents thought that was sweet and they couldn't turn down the invitation. It will be great."

"And we're staying...?"

Gemma frowned. "I thought you had that covered?"

"That wasn't on the list."

"We sure aren't staying at your parents' house the night of our wedding. Hello."

Asher rubbed his temples. "So the to-do list is still incomplete."

"Can you figure that out for us, please? Get us a room somewhere for that night before we leave for our honeymoon?"

"Our honeymoon," Asher remembered. "I forgot to do that."

"Oh, don't worry," Gemma said with a smirk. "I booked our flights and accommodations in Bora Bora."

Asher felt a twinge. "You did? How much was that? Wait, I don't want to know."

"Babe, I told you—I got a *huge* promotion. It's on me." She beamed. "You're going to love it."

It didn't make Asher happy thinking that his fiancée had paid for their honeymoon herself. It felt sort of, well, emasculating. But he shook it off.

"So then book the inn for us the night of, and that's it?"

"Write vows," Gemma said. "Don't forget to write vows. Otherwise, yeah. That's it."

Asher nodded. Vows. "Okay. I'll see you Friday?"

"I can't wait to be Mrs. Wolf." Gemma giggled. She blew him a kiss. "Bye, babe. Love you."

"Love you," Asher said. They hung up.

A shaman? Really? He supposed he'd have to deal with it, considering the rest of the wedding he had planned to suit his desires. Well, Lauren had designed it based on her perception of what they both thought Gemma would like. He'd have to deal with a shaman, whatever that was.

***

Monday, October twenty-ninth, Asher spent his lunch break calling the four different inns and hotels in the area.

"You're completely booked?" he asked the receptionist at Pine Lodge Inn, a beautiful hotel on Pine Lake.

"Yes, sir, I'm sorry. The rooms that were blocked off for the wedding of Asher Wolf and Gemma Turner are completely booked, as well as the other rooms we had available. It appears that the wedding is going to be quite a large event." The receptionist had no idea she was talking to the groom.

"Thank you. I appreciate your time," Asher said, hanging up.

That was the fourth and final inn he called. All booked, mostly with guests for the wedding. Asher reluctantly called the chain hotels and motels along the highway in the surrounding area, but even those were booked solid for Saturday night.

Where could he and his bride stay? Gemma had booked their honeymoon flights for the next day, Sunday, November fourth, and it was a long trip—they'd spend over a day flying across the United States, and then flying from Los Angeles to the Pacific Islands. They'd need all of Sunday to get there, which meant they certainly wanted to get some sleep Saturday night. Not to mention, a bride and groom tend to want their own private room the night of their wedding. And a luxurious one at that. It didn't matter, though. Even the roach-infested motels had zero vacancies.

Maybe there was somewhere he was missing. Asher wasn't entirely familiar with the new and improved Pine Lake, so it was possible someone owned a bed-and-breakfast somewhere Asher didn't know about.

But who would know that?

Lauren.

Standing with tears in her eyes was the last image he had of Lauren. It'd only been two days since their revelation, but Asher felt like it had been a lifetime. When one discovers something life-changing, time moves slowly, thoughts blur, and everything seems like a dream. Or a nightmare, rather.

If anyone knew about newly opened bed-and-breakfast spots or unconventional inns, it would be Lauren.

Picking up his phone, Asher knew he had no choice but to call her. But to call her seemed to be too impersonal, too casual, after all they'd been through. And maybe Asher wanted to see her again. To look into her big, beautiful, innocent eyes and discover his feelings. Was he being passive again, hoping Lauren would initiate their next move? Was he waiting to be steered in a specific direction?

Refusing to be passive any longer, Asher asked his mother if he could borrow her car—home from school, she was busy cleaning their house from top to bottom, dusting furniture, washing curtains, painting things, all to impress Gemma's parents and the many wedding guests she anticipated would be stopping by this wedding week—and after she said yes, Asher got in and sped down the country roads toward Lauren's house.

Lauren was unloading groceries from her van when Asher arrived in the driveway.

"Sorry to come over unannounced," Asher said, grabbing a bag from her trunk. She looked surprised to see him. Her eyes looked hollow.

"That's okay. I won't say no to help," she said, handing him more bags.

As they walked up the front steps, Asher took a peek inside. Both bags he carried were heavy, packed with frozen chickens.

"For the wedding, or are you hungry?" He smiled.

Lauren didn't. "For the wedding. Those will go in the freezer in the pantry."

Asher nodded, smiling, feeling awkward. He followed Lauren into the panty, a large galley closet off the kitchen near the laundry room. A tall freezer held dozens of jars and tins of frozen things. Lauren truly was keeping her word about being a homesteader. She was able to pickle and preserve anything. The fact that she'd grown and raised most of the frozen things made Asher feel proud of her.

"How's the business going, aside from the wedding venue hosting?" he asked as they stuffed frozen chickens into the freezer.

"Good. I've decided to make a few changes," she said, making sure not to meet his eyes.

"Oh? Like what?"

"Like, I've decided that I'm only going to make goat milk lotion, soap, and candles, and sell those."

"Instead of...?"

"Instead of what I was doing before, which was making chocolates and caramels from the goat milk and selling those. And trying to sell hens' eggs. And thinking about slaughtering chickens."

Asher smiled. "So, you're taking my advice is what you mean?"

But it didn't seem like Lauren was in the mood to find humor in this situation. "It makes sense. My main source of profit should be selling my homestead space—the barn—as an event venue. That's the biggest moneymaker. But I enjoy making lotions and soaps and candles from goat milk. That is a side hustle. And, like you said, drinking goat milk, making yogurt and candies and chocolates, gathering my hens' eggs, well those are added bonuses of owning a homestead. They're for me, only. Not a moneymaker." Having stuffed the last frozen chicken in the freezer, Lauren shut it, standing, facing Asher. She looked different— something had changed inside of her. She wasn't plastering a smile upon her face for his pleasure any longer.

"I think that's a smart idea, Lauren. I think you'll spend less time working and earn even more money."

She nodded. "I do, too. So, thanks for the idea," she said curtly, breezing by him and out the back door, headed for the van, Asher on her heels.

More bags awaited them, filled with spices and oils, butter, herbs.

"How are you going to make all of this food?" Asher asked when they returned to her kitchen, where he stood handing Lauren the groceries, watching her put them away neatly. Everything had its place in her kitchen.

"I don't know," she said, sighing. Lauren averted her eyes, continuing to put away groceries.

"What?" he asked. Did he say something wrong? Was there something on his face?

"Nothing, never mind," Lauren said.

"Gemma's getting a shaman to officiate our wedding," Asher said.

Lauren spun around, her face bright with laughter. "A shaman?"

That made Asher smile. "Yeah. Weird, right?"

She chuckled. "Totally." A frown quickly replaced her smile. "I hope I didn't screw up."

"What do you mean?" Asher stepped closer to her.

"Nothing," Lauren said. She shook her head. "Well, does it bother you, having a shaman?"

Yes.

Asher shrugged. "I've planned so much of this without her. Best to let her have her say."

Lauren nodded. "So that's it, right? All the boxes are checked?"

"That's what I wanted to talk to you about," Asher said, watching Lauren tense. "The last thing I need to do, besides write vows, is to find us a place to stay the night of our wedding. We overlooked the bride and groom suite."

Lauren gasped, covering her mouth. "Shoot. I forgot about that too."

"Well, we had a long list. Anyway, I called every single inn and hotel and motel in the area. They're all booked. You wouldn't happen to know any B&Bs or hidden inns around town that might have availability?"

Lauren's brows furrowed as she thought. "You tried my dad's? Lakeside Inn?"

Asher nodded. "Booked."

"And Pine Lodge Inn?"

"Booked."

Lauren frowned. "I don't know of any others, I'm sorry."

Asher nodded. "That's okay. I only wanted to check."

Lauren stared at him. "You two could stay here."

Asher almost laughed at the idea. "What? Are you crazy? No way, Lauren."

"Of course, I would leave. You could have the house to yourself. Stay in the guest bedroom. It's a double bed, but I assume on your wedding night you'd want to be close together anyway..." she said sadly.

"Lauren, we're not staying here, end of story."

"I'll stay at Sage's."

Asher waved his hands. "No way. That's too much to ask. It's also awkward."

She rolled her eyes, which was the first time he'd ever seen her do that. "What's the difference? You're getting married on my property."

"That's beyond generous, Lauren. It's saintly. You shouldn't offer that."

"I shouldn't offer that? Says who? And why?" Her voice rose angrily.

"I say it. I don't think you should do that to yourself."

"Do what to myself?" She stepped closer to him. Little Lauren, the epitome of sugar and spice and everything nice, stared up at Asher, her eyes aglow.

Asher was speechless. Maybe it was time to be honest.

"Fine. What I mean to say is…well, that I can't do that to myself. I can't sleep here with my bride. Not in your house, Lauren."

Lauren blinked, her face suddenly emotionless. "And why not?"

Asher's heart began to race. She was frozen, standing so close to him, her lips within such a short distance. Heat rose to Asher's face. Words clamored in his head. Words he needed to say. Words that haunted him, that wouldn't leave him. They had to escape.

"Because I still love you," he said, wrapping his hand around her delicate chin, crushing her lips with his.

For a split second, everything was right in the world. Asher was transported to childhood, to adolescence. Memories flooded his mind. Bright, happy faces. Warm embraces. A feeling of safety. Of understanding. That everything was where it needed to be. All the stars were aligned, the moonbeams shone in through windowpanes, stardust sprinkled upon them. It sounded insane to Asher's logical mind, but his heart, his gut, felt still, at peace. Synchronized with all the energy in the universe.

Her lips were soft and warm and tasted like honey. It was her beeswax lip balm, Asher thought, in the few seconds his mouth latched onto hers.

When he pulled away, Lauren's cheeks were rosy, her mouth ajar, her doe eyes stunned.

"I'm sorry," was the first thing that Asher said. But he wasn't apologizing to Lauren. He was apologizing to Gemma, thinking that an immediate apology would wipe clean his sin.

Lauren shook her head, touching her lips. "You shouldn't have done that."

Bewildered, Asher nodded. "I know. I'm sorry."

"Why did you do that?" Lauren asked, her chin beginning to tremble.

Asher reached out, his hand gently grabbing hold of her forearm. "I wasn't thinking. I had to be honest. Lauren, I still love you."

"I heard you," she said, backing away from him, his hand falling. "Please get out of my house."

"What?" Asher stepped closer, wanting to cling on to her, not let her go. "No, wait. Don't be mad."

"You're going to marry Gemma, aren't you?"

Asher stared at her. He couldn't say anything.

"Asher," she said, her voice gaining stability. "You're marrying Gemma. Right?"

Asher closed his eyes. "I don't know, Lauren." Opening them, he saw her expression of revulsion.

"You don't *know*?"

Asher's emotions and thoughts swirled inside, but he pushed them down. His brain took over. "Yes, I'm marrying Gemma on Saturday."

Accepting this, Lauren nodded stoically. "Okay, then. Please leave."

Shame engulfed Asher. He stared at her, his mouth open. "But, Lauren, please. Let's talk about this. Please."

She shook her head, turning to walk out of the kitchen. "There's nothing to talk about. The past is the past. The future is you and Gemma. Bye, Asher." And then she was gone.

Alone in her kitchen, Asher replayed the last few minutes. Never had he seen Lauren so in control, so poised, so assertive. She had total confidence. She was unshakable. Something had changed within her. Perhaps she'd turned to stone, her internal sweetness hardening like crystallized sugar.

With his head low, Asher left Lauren's house, driving home, full of regret and grief. He had done something that would hurt Gemma for years. But he had lost something that would hurt him forever.

Chapter Thirteen

Lauren

Looking at herself in the mirror, Lauren saw hollow eyes staring back at her, her heart a heavy weight dragging her down. Perhaps this was closure, this feeling of knowing she had said her truth, expressed her feelings, asserted her demands, and now there was nothing more to do.

I should be proud of myself. I began the discussion and actively tried to solve the mystery. I stood up for myself.

And she'd found out what happened between them. She'd fought for him. She'd asked him tough questions. Weeks ago, Lauren was ready to fight for Asher, to win him back. But that all seemed wrong now. He was marrying another woman. She couldn't tear him from her as much as she wanted to. And now, she was angry with him. Why had he kissed her? Why was he torturing her? And what would Lauren do about it?

It was time to give it up. Let go. Yes, she still loved Asher, but now it was clear that he was no longer hers and never would be again. It was officially over and they were done. It was time to leave it in the past and move on. Lauren had much to be grateful for. A loving family, wonderful friends, her own home, a bountiful farm, a career she loved. To want more would be greedy, selfish. And to want another woman's man? That was disgraceful.

So, from Tuesday until Friday, Lauren prepared for the wedding.

***

Wednesday was Halloween, one of Lauren's favorite holidays, but she was too busy to enjoy it. She hadn't put up too many decorations this year, only a few ghosts and spider webs on her front porch, because the less she put up, the less she had to take down a few days later for the wedding.

Rather than having children trick-or-treat along the stretching rural highways, Pine Lake hosted an annual Halloween party every year on Halloween at Town Hall, where every adult in town supplied candy, food, games, or crafts. The children spent hours enjoying the holiday. Later, adults drank wine and hard cider, enjoying Halloween in their own way. Lauren stopped by the party, happy not to see a single Wolf, and shared her goat milk chocolates and caramels with many happy children and adults.

As each day passed, the more Lauren got done, and the more she noticed the trees on her property were bare, their leaves completely dead and fallen onto the earth. Halloween had seen a light flurry of snow, none of it sticking to the ground, but the air had chilled, remaining at a cold forty degrees. It wasn't the most pleasant weather to be outside in, but Lauren had hopes for a miracle on Saturday. Anything above forty would be welcomed. And, of course, no snow. But this was up north. Anything was possible.

Day by day, she gathered boxes of white fairy lights, tiny little bulbs, and wrapped them around the rafters, the posts, and the doors inside the barn. Dozens of votive candles and tea lights lined the twenty wooden tables, waiting to be lit. On the tables inside the barn, tiny pumpkins became holders for table numbers. A tall wooden bar counter stood against the back wall. On the side where the bartender would stand, dozens of bottles of wine were stored, three kegs would be delivered the next day. Outside, generous donations of hay bales, pumpkins, and gourds from neighboring farmers were stacked artistically in front of the barn. A vintage dresser sat a few yards in front of the barn, blackboards declaring in calligraphy a "Hot Apple Cider Station," where guests could serve themselves. A stainless steel drink dispenser would hold hot cider the next day. Paper cups, spoons, and cinnamon sticks in lidded jars would complete the station. There were so many beautiful details Lauren had thought of for this wedding. It was going to be stunning. It was going to be *her* dream wedding, something she was only beginning to realize.

On Friday, Sage and Will helped Lauren erect the wooden pergola on the lawn next to the barn, where the ceremony was being held. They lined up the two hundred rustic chairs in rows, with the pergola at the center. They'd have to move the chairs back into the barn between the ceremony and the reception.

"What if it rains? No, what if it snows?" Sage asked, placing the last chair in the last row, watching Will triple check the pergola's security.

Lauren looked up at the overcast sky. "Well, I checked the weather and it says a twenty-five percent chance of snow. Otherwise, it should be partly sunny and thirty-nine degrees." She frowned at Sage, who scowled back.

"Thirty-nine degrees." She shook her head. "What happened to our fall?"

Lauren put her gloved hands on her hips. She was sweating underneath her down feathered coat, her chunky scarf, and hat. "This is what happens every year, Sage, which is why you should never have lied to Gemma and promised fall weather for her wedding."

Sage shrugged. "It could change." She watched her breath become visible in the chilly air.

Will approached them. "I think we're set. What else needs to be done?"

Lauren looked around the property. It was all coming together. "That's it for out here, for now. Tomorrow, the florist will bring all the flowers, wrapping them around the pergola and the tables. And then, of course, there's the food…"

Will and Sage looked at Lauren, whose face was twisted with worry.

"I still haven't figured out how I'm going to cook seventy-five chickens for two hundred people."

Will and Sage exchanged expressions of panic. "Seventy-five chickens?"

"And I have to bake at least three different desserts, at least three of each to feed everyone."

Will covered his face with his hands.

"And," Lauren continued, "roast vegetables. Throw together a salad."

"You seriously haven't figured this out yet, Lauren?" Sage said aghast.

A crushing feeling of doom descended upon Lauren. "I've been busy."

"One person and one oven can't do all of that. Are you crazy?" Sage threw her hands in the air. "We need to figure this out."

Sage grabbed Lauren's hand and dragged her to her pickup truck. Confused, Will followed.

"What are you doing?" Lauren asked, petrified in the passenger's seat. Will hopped in the car next to her, pushing Lauren to the middle.

"I'm going to fix this problem." Sage started the car, peeling out of the driveway and onto the country roads, headed toward town.

***

Lakeside Inn was a large restaurant, able to serve over two hundred guests at a time. It was rustic chic, its log cabin interior and exterior decorated beautifully, thanks to Lauren and her mother's influence. Its kitchen was filled with dozens of industrial-style ovens and stovetops, sinks and counters. A massive freezer stored all of the restaurant's food.

Michael Anderson, Lauren's father, stepped out of his office to greet his daughter and her friends, wrapping his strong, sturdy arms around Lauren in a much-needed embrace. She held tightly onto him, smelling his signature musk cologne. A tall man, Michael was fit-looking for his age of fifty-five. His dark brown hair was thick. But it was Tabitha, Lauren's mother, who happened to be at the restaurant that day, from whom Lauren had inherited her doe eyes and brunette hair. Lauren was the spitting image of Tabitha, who, at fifty-four, was still filled with energy.

"Sweetie." Tabitha smiled, hugging her daughter. "So good to see you. Aside from the accident, you've been radio silence the last six weeks."

Sage looked at Lauren, then looked at Tabitha. "You mean, she hasn't told you?"

Tabitha cocked her head to the side, confused. "Told me what?"

Lauren sighed, avoiding eye contact with her parents. "I'm hosting a wedding on my homestead. Getting paid for it. As a venue, like what we all discussed in terms of profitable endeavors on my property."

"Oh, wonderful, Lauren." Michael gently knocked Lauren's shoulder encouragingly.

Tabitha hugged her daughter again. "How fun."

"And she planned the wedding, too," Sage said.

"I bet you enjoyed that." Tabitha smiled.

But Sage wasn't finished. "And it's Asher's wedding. Asher is getting married to a woman named Gemma. Saturday. Tomorrow."

Michael and Tabitha grew quiet, ever so subtly turning to look at each other, exchanging a telepathic thought. They stared at Lauren, who finally looked up.

"It's a long story, and I should have told you, but I wanted to do this on my own. I wanted to succeed at my first huge business endeavor on my own. The thing is, I think I've bitten off more than I can chew."

Michael cleared his throat. "Honey, we know about Asher's wedding."

Lauren furrowed her eyebrows, gazing at them.

Tabitha nodded. "Yes, sweetheart. It's a small town. And... we were invited."

Lauren's eyes widened. "So you knew about all of this?"

"I've been talking to Heidi," Tabitha said. "But I didn't want to pry. I wanted you to come to me when you were ready to talk. That is if you wanted to talk."

A silence fell upon Lauren. This was how her parents had always been—hands-off. They'd always wanted to foster independence and strength in Lauren. Always encouraging, proud, and helpful, but only when Lauren asked. Otherwise, her parents trusted Lauren enough to know that when she wanted to talk, or when she needed help, she'd come to them. She appreciated their trust in her competence.

"Well, I don't want to talk about it, but only because I don't have time. Right now, I need your help." She looked at her father, her eyes full of humility. "Dad, can I borrow your kitchen tomorrow?"

Michael smiled graciously. "Absolutely."

Lauren smiled, feeling like she'd shaken a ton of bricks from her shoulders.

***

Feeling relieved, Lauren peacefully loaded the seventy-five frozen chickens from her deep freezer back into grocery bags, carrying them out to her van. Thankfully, Sage was helping.

"It's really happening, huh?" Sage looked at Lauren, hoping for a reaction.

Lauren shrugged. "Yep."

Sage was on Lauren's heels, quickly going up the stairs, through the house, loading bags, trotting down the stairs, loading the van. "I bet you're glad I forced you to ask your dad for help."

Lauren nodded. "Thank you. You know I don't like asking for help."

"Which is weird because you love helping others. I mean, you'll never say no to anyone. You'll support everyone else. But you are afraid of asking for your own help."

"I don't want to bother people. To annoy them."

"Asking for help every once in a while is not a bother, Lauren," Sage said.

"Well, this will be the last time I ask for help."

"What does that mean?" Sage asked.

Lauren stopped, looking at her. They were outside now, by the van, their arms empty. Night had fallen, darkness and frost had shrouded the fields surrounding the house. The crescent moon was bright in the sky.

"It means I've learned my lesson. And Asher was right," Lauren said, nervous to admit that. "He said I was doing too many things. That I would never make a profit if I sold too many things. He was right. That's why I'm giving up catering the venue. And I'm giving up trying to sell everything I can make with goat milk. Big Heart Homestead will make income through two ways. Being a venue and making goat milk lotions, soaps, and candles."

Sage looked disappointed. After a pause, her voice quietly left her. "But where does that leave me?"

Lauren's heart swelled. She smiled sympathetically. "Oh Sage. I would never get rid of you." She threw her arms around her best friend. "I'll still be growing produce and taking care of the goats and chickens. I'll need your assistance. And the venue—I'll still need manpower—womanpower—to get it ready for weddings. You're not going anywhere."

Sage smiled. "Phew." She thought, then continued, "Are you sure you don't want to continue planning weddings, too? You're good at it. And that's a whopping amount of money you can make for each wedding."

A smile tugged on Lauren's lips. "Maybe." The smile grew into a grin. "To be honest, I have loved planning this wedding."

"That's because it's *your* dream wedding," Sage blurted.

Lauren sighed. "Oh no, Sage. Is it that obvious?"

Sage shrugged. "I mean, you're pretty basic, so I'm sure it's every girl's dream wedding, so at least there's that."

Lauren swatted Sage playfully, narrowing her eye. "Brat."

Sage laughed. "Just kidding."

After another deep breath, Lauren whispered, her words forming into steam in the cold, night air. "Asher kissed me."

Sage's mouth hit the ground. "No. What?"

Lauren nodded. She replayed the entire conversation after the hospital, when Asher and Lauren discovered they had never officially broken up, as well as the scene in Lauren's kitchen.

Sage was speechless, if only for a short while. "He still loves you?" Lauren nodded. Sage went on, "But he's going to marry Gemma anyway?"

"I told him to," Lauren said.

"Why?"

"Because it's the right thing to do. So much time has passed, Sage. Our relationship was the past. We can't cling on to it any longer. I can't, anyway." Her voice was sad, quiet.

"You're over him?" Sage was skeptical.

"I'm ready to work on getting over him. I got my answers. I can look back on moments and understand why. I'm not going to be wondering what happened for the rest of my life. I know now. So that means I can move on."

Sage frowned. "That seems like an awful ending."

Lauren's eyes were dark. "I wasn't the one who chose it." Lauren slammed the trunk of the van shut, walking to the driver's side. Sage watched her, sadly heading toward the passenger's side. The ride to Lakeside Inn was a long, contemplative one that evening.

Chapter Fourteen

Asher

If there was anything Asher wanted to do that Friday night, it was to get out of that cramped house. He was happy when he stepped into his mother's car that brisk evening, driving carefully down the pitch-black highways, headed for the airport like he had done the night before. Only instead of picking up Cyril and Rose Turner, Asher was going to collect his bride.

Heidi had done a perfect job cleaning every inch of the four-bedroom Victorian house. When Asher arrived home with impeccably dressed, investment banker Cyril and equally elegant charity-organizer Rose, Heidi had made sure not a hair was out of place on her head, not a speck of dust in the house. She led them to Asher's bedroom, which had been thoroughly cleaned, and his masculine bed sheets had been swapped out with a flowery duvet. Cyril and Rose plastered on their most polite smiles for the remainder of the night, during dinner and conversations about Asher's childhood. Heidi and Fred did Oscar-worthy performances, avoiding any truths about Asher and Lauren, the wedding planner, as Cyril and Rose referred to her.

Friday, Heidi took off work and showed Cyril and Rose around Pine Lake, Asher tagging along. Cyril and Rose used the words "cute," "adorable," and "sweet" whenever they saw homes, buildings, and even Pine Lake—places Asher would describe as grand and breathtaking. But they were from New York, used to ostentatious and luxurious design. It was a small town in Fly Over Country to them.

As Asher approached the arrivals terminal at the airport, his heart raced. Six weeks had passed since he'd seen Gemma in person. Six weeks since they'd embraced. Six weeks since his lips had touched hers.

It had been four days since his lips had touched Lauren's. Yet, the longing he'd felt in those four days had far surpassed the longing he'd felt in six weeks.

What did this all mean?

Asher knew what it meant, but he refused to acknowledge it. His shameful behavior seared through his heart, burning in the pit of his belly. Repugnant. That vow he had taken to himself, the words he had promised Elias, the belief his boss Tim had of him, they were all worthless. He was not a man of integrity. He was a cheater, as quick as the cheating kiss had been.

Should he tell Gemma? Would he tell Gemma?

If he told her, she might end their engagement, cancel their wedding. Maybe that's what Asher wanted. Perhaps he had sabotaged himself or was being passive again, doing something lazy so that someone else would actively choose the tough decision.

Was this how he'd been living his life all these years? Why hadn't he pursued other jobs? Or even pushed for a higher title, a bigger pay raise? Going to grad school in the big city and working at the same job for seven years didn't exactly earn him the title of risk-taker or dream chaser. Was he doing what he loved? What he found meaningful? Or had he stumbled into things, a career, a new girlfriend, without making any decisions himself? Perhaps the fact that he was asking these questions was enough to reveal their answers.

When Gemma stepped through the sliding doors, her long, blonde hair bouncing, her blue eyes piercing, her lips glistening with gloss, her knee-high boots clacking against the sidewalk, Asher's mouth opened. She was something spectacular—she was stunning. His eyes lit up, the corners of his mouth nearly reached his ears. He was happy to see her.

The first thing he did when she arrived at his side was to pull her into his arms, clamping his mouth onto hers for a long, passionate kiss. Her sticky, sweet lip-gloss got onto his lips, which he hated, but the kiss was beautiful.

"It's freezing. Oh my gosh, *why* is it so cold here?" Gemma's first words were as icy as the air.

"I've missed you so much," Asher said, staring into her eyes.

"Aww, I missed you too," Gemma replied, a smile crossing her face.

Asher threw her luggage in the trunk of the car, making sure she was in the passenger's seat safely, then got in, taking off for their long drive home.

Gemma talked for twenty minutes straight about Japan. It was fun, wild, weird, and exhausting, she said. She loved all her Japanese colleagues. She'd made new friends, seen so much of the world, and led a team with more confidence and competence than she knew she possessed. Proud of herself, Gemma wanted more experiences like that.

"I think leading companies, training employees, making decisions, I think that's all in my future." She looked ahead through the windshield, but there was only a dark wilderness. Her eyes were looking beyond it, to her dreams. "I have so many ideas, Asher. So many things I want to do. I want to travel more. I want to open more companies. Speak at conferences. I want the world, Asher, and I believe I can have it." She turned to him, nearly giggling. "Do you think I can?"

He looked at her quickly, observing her giddiness, and as quickly returned his eyes to the road, the trauma of the crash forever haunting him. "Yeah, I do. Definitely."

"Do you want that, too?" Something in her voice was unsettling to Asher, as if she knew the answer to that question which wasn't a question at all.

"Do I want the world?" He could see her nod from his peripheral view. "Uh, well, I don't think I've ever dreamed of being a CEO of some major company."

"Do you have many dreams, Asher?"

She was beginning to sound like a self-help guru, or a motivational speaker. Her voice floated on the air, dreamlike, as if she weren't his fiancée. As if she were still thousands of miles away.

"Like, goals?"

"Dreams, Asher. What do you want to do, what do you want to be? How will you shape the world? Hello." Now she sounded a bit more like Gemma. *But still,* Asher thought, *something is off.*

"I want to have a family," Asher said. "And live a happy life. A simple life," he heard himself say. Although he had made fun of Lauren weeks before, telling her a simple life wasn't possible, six weeks living in Pine Lake had shown him it was possible, and it was indeed appealing to Asher.

"Simple lives don't change the world. That's what Riku said."

"Riku?" Asher looked at her, then back at the road. She was beaming.

"Riku. I met him in Tokyo. He's amazing, so inspirational. He was head of marketing. Incredible guy."

Asher's jaw clenched. He had a strange feeling about this Riku character. Yet, jealousy was not the feeling. Skepticism, distrust, cynicism. Those feelings swirled inside of him. The idea that Gemma could have possibly cheated on him did not. For some reason, he wasn't worried about that. Or, maybe, he had no feelings about it at all.

"Well, I guess I'd have to think more about it. Right now, I'm a little preoccupied with our wedding. Aren't you?"

She chuckled. "Of course, silly. Did you ever figure out where we're staying tomorrow night?"

Asher nodded. "Lauren's dad found out we were desperate, and he figured out a way to get us a room. We'll be staying at Lakeside Inn. It's a cute little inn downtown."

Gemma huffed. "In town? We'll be staying in town the night of our wedding?"

"What were you expecting? The Plaza Hotel?"

Gemma rolled her eyes. "Whatever. I guess it's only for one night."

"All that matters is that we're together," Asher said, reaching for her hand.

She let him hold it. Her hands were cold. Her engagement ring—the two-carat diamond Asher had saved up for eight months to buy—was freezing. He fumbled, finding the best way to clasp her hands in his. It felt awkward, but he tried to ignore that feeling and focus on driving. They'd be home soon. They'd spend the remainder of the evening sipping cocktails with his parents and her parents, attempting to relax the night before the wedding as they slept on a blow-up mattress in the living room. But they would get married the next day. Asher was sure of that. This was his life now. And he planned on living in the present.

***

Sunrays cast down through the dining room windows, illuminating specks of dust that danced like ballerinas along the hot, forced air. If Heidi saw this dust, she'd feel embarrassed, but only Asher's eyes witnessed this betrayal. While everyone continued to slumber, Asher sat at the dining room table in his pajamas, staring at a blank page of paper. The blank page stared back at him. He still hadn't written his vows.

It was six-thirty in the morning on the day of his wedding. The sun was shining, but the weather called for a possible snow flurry. A cool thirty-two degrees at the moment, the temperature could be expected to rise to forty-two degrees by two o'clock, the start of the ceremony, before it dropped to an icy thirty-five by seven o'clock. Thankfully, heaters were stationed in every corner of the barn. With two hundred bodies warming the space, Asher wasn't worried about the cold. He also knew that his Wisconsin friends and relatives wouldn't waste a shiver on that temperature. It wasn't until it reached below zero when Pine Lake residents started complaining. New Yorkers, though, could find anything to complain about.

Gemma, Asher wrote onto the paper in his chicken-scratch handwriting. He stopped, looking up again, out the window, watching snowflakes fall lazily. What should he say? What were vows supposed to express? What did he want to say?

I promise to be a good husband, Asher wrote. What did that mean? Did that mean he wouldn't cheat on her? Too late.

So would any of his vows be meaningful, then? Could any of his promises be kept? Were his words worthless?

Asher thought about all the things he had expected to say at the altar. He imagined himself standing in a church, surrounded by people, staring into his bride's eyes. He imagined telling her that he loved her, now and always, from here until death—no, beyond. Eternal love. He imagined expressing how his life had been made better simply by knowing her. How he felt inspired to be kinder, gentler, more giving. How she'd taught him to help others whenever he could. How she believed in him, encouraged him, pushed him to do more in the world. How she'd loved him, despite his many flaws. How she'd been there for him through so many of life's celebrations and challenges. How he'd been there for her, and always would. How merely the sight of her sent tingles throughout his body, shivers down his spine. How her smile and bright eyes lit up every room she entered. How her grace and humility was unmatched. That's what he imagined as he looked into her eyes and told her that they were meant to be. That they were soul mates. That nothing could ever tear them apart. Because you can't tear apart a soul.

He would tell her, "I am yours, and you are mine, and this we will be until the end of time." He didn't even know where that came from, but he heard it, the voice bubbling from deep within him.

But the bride he imagined in his head declaring these words of love was not the bride he'd be marrying that day.

His heart broke as his brain gently reminded him that reality was different from dreams, from imagination. And people had to learn to move on. To let go. To be brave.

For once, he would have to be active. For once, he would have to make a decision, instead of letting life decide for him.

Yes, he would be active.

Asher stuffed the piece of paper into his pocket, rushing out of the dining room and toward the foyer. He opened the closet, throwing on his coat, stepping into his boots, without even grabbing a scarf, and entered the frosty outside. He crept into his mother's freezing car and sped down the highway, his mind and heart finally in sync.

***

Lauren was wide awake, showered and dressed, her hair perfectly blow-dried and curled, a full face of makeup, wearing a casual cotton sweater dress, when Asher arrived at her front door, despite it only being five minutes past seven o'clock in the morning. She was a farmer, Asher remembered, and she was a woman with a strong sense of duty and responsibility.

"Is everything okay?" Lauren asked, ushering Asher into her warm home. It was perfectly tidy and smelled like cranberries. He spotted one of Lauren's cranberry-scented candles burning on the kitchen counter.

"No," Asher said. Lauren leaned back against the kitchen counter, her eyes wide as she watched him pace in the kitchen before her, his coat open, pajamas showing. "I mean, yes, everything is okay. Everyone is okay, for that matter. I need to say something to you, Lauren."

She stood up, straightening. "Asher, don't. Please don't."

"I have to," Asher said.

"But you've already told me enough and I don't think I can handle any more." Her eyes were pleading.

He took her hands in his. They were warm, soft, delicate. He memorized that feeling. "I love you, I always have, and I always will. I'll never stop loving you. Lauren, you're... we're..." He took a deep breath. *Make a decision. Be active, not passive.* "We're soul mates." He watched her eyes defrost. Her cheeks grew rosy. "I know you believe that too."

She swallowed. He could feel her pulse quicken as he held her hands. "I believed that, yeah, I did. When we were young. When we were together. But if we were soul mates, you wouldn't be marrying Gemma."

"That's the thing," Asher said, feeling his words slip out of his mouth like a slimy fish, unable to catch them, "I don't have to. I don't have to marry her."

Lauren was still. She was thinking without showing it. Then, she said calmly, "Yes, you do. You do have to marry her. Because I think you love her, too."

"Not the way that I love you." He searched her eyes. He could see a glint of pain cross them. "I love her because I care about her. She's a good person. We've shared memorable experiences. I love her in a way that is nothing compared to the way I love you. I am *in* love with you. I am connected to you through, though my soul— through my heart. We're..." Asher combed his mind for words but failed. "I can't even explain what we have, Lauren. You're the only one for me. You're my true love, as trite as that sounds. Please, I'm doing everything in my power to be decisive. To choose you, and to go after what I want. To make sure I'm not failing at this again. To make sure that I don't lose you again."

Lauren's eyes welled with tears, but she held them back. Her Viking roots seized her. She was impenetrable.

"It's over, Asher. We're over." She let go of his hands. "Marry your bride. That's what I want for you." She stepped away from him.

All the color drained from Asher's face. Blood rushed from his head down to his feet. He became empty.

"Please, don't do this, Lauren. I'm fighting for you."

She nodded slightly. "I know, Asher. But it's too late." She sighed, opening the kitchen door for him. "Go get ready. You're getting married today. And there are two hundred people who will be watching, including me."

"No." Asher stared at her, the wind whipping at his back.

Her hands shot to her hair as if she couldn't stand holding back any longer. She twirled. "I love you too, okay? But this is wrong. And I won't be part of this. It's wrong." With her farm girl strength, she shoved him out the door, slamming it behind him. He heard her let out a cry, then nothing.

He stood in the cold, snow covering his bare head and reddened ears, until he felt the snow gods had punished him long enough.

***

"You should be getting ready, honey. The photographer will be here soon to take photos of you and your groomsmen," Heidi said as she entered the house, her hair flipped and curled in every which way. She smelled like gasoline, or maybe that was hair spray, Asher concluded. Having returned from the beauty salon, Heidi's hair and makeup were immaculate—and dramatic in Asher's opinion—yet she wore a velvet sweatsuit.

He was sitting at the dining room table again, attempting to write his vows. It was nine a.m. He stood up, walking into the kitchen to look at the schedule hanging on the fridge Lauren had written up and printed out. Such a detailed list of things to do for the day, starting at eight a.m.—all for a ceremony that didn't even start until two in the afternoon. Asher had come to realize weddings were a lot of work. They weren't something one would want to do more than once. Would he?

"Your brothers are on their way, as I assume Lukas is, to get ready here." Heidi walked up to him, staring. When he turned to make eye contact with her, she smiled. But her smile masked concern. "Are you excited, sweetie?"

Asher looked into his mother's eyes, noticing them search his face for a hidden answer. "Yeah."

"You're marrying the love of your life today," she said, her eyes lingering on his.

"I'm trying to stay calm," Asher said. "Everyone around me is so stressed. It doesn't even start until two."

Heidi laughed, touching his face with her manicured hands. "Oh honey. I'm glad you're calm. You're happy, right?"

Asher smiled so that his eyes crinkled. "Yes, Mom. I'm happy."

She kissed his cheek, leaving a lipstick mark. "Well, that makes me happy then. It will be a beautiful wedding. I'm sure of it." She squeezed his arm, then trotted off as Fred ambled in the kitchen.

The sight of his father usually made Asher tense up, prepare to be judged and criticized, but at that moment, Asher felt so empty inside that he had no reaction at all. It was clear Fred had recently shaved. Tiny pieces of toilet paper were stuck to his face, little red dots holding them in place. He wore a white undershirt and his black suit pants.

"Have you seen my white shirt?" he asked his son.

"No, Dad." Asher leaned against the kitchen counter.

Grumbling, Fred shuffled around the kitchen. Suddenly, he looked up at his son with tenderness. "You're getting married today," he said. "How do you feel?"

Asher's smile was mellow. "Fine."

Fred furrowed his brows. "I suppose that's better than having cold feet."

A puff of laughter snuck out of Asher's mouth. Something inside of him snapped. "Dad, do you think I'm less of a man because I don't work with my hands like you and my brothers?"

Astonished by this question, Fred stood still, his face blank. "Where'd you get that ridiculous idea?"

Asher sighed. "Oh, I don't know, probably from the dozens of times you, Duke, and Tyler talk about your jobs, how there's nothing like working with your hands doing something masculine."

Fred scowled. "Sure, but we're only saying what we feel about our jobs. We never meant to criticize you by saying that."

"You sure about that?" Asher was skeptical.

Nodding fervently, Fred replied, "Of course, Asher. We're proud of you. You're the smartest one in the family. You got into NYU.

You do good work. Why wouldn't we be anything but proud of your success?" Fred's sincerity was apparent in the way he looked at Asher. Asher soaked it up.

"Really?"

"Yes, son. Really."

Asher smiled, feeling a weight lift from his chest. "You don't think I'm a big fish in a small pond here, do you?"

"Son, I don't even know what that means," Fred said, chuckling, causing Asher to chuckle back.

"Do you think I could make something of myself here? Would you still be proud of me if I moved home and did something," Asher paused to think, "I don't know, not as impressive as being a director of operations in New York?"

Fred stepped forward, placing his hand on Asher's shoulder. "I will always be proud of you, no matter what." He kissed his son's forehead, patting his back, and walking away. But then he stopped, turned, and looked back at Asher before leaving the kitchen. "Besides, *you* get to decide who you are, what you'll be, whether that's a big fish or a little fish. It's up to you." And then, he was gone.

***

Dressed in his suit, Asher stood in front of the full-length mirror in the second-floor bathroom.

"Looking good," Duke said, standing in the doorway. "How do you feel?"

Asher stared at his older brother. Never had Duke asked him that question. And maybe this time, he was simply being polite. But Asher was desperate. He was searching for answers, hoping that everyone in his life would offer up a solution so that he didn't have to.

"Honestly, I'm feeling weird."

Duke frowned. "Maybe your belt's too tight." He stepped in the bathroom, reaching for Asher's tie. "Or your tie is wrong. Yep, it's your tie." Duke's meaty fingers, rough with calluses from working with his hands, fumbled with Asher's tie, loosening and lengthening it. "Gotta say, the navy blue suits and brown shoes do look sharp."

"Lauren did a great job." Asher took a deep breath. "Duke…"

His brother looked down at him. "Yeah?"

"Do you think it's possible to love two different women at the same time?"

Duke finished with Asher's tie, standing back, arms crossed. Intensely, he stared at Asher. "No."

"What? Really?"

Duke shrugged. "That defies the meaning of the word. I mean, well, okay—love is something you're supposed to feel a lot of, right? Like, uh, let's see. I love Mom, and Dad, and my kids, and you, I guess." He chuckled, gently punching Asher's shoulder. "So I guess in that sense, you can love a lot of people. But, the romantic sense? Nah. That would be something else."

"Maybe nostalgia?" Asher asked, hopeful.

"Nostalgia? Yeah, I mean, maybe you're reminiscent of the love you used to feel. Confused."

"Or it's not loving, but a deep caring for someone?"

Duke nodded. "Sure. Maybe that."

"So you don't think you can love two women at the same time?"

Duke sighed. "I don't think you can be *in love* with two women at the same time. I think you can care about another. Dude, I don't know. I've only ever loved Jenny." He took a long look at Asher. "And I can't tell you what to do or how you feel, man. That's something only you can figure out. But if you're having second thoughts—"

"No, no. I'm not." Asher attempted to steady his voice, sounding confident.

"Okay, then. Well, good luck. I think it'll be a great wedding, Ash." Duke smiled at his brother, and then left.

Can't be in love with two women at the same time, Asher told himself. So which one was he in love with?

Chapter Fifteen

Lauren

At one-thirty, Lauren was pacing in her kitchen, nervous. She wore a plum-colored, A-line dress. It was floor-length, its sleeves three-quarter length. The top was a V-neck, the material lacy. The skirt was chiffon, pleated out like a princess dress. She looked stunning, but she felt miserable. Even though her hair was curled in long, loose curls, and her makeup was dramatic but elegant, Lauren felt like an absolute mess. Worries of all sorts crept into her mind, but she didn't have the experience to quiet them, to reassure herself that it would all work out.

Sage was at Lakeside Inn, ordering the chef and sous-chef to follow Lauren's recipes for dinner and dessert to a T. They would be preparing to cook now, cooking at two-thirty, and having dinner arrive by three forty-five to serve at four.

Outside, the chairs faced a wooden pergola, wrapped in autumnal flowers and garland by the florist. Bouquets of burgundy ranunculus, beige and cream hydrangeas, dark plum peonies, peach and coral garden roses, rust orange mini roses, wild wheat, lavender thistle, and burgundy berry sprays were placed on every table and at the end of every row of ceremony chairs. The bride's and bridesmaids' bouquets were in vases of water waiting on Lauren's dining room table. The cider was steaming hot in its stainless steel dispenser, displayed on the vintage dresser outside for the guests who were beginning to arrive.

The air was a chilly forty degrees, a few degrees warmer than predicted. No signs of flurries, but the sky was overcast, the clouds fluffy and heavy. Not a single leaf remained on tree branches. But the air still smelled like candy corn and bonfire. Sweet and lovely, crisp fall scents breezed by.

As she wrapped a faux fur shawl around her, Lauren took a deep breath, finally leaving the comfort of her warm home, and entering the brisk outside, heading straight for the cider station. There, she gave ceremony programs to guests as they arrived, telling them to fill up their to-go cups with hot apple cider and cinnamon sticks. She also encouraged guests to take a plaid-colored scarf—Lauren's idea for a wedding favor—in case they got cold outside. Every single guest loved the idea of the scarves and the apple cider. They praised Lauren for the beautifully decorated venue. Some even said they felt they'd stepped into an autumn wonderland. Pride swelled inside of Lauren, masking her feelings of heartbreak, if only for a little while.

"Whoa, this is awesome," Lauren heard a mellow male voice say. She turned to see a tall, shaggy-haired man. A white, rhinestone-studded jacket fell to his knees, a rainbow-colored scarf wrapped around his neck. His clothes beneath his jacket looked like traditional clothing from the Far East, even though his skin was pale and his eyes ice blue. He stood out like a sore thumb.

"Hi, welcome to the Wolf-Turner wedding." Lauren handed him a program.

"Thanks. I'm Shaman Duju." He smiled peacefully, closing his eyes.

"Oh. That makes sense. Hello. So nice to meet you." Lauren smiled wide, shaking his hand.

"Where should I set up?"

Lauren pointed to the pergola. "That's where the ceremony will be held. Is there anything I can do to help you?"

Shaman Duju brought his hands together in prayer, bowing slightly. "Be you, and exude peace and light." After a quick nod, he left Lauren's side, heading for the pergola.

As Lauren was greeting more guests, a white stretch limo pulled into the driveway. Digging her heels against the cold gravel, Lauren rushed to the limo, opening up the door. She peered inside, ready to help.

There was Gemma, glowing like an angel. Her freshly highlighted hair was in an updo, curls cascading down her bare shoulders. Her strappy, form-fitting wedding dress was sensual, making Gemma look like a model. Her makeup was minimal but accentuated her naturally stunning features and strong bone structure. Looking at Gemma, Lauren felt her feelings of inadequacy return. But as soon as they arrived, Lauren shook them away, reminding herself of her value, clinging onto her feelings of pride. *I am worthy*, she told herself.

"Happy Wedding Day," Lauren sang, extending a hand to help Gemma out of the limo. Her three gorgeous bridesmaids, wearing hot pink dresses, piled out of the limo. Looking at the bridesmaid dresses, Lauren felt a sting of worry. Her eyes were glued to Gemma's face, studying her expressions.

"Cute," Gemma said without any emotion as she quickly surveyed the grounds while rushing up the front steps of Lauren's house, hoping not to be seen by any guests.

Leading Gemma and her bridesmaids inside, Lauren shut the door behind them, ushering them into the living room.

"Thankfully, I don't think anyone saw you. You'll be able to make a grand entrance down the aisle." She smiled at Gemma, who looked at herself in a mirror on the wall. "You look so beautiful, Gemma."

Gemma looked over at Lauren, forcing a smile. "Thanks."

"Do you like the setup?"

Gemma smiled mechanically. "Uh-huh."

Lauren's finger shot to her hair, ready to twirl, but she stopped herself. "Okay, well, make yourself at home. We have fifteen minutes until the ceremony begins. I'll send your dad over when we're ready to begin."

Gemma focused on her reflection, paying no attention to Lauren.

Don't worry. It'll all be okay, Lauren told herself, shutting the door behind her as she went back outside.

Her worry was put to ease when she spotted most of the chairs filled with guests, almost all of whom happily sipped hot cider, wrapped in plaid scarves. Don Carlson was already snapping photos. Local musicians—a last-minute addition—played classical music on violin and keyboard.

In a gorgeous navy blue gown and white faux fur shawl, Heidi approached Lauren, her arms open in a loving embrace. Lauren took comfort in her hug.

"Honey, this looks amazing. I'm so impressed with your wedding planning skills. Every inch of this farm looks gorgeous. All the little fall details." Heidi let go of her embrace, looking Lauren in the eyes. "You are a special person, Lauren, to do all this for my son."

"I was happy to. I want to see him happy." Lauren watched as Heidi's smile turned downward, her eyes welling with tears. She quickly wiped them away.

"I do too," Heidi said. "And I hope she makes him happy." She sighed, pursing her lips, contemplating something. Finally, she leaned in and whispered, "But you'll always be my favorite. I'll never love her the way I love you, Lauren. You know that, right?"

"Mrs. Wolf," Lauren whispered back, "I..." But what was the use? Lauren grinned. "I know."

A wink, and then Heidi was gone, finding her place in the barn for the walk down the aisle. A loud noise buzzed behind Lauren, and she turned to see a black stretch limo arriving down the driveway. Soon, Asher, Duke, Tyler, and Lukas piled out, all handsome in their navy suits. Asher looked more handsome and refined than ever. And, Lauren realized, he looked exactly as she'd always hoped he'd look on their wedding day.

Have I planned my own wedding, Lauren wondered, surveying her homestead. Bursts of autumn colors delighted the senses while pumpkins and hay bales decorated every corner. The weather was perfectly nippy, the atmosphere undeniably romantic. And there, walking toward her, her once-groom was looking like a dream.

"Lauren, this looks amazing," Asher said, approaching her. "And you..." He looked her up and down, his hand instinctively shooting to her face, gently brushing his knuckles against her soft cheeks. "You look breathtakingly beautiful."

She felt herself blush. "Thank you. You look wonderful."

He drew a deep breath in. "Thank you. Thank you for all of this."

A slight smile twisted her lips, but she couldn't help looking at him with sad eyes.

"Lauren," he began, turning his head to make sure no one was in earshot. "I want to tell you, one last time, that if there's any chance, any way we can—"

But Lauren cut him off, backing away from his gentle touch. "Go marry Gemma, Asher."

His blue eyes iced over, and his hands dropped to his side. With a nod of resignation, Asher walked past Lauren and slipped into the barn, disappearing in the darkness.

Taking a deep breath of courage, Lauren looked around the front lawn and the barn, toward the house and the surrounding fields. Every chair was filled with guests. It was time.

She nodded to the musicians, who began playing "Canon in D," signaling the groomsmen and Asher to file into their places. Heidi and Fred walked down the aisle to their seats, with Rose Turner being ushered down the aisle by a friend of Asher's. Lauren looked over to the side of the house, where a bridesmaid looked out the kitchen door window. Lauren nodded, and the bridesmaids elegantly stepped out, down the aisle, their bouquets in hand. But when the musicians seamlessly transitioned into "The Wedding March," Gemma was nowhere to be found.

Heart thumping wildly in her chest, Lauren searched the farm, her eyes darting from the barn to the house.

No sign of Gemma.

No sign of Asher.

Lauren could feel the burning gaze from guests on her.

What was happening?

Chapter Sixteen

Asher

In the barn, the vintage chandeliers that hung from the ceiling and the Christmas lights wrapped around beams created a romantic ambiance, the rustic tables and autumn décor adding to the warm feeling.

But where Gemma and Asher stood, facing each other, the feeling was anything but warm.

"You got my text?" Asher asked.

He'd sent Gemma a text to meet him before the wedding because he wanted to tell her something. After he'd sent it, he immediately regretted it. What was he thinking? Telling a woman he wanted to tell her something before the wedding. He must have panicked her...but for a good reason. He couldn't save her from the hurt she was going to feel. Asher couldn't do this. He couldn't marry her. Not with what he knew. Now that he knew Lauren still loved him. That he'd messed up. He had to tell Gemma the truth.

"They're waiting for us," Gemma said, her expression weary. "I feel so bad."

"Thanks for meeting me in here," Asher said. "I have a knot in my stomach right now, but—"

"So do I," Gemma confessed, pacing before him.

"So then, you must know what I'm feeling?" Asher's voice was quiet, subdued. Heart heavy, he looked at his stunning bride-to-be. She truly was beautiful.

Immediately, Gemma burst into tears. Asher rushed to her side.

"Gemma? Are you okay? I'm so sorry."

Dropping her hands from her face, Gemma revealed puffy eyes, her mascara leaving black trails down her cheeks, her mouth turned downward. "Of course I'm not okay. I'm standing in a barn with my groom, letting him see me before I walk down the aisle while all those people are waiting on me. I can even hear the 'Wedding March.'"

He tripped over his words. "I have to tell you something." Oh, Asher could feel the weight of the world on his shoulders. Why had he let it go this far?

"I have something to tell you, too." Gemma sniffled, catching Asher off guard.

"What do you want to tell me?" Asher asked, but Gemma kept crying. Finally, she composed herself.

"First of all, this isn't my wedding," she cried, trying to catch her breath.

"What are you talking about?"

"That isn't my dream wedding. This is Lauren's dream wedding. It's not me." Her tears ran angry, her forehead creased. "It's like you and Lauren planned your *own* wedding."

"What do you mean? We ran everything by you. You said you trusted us to plan the wedding you wanted."

"It isn't a fall wedding. No leaves on the trees. It's so cold I can see my breath. It's freezing. And this barn is so primitive. I don't like the plaid scarves. It's…it's not me, Asher."

"I'm sorry, Gemma. Maybe we should have consulted you more." He shook his head. What did it matter? "But it doesn't matter because, Gemma, I can't…I can't…do this."

"I can't do this either," Gemma said, surprising Asher. She stared at him, her eyes brimming with tears. "I love you, Asher, but I don't think we're supposed to be married."

Asher felt his chest tighten. Even though he felt the same way, it still hurt.

"Gemma, there are so many things I regret not telling you. I should have told you that Lauren wasn't only a friend in high school—we were deeply in love. I'm sorry. I kept that from you."

Gemma looked down. "I could feel it, Asher. It's hard not to notice that between two people."

"I'm so sorry." Asher stepped closer to her, grabbing her hands. "So you don't want to do this?"

"Do you?" She looked up at him, her eyes wide and innocent. Asher had never seen her so vulnerable before.

"I'm still in love with Lauren. I'm so sorry." Hearing the words tumble from his mouth, Asher felt ashamed. "I wish I had realized sooner. Saved us both from this whole mess."

Gemma's lip trembled. "It's my fault, too."

"Your fault too? How?"

Gemma took a deep breath. "I fell in love with Riku," Gemma blurted.

"What?" Asher blinked, frozen. "The shaman?"

"No. That's Duju. Riku was my Japanese coworker in Tokyo. He's my soul mate," Gemma said, staring at Asher with wet eyes. "I didn't cheat on you, but I fell in love with him."

"Oh. Okay..." Asher was completely surprised. He was overwhelmed with all the feelings expressed in the dark barn. A strange feeling seized Asher. Was he relieved? Disappointed? Hurt? Even though he'd discovered he didn't love Gemma the way he loved Lauren, it still hurt to hear Gemma had fallen in love with someone else. Should he be angry?

Asher looked to Gemma. Sadness hung heavy on her face. She'd been such a beautiful bride, stunning in her dress and makeup, but she'd only been performing—and at a wedding she didn't even want to have, a marriage that wasn't even planned to her liking.

"So, we're not getting married?" Asher asked again.

"We're not getting married." Gemma's tone made it clear to Asher she was struggling with these complicated emotions as well.

Asher took her hand and kissed it. "I care about you. I love you, but not in that way," he said.

"Same," Gemma said, slightly smiling.

"I guess this is good, right?"

Gemma nodded. "This isn't ideal by any means. I wish we hadn't gotten this far. I think we were both a little confused. Wrapped up in our own lives. I'm sorry, Asher."

"We have to tell everyone," Asher said. "Everyone is waiting on us. I only want to make sure you're okay. That I'm not alone here in my feelings?"

Gemma nodded. "I don't mean to hurt you when I say this, but I don't think I knew what love was until I met Riku."

Asher's ego deflated. No matter his feelings for Gemma—or his lack of feelings—that still stung.

"I care about you, of course, and up until Japan, I was ready to marry you," Gemma took Asher's hand, "but when I met Riku, I felt something I've never felt before. Not with you, not with anyone. I still went through with planning the wedding because I knew how much work it had been for everyone involved, but I knew in my heart our marriage wouldn't last."

Asher shook his head. "Wow. If only we were honest from the start."

"I don't think it's that easy, honestly," Gemma said, shrugging. "It's scary to disappoint people, to completely change your life with such certainty. It's complicated."

Asher nodded. "What will we tell people? Your parents?"

"Let me handle that. Poor Lauren. All her work." Gemma's eyes brightened. "Maybe we can still throw an awesome party?"

Asher wasn't sure how to feel about that. "What about the honeymoon?"

"Uh, yeah, I'm going on that tomorrow." Gemma bit her lip, looking coyly at Asher. "I'm going to have Riku come with me."

A pang of jealousy and hurt rippled through him after that comment. He couldn't help it—he was human, after all.

"Okay. You paid for it, so that's only right."

Gemma's father arrived at the door outside the barn, loudly clearing his throat. "Is everything okay?"

"It is now, Dad," Gemma said.

Asher smiled, reaching over, embracing Gemma for the last time.

Chapter Seventeen

Lauren

When Lauren finally saw the barn doors slide open, she was shocked to see Gemma and Asher holding hands, Gemma's eyes puffy from crying. As Gemma and Asher walked down the aisle together, audible gasps rippling throughout the lawn. The musicians looked to Lauren for direction, but she didn't know what to do. They continued to play until Asher and Gemma arrived at the top of the aisle.

Asher smiled at Shaman Duju, taking the mic from his hands.

"Hello, everyone," Asher said, a crack in his voice.

Lauren could see heads whipping left and right, guests trying to get a sense of what was happening. Gemma's parents looked beet red. *This can't be good*, Lauren thought, embarrassed.

Gemma leaned over to share the mic with Asher.

"Thank you all for coming today. It's so wonderful to see so many of our loved ones gathered here to celebrate Gemma and me on our big day. It's only… the thing is…" Asher looked at Gemma, who, never one to turn down attention, grabbed the mic, letting a positive smile bloom onto her face.

"We've decided not to get married." Gemma's tone did not match her words. With that charming energy of hers, she was able to spin her news into something exciting. "Asher and I have thought long and hard about this, and although we care about each other deeply, our hearts belong to other people."

More audible gasps. The audience wasn't sure what to do. Whispers rang through the crowd.

"Gemma…" Rose Turner whispered, although it sounded more like a feminine growl. "What are you doing?"

Lauren watched this from where she stood, off to the side, near the musicians. She was frozen.

"It's okay, Mom," Gemma said. "Asher and I both agreed to this. I'm sorry to do this to you all last minute. And, Lauren," Gemma said, eyes locking onto Lauren's deer-in-headlights gaze, all eyes turning to her, "I'm so sorry. You've created such a beautiful wedding, and I think you're the best wedding planner in the Midwest. How about a round of applause for Lauren's wedding planning skills? And this gorgeous venue?" Gemma's smile was enough to compel the audience to applaud. Lauren's cheeks grew rosy.

What the heck is happening? Lauren felt like she was having an out-of-body experience.

Asher grabbed the mic. "We won't be having a ceremony, but we'll still be having a reception. We won't send any of you home hungry or without having danced to 'Twist and Shout.' So why don't you all gather yourselves and meet us in the barn." Asher smiled, then handed the mic back over to Shaman Duju.

"Well, uh, all right. Let's get this party started," he said, gesturing for the crowd to get up and head to the barn.

Lauren couldn't move. Had Asher and Gemma mutually called off their wedding?

Relief and disappointment simultaneously washed over Lauren. Although she took solace in knowing Asher had called off the wedding, she couldn't deny disappointment that so much time had passed between them. Lauren made a vow to herself. Never again would she pretend to be happy when she wasn't, never again would she put herself last, and never again would she ignore her authentic self, deny her heart's wishes. She would stand up for herself, pursuing her dreams and desires without any guilt.

As guests were herded into the barn, Lauren decided she'd hang back, hoping to make sense of everything that had happened. Asher was swallowed up into a sea of people, who Lauren guessed were asking him was going on.

Music played inside the barn. Gemma's wedding playlists, Lauren recognized the songs. It was supposed to be the song Gemma and Asher were going dance their first dance to. *What would our song be?* Lauren wondered. They had so many songs together, and there were too many memories to choose from. It would be something folksy, with whimsical lyrics and soulful music, the type of song that carries you away into a dream. The kind of song that envelops you. This was not that kind of song.

She couldn't stand being in the barn, so Lauren rushed off to her kitchen to grab the desserts. Was Asher going to try to win her back now? What was Lauren feeling? Did she want it to happen this way? Had everything been tainted now?

It's almost over. You can do this. The night is almost done. She encouraged herself as she stepped out of the kitchen, returning to the barn, happy to see everyone had begun eating dinner. Setting up the pies and cake on a display table, Lauren avoided eye contact.

Sage took control, cutting the cake despite the fact no marriage occurred. With music playing in the background, Sage passed around slices of cake and pie, and guests returned to mingling and drinking. Don Carlson had snapped photos, and guests rushed the dessert table, loading up. Despite the strange events, people were still having an amazing time.

Lauren heard someone say, "This is the best non-wedding I've ever been to."

Smiling to herself, Lauren slipped outside, alone in the brisk, dark autumn evening still able to hear happy murmurings while everyone enjoyed their dinners.

She listened to the sounds of crickets singing, the night breeze rustling falling leaves on the ground. If she could do this for the rest of her life—host weddings, not watch the love of her life almost marry someone else—she knew she could be happy. Life would be simple. But it would be happy.

Finally, the frosty night air was becoming too much for Lauren, despite her heavy shawl. As she reached to open the barn doors, a hand gripped her shoulder.

"Jacob," Lauren said, surprise flashing across her features.

Jacob stood across from her, his expression was somber. A twinge of fear crossed through Lauren's body.

"Is something wrong?"

Jacob shook his head. "No, and don't worry. Do you feel the same about me as I do about you?"

Be honest, Lauren told herself. *Be brave.* She couldn't avoid Jacob any longer. What was there to be afraid of anymore? Her life had taken a vastly different path than she'd imagined. Fear could not control her any longer. But she was adamant she could tell the truth without hurting Jacob like she was hurting.

"Jacob, I have to be honest with you. It's only right. But you're not going to like my answer." Lauren stepped closer to him. "I care about you, Jacob, and I've always loved you as a friend. But I don't love you romantically. I never have and I never will. And I'm sorry. I've never wanted to hurt you, which is why I've probably avoided telling you this for so long. But that's only hurt you more, and for that I'm sorry, too. You deserve the best—a woman who loves you back. The thing is, I don't want to stop being your friend. But I can't be anything more."

Jacob nodded, absorbing her words as if he understood it was coming. "That's what I figured," he said, scrubbing his face with his hand. "I guess it's not because of Asher, either?" Jacob gestured toward the barn. "You weren't holding out for him?"

Lauren's shoulders fell in defeat. "It has nothing to do with Asher, Jacob. You and I simply aren't meant to be."

Jacob nodded. "Okay then. I only wanted to hear you say it."

Silently, Lauren watched him turn and begin to walk away. He stopped, turning around. "You don't have to avoid me, though. We'll never be able to be close friends, but don't avoid me, okay? I won't make things weird. I promise."

Lauren nodded. "Okay."

A smile lit up Jacob's face. "And I won't sing you any more love songs in public...or in private."

Lauren chuckled. She waved, and Jacob waved back, hopping into his truck and driving away. She looked back into the barn. Everything was going smoothly, and there was nothing else Lauren would have to manage at this point, besides cleanup. Out of the corner of her eye, she saw Asher and Gemma smiling with guests on the dance floor.

For a non-wedding, they certainly were having a good time.

Lauren needed a break.

She got into her car and drove away.

Chapter Eighteen

Asher

Asher had been searching for Lauren all night, but every time he caught a glimpse of her, she scurried off. Didn't she know he was doing this for her?

Finally, when guests began to yawn, ready to head out, Asher stood alone for the first time. He hurried from the barn to Lauren's kitchen door, peering inside. Darkness. Opening the door, he entered, calling out her name.

"Lauren. Are you in here?" But the house was quiet.

Asher ran back into the barn, only to see Sage and Will stacking chairs and clearing tables. Lukas was helping.

"Is Lauren here?" Asher asked, his voice startling the three. All six eyes stared at him.

"Isn't she in the kitchen?" Sage asked. "That's where I last saw her."

Asher walked closer, searching the barn, feeling heat rise inside of him. He was beginning to feel like time was running out. *Hurry*, something inside of him was telling him. He'd waited too long before. Was she willing to give him a second chance?

"She's not there. I need to find Lauren right now," he told them.

"She went for a drive," Lukas said. "That's all she said."

"Did she seem upset?" asked Asher.

Lukas turned to Sage, who frowned. "You know Lauren. She never *seems* upset."

Nodding, Asher turned on his heel, ready to find her, but he spun right around quickly. "Wait, I don't have a car. Um, can I—"

Keys flew through the air, almost hitting his face, before Asher even realized Lukas was throwing them. "Good luck, brother," Lukas said, smiling.

"Thanks," Asher said, jogging out of the barn.

As he opened the driver's-side door of Lukas's pickup truck, a hand gripped his shoulder. Turning around, Asher saw cloudy eyes. Don Carlson, holding his camera, smiled at him.

"Asher."

"Hi, Mr. Carlson. Um, I'm actually in a rush—"

"I want to show you something," Don said, turning his camera's display screen toward Asher, clicking through a series of photos of Lauren. She was stunning. And her eyes were on Asher. Don had caught her staring at him, her eyes full of longing and melancholy. "That is the look of a woman madly in love with someone she can't have." Don's eyes flicked up to Asher's. Then, he clicked through a few more, this time of Asher looking at Lauren from across the room, unbeknownst to her. "And that is the look of a man madly in love with someone he can't have."

Asher smiled. "You're only half right, Don. I'm going to go fix that last part."

Don chuckled, patting Asher on the back.

"I was hoping you'd say that."

***

Driving down the dark country roads, Asher felt a sense of urgency and panic overcome him. What was Lauren thinking? What was she doing? Where was she?

And as Lauren's beautiful face floated in his mind, another image entered.

He knew exactly where she'd be.

Chapter Nineteen

Lauren

By midnight it was so cold Lauren had to wear her winter coat. She'd changed out of her dress and heels and into jeans and a sweater. Her winter boots kept her warm as she stood on the frozen dirt next to the tree. *Their* tree. How could she ever call it anything else?

It was time to say good-bye. Good-bye to this tree, good-bye to Asher, good-bye to any hope of a future together. It was time to shed the past's mistakes, forgive Asher and herself for failing at their relationship.

You can't think like that anymore, she told herself. It didn't help to comb through her memories with Asher, especially that last year, and continue to analyze everything they could have said or done differently that would have kept them together. That was it. She had to be done thinking this way. It was time to let it go. Let him go. Time to move on and only look ahead.

Maybe, Lauren thought as she pulled off her gloves and placed her bare hands on the jagged trunk, *our love was only meant to last so long, like everything in life. Like this tree, which will eventually die and fall over, our love was not everlasting. Maybe there's another man out there for me, for my second chapter in love.*

It was so hard to believe that, though. That's the thing about faith, Lauren reminded herself. It's not based on evidence, not based on knowledge, but based on a simple belief, a confidence in the unknown.

She stared up at the tree, at its diverging trunks, and closed her eyes.

Good-bye, tree. Good-bye Asher. I'm letting you go.

A warm feeling on her hands frightened her. Her eyes shot open and she pulled her hands away from the tree in fear. As adrenaline shot throughout her body, Lauren slowly recognized the hands, then the body, then the face that stood before her.

"I knew I'd find you here," Asher said, smiling. He was still in his wedding suit and dress shoes, and Lauren guessed he was freezing.

"What are you doing here? How did you know? I didn't even hear—" Lauren was so full of questions, feeling disoriented.

Asher stepped closer to her. "I am in love with you, Lauren. I always have been, and I always will be." He took her bare hands in his. "I know there was so much that happened that didn't have to happen. But that's in the past. I want to move forward, focusing on you, and our love together. We're meant to be, Lauren. We're soul mates."

His eyes were sincere, gazing into hers. She felt love emit from his body. His hands gripped hers with tenderness.

"But... it's too late, Asher."

"No, it's never too late. Don't say that."

She looked at him sadly. "You almost married her. You were about to walk down the aisle."

"But I didn't. Don't you see? I didn't. I know it was last minute, but I couldn't go through with it. And Gemma doesn't love me either. She fell in love with a man in Tokyo. It's over, Lauren. You and I can finally be together after all these years. And I'm trying to be as communicative with you as possible now. I know, it's confusing and it's sudden—"

"But you almost married her," Lauren said emphatically.

"Only because you told me to," Asher replied. "I tried to tell you before the wedding that I wanted to be with you. But you told me to marry Gemma." Lauren didn't know what to say. "But look—people still got to enjoy your wedding. You did an amazing job."

"But my first wedding ever was a disaster," Lauren blurted, covering her mouth once she realized what she'd admitted.

"Your *first* wedding *ever?*" Asher asked, incredulous.

"Oops." Lauren smiled. "I mean, well, yeah. I guess it's time to be open and honest with each other. This was my first time hosting a wedding on my property."

Asher smiled. "Despite the circumstances, you still did an amazing job." Asher stepped closer. "I love you, Lauren. We're meant to be together."

He's telling the truth.

"But what about all the miscommunication? All the hurt feelings? All the years that we've wasted?" Lauren wondered aloud.

"What about them? There's nothing we can do. It's in the past. All we can do is vow never to let that happen again. I'm ready to take an active role in our love, Lauren. I'm ready to win you over every day."

That sounded good to Lauren. She smiled. "So, what does this mean?" Lauren asked.

"I'm moving back to Pine Lake. To be with you."

"What? What about your job in New York?"

"You were right. I don't find meaning in it. I think there's a more meaningful job here for me in Pine Lake. I'm sure I'll find it. Loving you brings meaning to my life. Being around my family and my community brings meaning to my life. I know I will find my purpose here, too."

"Really?"

"One hundred percent." He smiled. His eyes stared directly into hers, full of passion and longing. "Do you love me, too?" His voice was almost nervous.

Lauren smiled, extending her arms over Asher's shoulders, feeling his hands rest around her waist.

"I love you more than ever, Asher."

She reached up and met his lips with hers. Finally, after all these years, she could feel his warm, soft lips against hers, feel loved again by the only man for her. They *were* meant to be. And like the tree, they were entwined together eternally. Soul mates.

When their lips pulled apart, but their faces remained close, Lauren grinned and said, "About that job in Pine Lake. I know a business that is in desperate need of a business operations director."

Asher grinned back. "That is exactly the job I was hoping for." He pulled her into his body, locking his lips onto hers, wrapping his arms around her.

They'd never let go again.

ABOUT THE AUTHOR

Brigit Stacey is an author and screenwriter. She's sold three screenplays to the Hallmark Channel, including *A Valentine's Match, Country at Heart,* and *Love at the Inn.* Her novel *An Inconvenient Wedding* is set in Brigit's favorite place on earth, the Northwoods of Wisconsin, where she likes to spend every summer. When she's not writing, she enjoys reading outside while drinking a glass of Pinot Noir. She resides with her husband in Chicago.

CONNECT WITH BRIGIT:
website & blog: BrigitStacey.com
Instagram: @brigitstacey

www.BOROUGHSPUBLISHINGGROUP.com

If you enjoyed this book, please write a review. Our authors appreciate the feedback, and it helps future readers find books they love. We welcome your comments and invite you to send them to info@boroughspublishinggroup.com. Follow us on Facebook, Twitter and Instagram, and be sure to sign up for our newsletter for surprises and new releases from your favorite authors.

Are you an aspiring writer? Check out www.boroughspublishinggroup.com/submit and see if we can help you make your dreams come true.

www.ingramcontent.com/pod-product-compliance
Lightning Source LLC
Chambersburg PA
CBHW031334170626
46807CB00002B/695